PRAISE FOR
THE HEART OF ALL WORLDS SERIES

The Sidhe—Finalist, 2015 Foreword INDIES Book of the Year | Fantasy

The King and the Criminal—Finalist, 2016 Foreword INDIES Book of the Year | Fantasy & LGBT

"FIVE STARS… The book's dreamlike tone is a pleasant change from the grim and dark novels that characterize the modern fantasy genre."

—*Foreword Reviews* on *The Sidhe*

The Sidhe—Named Prism Book Alliance Recommended Read

"4.5 STARS… Ashe gave us a rich world filled with deep characters and stories hiding around every turn. I can't wait to return."

—Prism Book Alliance on *The Sidhe*

"A mix of fizzy romance and thorny politics."

—*Publishers Weekly* on *The Sidhe*

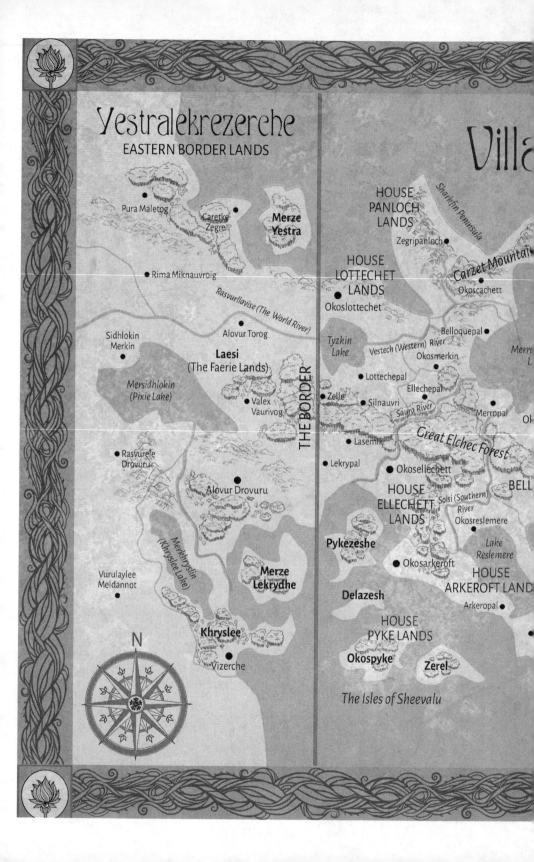

Yestralekrezerche
EASTERN BORDER LANDS

Pura Maletog

Caretke
Zegre

**Merze
Yestra**

Rima Miknauvroig

Rasvurllavise (The World River)

Sidhlokin
Merkin

Alovur Torog

Laesi
(The Faerie Lands)

*Mersidhlokin
(Pixie Lake)*

Valex
Vaurivog

Rasvurele
Drovuru

Alovur Drovuru

*Merkhryslin
(Khryslee Lake)*

Vurulaylee
Meldannot

**Merze
Lekrydhe**

N

Khryslee

Vizerche

Villa

HOUSE
PANLOCH
LANDS

Sharleln Peninsula

Zegripanloch

Carzet Mountain

HOUSE
LOTTECHET
LANDS

Okoscachett

Okoslottechet

Belloquepal

*Tyzkin
Lake*

Vestech (Western) River

Okosmerkin

*Merre
L*

Lottechepal

Ellechepal

Zelle

Silnauvri

Saura River

Merropal

Ok

Great Elchec Forest

Lasemik

Lekrypal

Okosellechett

HOUSE
ELLECHETT
LANDS

Solsi (Southern)
River

BELL

Okosreslemere

Pykezeshe

*Lake
Reslemere*

Okosarkeroft

HOUSE
ARKEROFT LAND

Delazesh

Arkeropal

HOUSE
PYKE LANDS

Okospyke

Zerel

The Isles of Sheevalu

THE BORDER

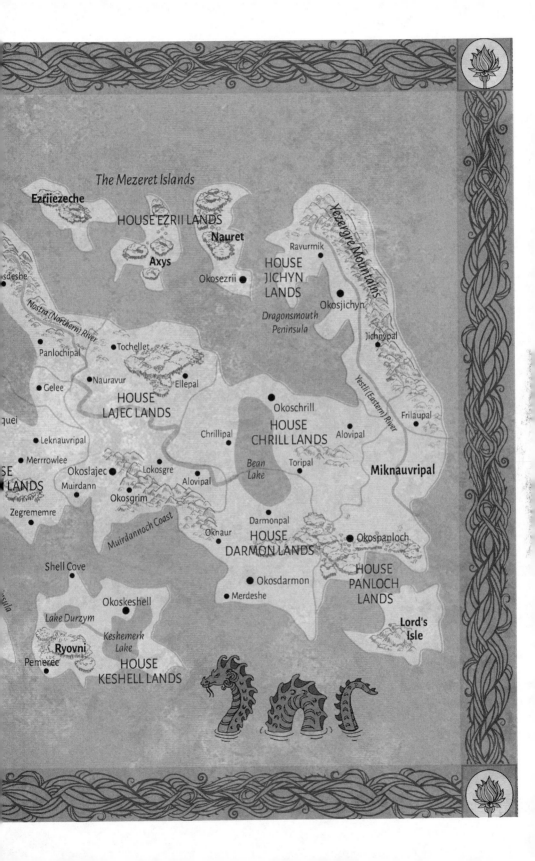

Before...

ONCE UPON A TIME, ON THE SURFACE OF THE SMALL BUT vibrant planet of Ullavise, in the nation of Laesi, The Sidhe shared their lands with humankind. While not overly fond of the creatures, they tolerated their presence, and some sidhe, those with the ability to compel the minds of lower creatures, chose to keep human pets. But over time, humans—as is their nature—rebelled and grew violent toward their elfin rulers.

Eventually the Royal Council of Sidhe Nations, troubled by increasingly aggressive humans and, to a lesser degree, concerned about the treatment of humans at the hands of sidhe people, sought a solution: they would sacrifice a piece of Laesi to the humans. In exchange for this, all humans must leave Laesi immediately and migrate to their new home. And so Es Muchator, the Great Change, came to Laesi.

The humans were given Villalu—a small portion of the Eastern Sea Lands of Laesi—as their own. And The Sidhe created a great magico-physical barrier, the greatest collective spell that their world had ever seen, to contain Villalu. Over time, this barrier came to be known simply as "The Border."

The Sidhe understood the purpose of The Border, of course, even those who didn't agree with the reasoning behind its construction. But human lives are short, and human memories are notoriously unreliable. After a handful of generations, the humans of Villalu had no memory of their former life beyond The Border.

As the centuries wore on, things began to change even more.

The Sidhe began exiling their criminals to a life beyond The Border, where they had to live in a land full of humans. With criminal sidhe among them, the humans had to learn methods of controlling The Sidhe. Humans learned that when bound in iron or drugged with verbena tincture, The Sidhe are nearly powerless. Armed with this knowledge, unscrupulous humans created a bustling slave trade in sidhe.

Villalu's wealthiest and most powerful people kept sidhe slaves as status symbols, and followers of the prophet Frilau began preaching that enslavement was the only way to save the souls of The Sidhe after death. Meanwhile, walled cities populated by sidhe in exile rose along The Border, and with them came a resurgence in the sidhe practice of keeping magically compelled humans as pets for their own amusement and pleasure.

Aside from the tiny republic of Khryslee, in which humans and sidhe managed to live in relative harmony, the two species seemed unable to coexist peacefully on Ullavise. And so The Sidhe's royal Council of Nations chose to simply turn a blind eye to all activity beyond The Border and adopted a strict policy of non-interference with the human government there.

And so it remained for fifty thousand years, with no sign that it would ever change.

But change it did. Change began with a sidhe slave, a servant, two princesses, a king, and a criminal, and now continues…

THE HEART OF ALL WORLDS, BOOK 2

the KING & the CRIMINAL

Charlotte Ashe

interlude press • new york

Copyright © 2016 Charlotte Ashe
All Rights Reserved
ISBN 13: 978-1-941530-86-3 (trade)
ISBN 13: 978-1-941530-87-0 (eBook)
Published by Interlude Press
http://interludepress.com

Book Design by Lex Huffman
Cover Design by CB Messer
Cover illustration by Sarah Sanderson
Map illustration by Sarah Sanderson and RJ Shepherd
10 9 8 7 6 5 4 3 2 1

interlude press • new york

For my dad.

My books may not have been your cup of tea, but I always knew how proud you were regardless; you told me whenever we shared a cup. I will forever drink tall glasses of chilled Tulsi Basil in your honor, and I will never stop doing my best to make you proud. Thank you for the gift of my weird and wandering mind, Dadster. I love you, and I miss you like hell.

A mighty flame followeth a tiny spark.

—Dante Alighieri

PROLOGUE

FIRAE SETTLED AT *B!Nauvriija*'s FEET, EYES FOCUSED ON THE offering he had brought with him. It was a branch of the *Lanafernaui*, the oldest known living tree in the Queendom. He had managed to sprout the sixteen varieties of blossom present in *B!Nauvriija*'s own woven crown from the branch, and it had been hard work. His powers of compulsion and summoning were a bit weak; his command of earth was mediocre at best, especially when using such a narrow anchor. But stretching himself and his own limitations was important. Especially for this Goddess.

The Sacred Weaver of Blossoms and Guardian of Trees was not an easy divinity to please. Her lessons were often stringent and difficult to navigate, and an offering that did not demonstrate his best work would not coax her to make things any easier for him.

He maintained his focus as the hallucinogen took effect. He did not let his eyes drift closed, but focused his energy on each blossom in turn, moving through them in the correct order before starting once again: setting the pattern, weaving his intent, over and over and over again, until the blossoms began to grow and multiply, reaching the cupped hands of the Goddess within the statue. Her eyes were alight with conscious wisdom by the time he raised his own eyes to meet them.

Still whispering the names of the blossoms, Firae stepped out of his body and faced her.

A silent question drifted to him from the eyes of the Goddess: *King Firae, First Child of Queen Gira of the Cloud Valley Feririar, what knowledge do you seek?*

Confirmation that he is the one, Firae replied. *That we will persevere, as trees intertwined, long after the frost of winter has carried away the fragile flower that captures his attention.*

"But blossoms *are* fragile flowers, Firae, are they not?" The voice behind him was unmistakable. "And the guardian of trees is also the weaver of blossoms. Perhaps they are not as incompatible as you might wish."

Firae's eyes widened, and he stared at the statue before him. Her eyes danced with something very like *amusement,* and, were it not blasphemy, he would have cursed her where she stood. *How—*

"Are you not even going to face me, my love?"

Firae turned slowly, hoping against all rationality that his ears had deceived him.

They had not. Before him stood Sehrys, barefoot and dressed in a wedding tunic, his wrists and ankles and ears and waist and throat adorned with a veritable rainbow of flowers.

Sehrys giggled, plucking one of the flowers from his belt and placing it behind Firae's ear. "Shall we go, then?" he asked, grasping Firae's hand to pull him along.

"What—I don't understand," Firae protested, though he allowed Sehrys to lead him into the bank of trees at the edge of the clearing.

"If you understood you would hardly need a *guide,* would you? Honestly, Firae."

Firae narrowed his eyes at his guide. There was something off about him, but he couldn't quite place it. It was Sehrys who was leading him, that much could not be mistaken, but he wasn't the same as—

"I'll race you," Sehrys whispered, bending close, and took off running with a joyful cry. Firae grinned and followed. It had been *so* long since he had seen this side of his betrothed.

And in the instant before the trees around them dissolved into a swirl of color, before billions of galaxies spread out before them and pulled Firae toward his own place in the Heart of All Worlds—in that instant, he finally understood.

When Firae found him there, sitting cross-legged in a spray of stars, Sehrys smirked. "You've gotten slow, old man."

"You—you're not him."

Sehrys cocked his head.

"What I mean to say is, you aren't Sehrys as he is now. You—you're Sehrys from before. Before he left for his first soul-walk all those years ago." Firae fought the painful swell in his chest. "Before he left *me*."

Sehrys's smile grew softer. "Perhaps not so slow after all," he conceded.

Firae swallowed. "I miss you so much," he whispered. He could not understand how he felt so heavy when his body was a million universes away.

"The Goddess heard your question." Sehrys's voice was gentle. "But she has one for you. Why is it, Firae, that you insisted upon nuptial soul-walks once again? He was ready to marry you without one. And surely you remember your last soul-walk, before you were meant to be married the first time. Six years isn't so terribly long between lovers, after all."

"I just wanted to be sure." Firae settled to face his guide. "So much has changed."

"And yet you refuse to face the biggest change of all." The guide held out his palm, passing the tiny light within it to Firae. As Firae took it into his own hand, a pulse shot through him, and a scene played out, clear as day: Within the Northern Tower, the lights of Brieden's cell flickered on and off. At the tower's base stood Sehrys. His eyes were like open wounds, his breaths came fast and hard, and his knuckles shone white against the frame of the outer door as he fought to keep himself from climbing the stairs. The desperation that radiated from his entire being was a punch to Firae's gut. He knew, without a doubt, that what he was seeing was real.

"Take it away," he ground out, his fists clenched, and he almost gave in and left the spirit-walk, forced his consciousness back into his body, and stormed the tower so he could tear apart the tiny, pathetic, inconsequential creature that had taken his Sehrys away from him.

"You know that it wasn't him," the guide said softly. "He didn't take me away from you. You do realize that, do you not?"

Real, physical tears stung Firae's eyes as he looked at the guide. "Before *him,* your heart was mine."

"Perhaps. But you also know that I am gone, and I am never coming back."

Firae closed his eyes. "He... is still you. He is still the same man."

Sehrys hummed. "He is and he is not. But do you truly believe that eliminating Brieden will bring him back to you? Turn him back into me?"

Firae opened his eyes and breathed deeply, casting his sight across the multiverse that swirled around him. It contained worlds in which Sehrys had never left, worlds in which they were happy, worlds in which time moved more slowly and it was not too late.

"I wish I could turn back the years," Firae murmured. "I still love him, even if he is you no longer. But if I could go back, stop him from leaving—" Firae sighed. "I miss the ease between us, the innocent sparkle in his eyes, the laughter. He laughs so little now. If only there were some way."

Sehrys cocked his head. "There is not. But there was. It was simply not the way you chose."

Firae stared at him. "What are you saying?"

"Why did you never look for me after I disappeared?"

"I... but I did! I sent envoys to the border cities. I did all that I could!"

"All that you could?" The guide's tone was neutral, but Firae could not help the frustration that rose in his own chest.

"What was I expected to do? The Non-Interference Doctrine—"

"Ah."

"Are you quite sure you're the Sehrys from *before?*" Firae muttered.

"I'm not truly Sehrys at all. You know that."

"I do." Firae sighed. "And unless I am mistaken, you are implying that I should have broken the very law that I have been entrusted to uphold."

"I have no opinion about what you should or should not have done. But I must ask you this: You are King Firae, Child of Queen Gira, descendent of Queen Tyzva the Liberator. Do you honestly mean to stand before me and say that you are helpless in the face of the *law?*"

"I am not helpless in the face of *anything*," Firae all but growled. "But had I gone in search of Sehrys, *truly* in search of him, I may not have survived. It would have meant leaving the Queendom without a ruler, alienating the Council, losing the respect of my people, facing sanctions upon my return, possibly even execution—"

"All of that is true. Now tell me, what did Brieden risk when he helped Sehrys escape his master?"

It was as if a large stone had been hurled against Firae's solar plexus, stealing all breath from his body. He opened his mouth to find no words upon his tongue.

The guide watched him with a neutral expression.

"It..." Firae was barely able to settle on a coherent reaction. *Brieden,* that lowly creature who had stolen Sehrys's heart away from Firae, that pathetic great wingless pixie who had touched Sehrys, held him, brought him the kind of pleasure that Sehrys had *never* sought with Firae, that *insect* of a man that he could not squash once and for all without losing Sehrys in the process—what could a being like that possibly know about risk? About love? About *anything* that mattered? He gritted his teeth. "It isn't the same."

"My question was not whether it is the same. My question was: What did he risk?"

Firae bit his lip against the vise that squeezed his heart. Even his own rage and prejudice could not completely obscure the truth.

"He risked everything," Firae whispered, and hung his head.

"Law is not inherent," the guide said gently. "Law is created by sentient beings in an attempt to bring reason to reasonless worlds. And like all things on the temporal planes, laws run their course. You have a choice, Firae."

Firae looked up at the guide, at the face of the man he loved more than any other in the world. "Every moment is choice," Firae recited. This was one of the most basic tenets of those who served the Sacred Weaver.

The guide smiled. "Yes. But I am referring to your life on a larger scale. You are at a crossroads, and the choice that lies ahead of you will determine the very fate of your world. Are you prepared for a glimpse of precisely what I mean?"

Firae nodded, his nerves alight with anticipation.

The guide rose to his feet and spread his arms wide. He threw his head back as light rushed forth from his hands, and before Firae could finish standing up to face him, Firae was assaulted by a wall of blinding light.

He saw a plethora of worlds, each a muted, spectral shadow of what might be—millions of tiny rainbows cast by the prism of the present moment. Two of the worlds were larger and brighter than all the rest. Everything moved very fast, and little was clear.

In one of the two brightest worlds, Sehrys was by his side. There was laughter and light. Sehrys cried in the moonlight far too often, and there was something in him that Firae could never quite reach. That world carried a constant ache, but the ache was offset by joy. Celebration. Lovemaking. Solace. *Children.*

It was a good life, even if Sehrys's eyes drifted too often in the direction of Khryslee, even if Firae slept alone too often, even if Firae's husband sometimes slept alone in a certain cell in the Northern Tower—a cell that Sehrys insisted remain empty and undisturbed at all times.

And in this world there was change. Sehrys was as fierce an advocate as he could possibly be, and the light dimmed in his eyes each time the Council overrode his proposals and dismissed his demands.

And then there was darkness. Something heavy settled over everything. And Firae knew, suddenly and inexplicably, that it was because The Border was gone and Villalu was gone with it.

In the second of the two worlds that glowed more brightly than the rest, there was heartache. There was pain and loneliness and crushing weight. But that was temporary, briefer than Firae could have imagined. And then there was… warmth and possibility, passion and fear, revolution and *risk*. There was Firae, the Child King, with a destiny stretched before him that could render him a hero. And there was still the possibility of joy, celebration, lovemaking, solace, *children*. There was a man whose eyes never lingered on the Northern Tower, but always on Firae.

The final outcome was less clear in this vision. He could remain a king. He could become a criminal. He could lose everything, or he could gain more than he ever imagined. This vision both beckoned him and filled him with terror.

And in both worlds he saw suffering: the suffering of humans and of sidhe; the torture and degradation that his own people turned their backs upon; the pockets of resistance rising up amongst the humans, who screamed for help until they were slaughtered and silenced by their own kind, ignored by the Queendoms of Laesi. He saw the true extent of his own power to do something about all of it. It came at a risk, but when had he become so risk-averse? When had that particular sort of confidence escaped him?

Sensing his line of thought, the guide led Firae away from the futures-that-could-be and back along the splintering path of his own life thus far, back to a moment that he rarely recalled but sharply remembered as it unfolded before him.

He saw himself as a young prince about eighty years ago, when the very shrine where his body now sat had been built. The original shrine to the Sacred Weaver in the Eastern Lands had been in Villalu, but it had been destroyed, along with other sidhe shrines, by a group of enraged humans. The shrine had been rebuilt in the Eastern Border Lands, and the Shrine of the Great Mother, the only one of the original eight that remained in Villalu, had been encased in a small border of its own to keep it safe.

The humans responsible for the destruction belonged to a religious cult that had gained prominence in Villalu over the years. The cult hated The Sidhe, were discovering ways to suppress sidhe power, and had helped the practice of sidhe enslavement to grow ever more prominent.

"Why are you letting them do this?" Firae had demanded, through tears of frustration. "You are the *queen*. You can go over there and make them stop!"

"It is not our place." His mother's voice had been far too calm. "It is our job to uphold and execute the law, not to disregard it when it is not to our taste."

"But you could go to the Council, you could *tell* them—"

"The Council knows, Firae. It is not our job to interfere with the governance of humans in their own lands."

"But they're *hurting* people! They're *enslaving* them!"

"It is also not our job to bring comfort to criminals." His mother's voice held an air of finality, but Firae was young and impulsive, and his blood ran with fire. He followed his mother as she walked away.

"They're not all *criminals*, though, Mother. There are innocent sidhe there, too. What about them?"

Gira turned to face him. "They know the risk they are taking. It is their choice to live with the consequences."

Firae jolted free of the vision; his mother's words rang in his ears.

Sehrys had spent six years as a slave. *He knew the risk that he was taking. It was his choice to live with the consequences.*

Firae felt sick.

He had loved his mother. He was her only child and had known no other parent. It hurt him to accept that perhaps, to some extent, she had been cruel. And perhaps, to some extent, he had allowed that very cruelty to seep into his own heart when he took the throne.

He thought of Sehrys, who stood with his hands braced against the door at the base of the Northern Tower, fighting to stop himself from climbing the stairs to his lover's cell. He thought of Brieden, how wide and bright and wet and desperate his eyes looked when Firae took Sehrys away from him. He thought of everything Sehrys had told him about what was happening along the Villaluan border.

And he realized, Nuptial Rite or no Nuptial Rite, this soul-walk hadn't been about Sehrys at all.

"Exactly," his guide confirmed, and Firae looked up, startled, at the change in voice. Before him stood his mother, just as he remembered her before her sudden death.

"You have more choices than you accept or acknowledge," she continued, beginning to fade even before Firae had the chance to drink her in.

"Don't leave," he whimpered, his eyes prickling.

"You don't need me." Cool and mistlike, she touched his hand.

"But what if I make the wrong choice?" He tried in vain to clutch her hand.

"There is no wrong choice. All worlds are born; all worlds die. Only the Heart of All Worlds is eternal. No choice you make can affect that."

And then she was gone.

Firae awoke at the foot of the statue of the Sacred Weaver, still chanting the names of the blossoms in *B!Nauvriija's* crown. He finished the chant; his voice was hoarse, his body heavy with exhaustion.

There was a flower behind his ear; he couldn't say how it had got there. He removed it and twirled it between his fingers, taking in the orange and gold shot through with green.

Firae turned his face to the east. The Border wavered in the distance.

Risk or security. A king or a criminal.

And for the first time since he had taken the throne, he truly considered his choices.

Chapter One

One Year Later

A rustle and too-loud whispers of tiny voices directed his attention upward, where three children with red knees and dirty feet watched him through the branches. When they spotted him looking back, they giggled and attempted to hide themselves amongst the foliage.

Tash chuckled. Between the younger Keshell siblings and the servants' daughters and sons, the palace was near to swarming with children. He headed for the tree, found purchase easily on the rough bark with his hands and bare feet, and climbed the trunk as fast as a cat. The children shrieked as he approached them.

"To what do I owe this pleasure?" Tash asked, settling himself on a branch facing Seleche, Brissa and Cliope's ten-year-old sister. Her younger brother Najet and the cook's son Raslee hid their faces behind her, though their sky-blue playsuits made them entirely visible from the neck down.

"Cliope said you can light things on fire," Seleche said.

"That's true," Tash agreed, pulling a leaf from a branch and eating it. "But not if they're too far away."

Seleche picked a leaf as well and made a face when she tasted it.

"What kind of stuff do you burn?" Raslee ventured. His cheeks went pinker.

Tash shrugged. "Anything that needs burning. Mostly I just make fire for heat and light when I need it, though."

"Could you burn this tree?" Seleche asked.

"I could, but I wouldn't want to. It's a nice tree, and I think we'd miss it, don't you?"

Seleche nodded.

"Could you burn down the whole castle?" Najet blurted, eyes alight.

Tash looked at the castle. "I don't think so. It's too big, and stone doesn't burn very well, at least not for me. But I know someone who might be powerful enough to do it."

This information seemed to cure whatever lingering nervousness the children had around him.

"Who?"

"Is he going to come here and burn it?"

"Why can't you burn it?"

"What would happen if you tried?"

Tash laughed. He had always liked children and, in his years as a teacher, he'd liked the younger ones best. They were excited and boisterous and so eager to learn that they *demanded* knowledge. "If I tried, it simply wouldn't work. My power isn't strong enough. But my..." *Friend?* Hardly friend, not really, but something like a friend, maybe. "The sidhe I know who could burn it is one of the most powerful elves in the world. But he wouldn't have any reason to burn the castle. He doesn't even live in Villalu. He lives on the other side of The Border."

"My mom said The Border is there so The Sidhe don't come and kill us," Raslee said from behind Seleche in a voice barely above a whisper. "She said that's why all sidhe on this side are slaves. To keep us safe from their magic."

"Tash isn't a *slave*," Seleche huffed, her tone that of a person burdened by her own wealth of knowledge. "And keeping slaves is evil. That's why my sisters are going to kill everyone who does it."

"It's not evil. The *Sidhe* are evil," Raslee argued, his eyes shifting toward Tash.

"Raslee, that's rude," Seleche snapped. "And if you think The Sidhe are evil, that actually makes *you* evil. I'm going to tell Cliope you said that, and she's going to have you executed."

"No, she won't," Tash interjected calmly when Raslee's eyes grew wide. "Your mother just believes what she's heard, Raslee, which is what everyone does when they don't understand something. But The Sidhe aren't evil. We're a lot like humans, actually. Some of us are good, and some of us are bad, and most of us are somewhere in between."

"Are you good?" Raslee ventured, eyes flitting between Tash and Seleche, who was scowling at him.

Surprised at the impact of the question, Tash took a steadying breath. "I'm probably one of those sidhe who are somewhere in between," he admitted. "But I'm trying to be good. That's why I'm helping Brissa."

"And because Brissa is queen of the whole human realm," Seleche added in a grand voice. She sat up straighter.

Tash smiled. "That too."

"Why aren't you a slave?" Najet blurted, and Tash couldn't help but laugh at the bold innocence of the question.

"I never got caught." Not entirely true, perhaps, but true enough. "Now, do you want to see some magic or don't you?"

At this, the children nearly fell from the tree in excitement. Tash held out his palm, and a small orange flame sprang to life in its center. It was simple enough to put on a little show, to make the flame rise to nearly a foot high before it shrank to the size of a bean, then divided itself into a dozen little flames weaving and dancing across his palm. The children fell silent, one by one, enraptured by the show of tiny lights.

"Tash, stop showing off for the children!"

With the flames still dancing in his cupped hand, Tash glanced down to find Cliope standing below. Her green-brown eyes sparkled with good humor. She had clearly had her hair trimmed that very morning; the tight black curls were cropped close to her scalp, and she was dressed in a loose, whisper-light ecru tunic and matching knee-length leggings. Her feet were clad in finely crafted cork sandals. Tash smiled at her.

It had been a more than a year since she found Tash and brought him into her fold, and nearly six months since their ship from mainland Villalu had arrived safely in Ryovni. Cliope had blossomed beneath the sun of her island home. It was still strange to see her so calm and rested, without bloodstained boots, protruding clavicles, or dirt-streaked cheeks.

"He's showing us his fire!" Seleche yelled. "Don't interrupt!"

Tash chuckled and allowed the fire to continue its dance. "You heard the lady, Cliope. I'm in the middle of an important demonstration."

"If you want fire, take the boys inside and light some candles, Seleche. Tash is needed."

"'Tash is needed,' is he?" Tash turned to the children and rolled his eyes, causing them to giggle. "If so, perhaps it would be wise to tell Tash what he is needed *for*."

Cliope heaved a loud sigh and addressed Tash by his full formal name. "Shall I grovel, O great *Tash Tirarth Valusidhe efa Lesette?* Perhaps craft a shrine to your brilliance and offer it a child sacrifice? Or *three?*"

"Mother said you're not supposed to joke about sacrificing us!" Seleche snapped. "It scares Najet!" The boy's eyes had indeed gone wide.

"Very well. No child sacrifices, then. I suppose I'll just have to tell you directly: Her Highness has summoned you. There is news from the southern coast that may be of some interest to you."

Tash snapped his hand closed. The fire dissipated without so much as a puff of smoke. The children made noises of protest all around him. "Lead the way," he said to Cliope.

BRISSA WAS SITTING AT THE TABLE ON THE BALCONY OUTSIDE HER chambers when Tash and Cliope arrived. Her chambers at Keshell castle were a stark contrast to those she had reclaimed from Dronyen in Miknauvripal. They were not as majestic, at least not objectively, but they held an undercurrent that Tash recognized from home—though less ornate, Keshell castle was certainly more lush. The castle was open to the outside air wherever possible, encouraging the cool mountain breeze to temper the near-constant heat of the lowlands, and thick flowering vines tumbled in from the walls outside. It didn't surprise Tash that Brissa's balcony was nearly twice the size of her sleeping chamber.

"Tash." Brissa's voice was warm as she rose to greet him, as if he were worthy of such regard from a queen. He cherished the way she had welcomed him into her fold with open arms, even if it still made him uncomfortable.

"Your Majesty." He greeted her with a deep bow before settling in the chair opposite her, where a place setting awaited him. Cliope took the chair to his right and immediately helped herself from the pot of fresh tea and platters of food at the center of the table. Tash eyed the fare appreciatively: the cheeses, chilled mussels, and smoked fish did not tempt him, but there were platters of mango and cherimoya, a large bowl of fresh tender leaves and sea vegetables in a rainbow of colors, and a large number of *karanoviches*, a Ryovnian treat Tash had grown to love. They were made of a sticky dried fruit paste rolled in crushed roasted nuts and drizzled with nectar of *novichene*, a rubbery plant that grew in Ryovni's drier areas.

"Thank you for coming to see me," Brissa said, settling back to her breakfast. In the morning light, Tash was struck afresh by her extraordinary beauty. The sun at her back made the glossy black curls that cascaded to her waist glow almost as brightly as her nearly black skin, and her deep green-brown eyes, the same color as her twin's, shone like polished jewels. Her long frame, while still lithe, had filled out slightly with the comforts of Ryovni at hand, and the subtle muscles in her slender arms had grown nearly as pronounced as Cliope's after many hours of sword practice. She wore a fine but simple pale green dress in a gauzy material, held up by two thin shoulder straps and belted loosely at her hips with a dark green sash.

"There has been a strange development on the south coast of Ryovni," Brissa continued, "and you may be the only one who can help us."

"I will certainly do what I can, Your Highness, but if my luck in opening the door is anything to go by, you may be mistaken on that front."

"You'll get the door open," Cliope insisted, popping a stuffed sournut leaf into her mouth. "We haven't really been here long in the grand scheme of things, Tash."

"Cliope is right," Brissa agreed. "But this is a problem of an entirely different nature. I have word from Pemerec that a man washed up on the beach there three days ago. He seems to have survived a shipwreck, though the bits of the ship that have washed up are like nothing we have seen before." Brissa took a deep breath. "And he's a sidhe."

Tash nearly choked on his mouthful of clothweb and sournut leaves.

"Is... has anyone spoken to him?" he managed to ask after he'd swallowed.

Brissa shook her head. "He is unconscious. All who have seen him are amazed he survived at all, but he won't wake up. And he appears to be languishing."

Tash braced his hands on the table. "What have they done for him?"

"They're doing their best to keep him warm; he's staying in the healer's cottage in the village where they found him."

"He shouldn't be in a bed or inside a human house." Tash's shoulders went tense at the mere idea, no matter how well-intended it may have been. He stood and paced the balcony. "We should send word immediately with a few basic instructions—first of all, he needs to be outside. They can lay him in the garden; it doesn't have to be anything special. He'll need to be stripped of his clothes." Tash braced his hands on the waist-high stone railing at the balcony's edge and looked out over the palace gardens. To find oneself cut off from all that can heal, like a sun-loving plant locked away in a pitch-black cupboard—the humans didn't understand. They *couldn't*.

Tash turned to face Brissa. "Tell them they can hide him from view however they like, if their human modesty requires it, but his bare skin *must* be in direct contact with the ground. And after breakfast I shall journey to his side."

Brissa smiled and waved at her handmaiden, who sat at a little table off to the side at work on her own breakfast. "Gejene, please fetch me a quill and some parchment. I must send instructions to Pemerec." She turned her attention back to Tash. "Thank you, Tash, I was hoping you might be amenable to a trip south."

"I can't promise anything," Tash responded, settling back into his chair. "My mother was a healer in our feririar, so I have learned some methods that can restore health when a sidhe's magic is depleted, but it may not be enough."

"I understand. Thank you, Tash."

REDEMPTION WAS A HARD GOAL TO PURSUE.

Tash wasn't entirely sure it was possible; he was under no illusions that a few acts of kindness and bravery could erase the damage he had done: the life he had taken, the humans he had treated as playthings. Most of those humans had surely been reduced to no more than *actual* playthings once they had moved on from his care. Few if any got their lives back or even their identities.

Nothing could fix it. Tash had no plans to try.

But if he was lucky, he had a good few centuries left. And even if he managed to get that door open, he might spend all of those centuries trapped in Villalu. He may as well do his best to remove suffering where he found it rather than exploiting or contributing to it. He may as well pretend to be good, because it was all pretend. Tash was not a good person.

Though he did genuinely like the Keshells, he had sworn his allegiance to them, in no small part, in order to save his own hide. They offered him a chance to live as comfortable a life as possible while trapped inside The Border. He wasn't enslaved, and he wasn't subject to the trickery and desperation of the border cities. He was lonely amongst all these humans, and the mysterious sidhe on the south coast of Ryovni might represent the companionship of another of his kind or possible competition for his coveted spot as the sidhe advisor to the rightful—if not official—queen of Villalu.

Tash needed to know. And he needed to know immediately.

Ryovni was not large, and most of its roads were well tended. The royal contingent that led the way as he and Cliope rode southwest to Pemerec ensured that their path was clear and that any onlookers were kept to the sidelines.

Ryovni was different from what Tash had seen of mainland Villalu; the pace was a bit slower, the air quite a bit hotter, and the cool sea breeze nearly constant. The greenery was lush, and trees he had never seen before bore delicious fruits of nearly every color.

Most of the homes and buildings they passed as they rode through villages were built of white stone or adobe and washed in pale blue, green, or lavender pigments, which reflected the aesthetic of the island's ruling House. The air was salty and fresh, and skinny boys and girls ran through the village squares on calloused bare feet to watch the royal procession. They were long-limbed and curly-haired; their skin color ranged from deep brown to midnight black.

There was a lightness here he had never felt in mainland Villalu, a careless joy in not just the children, but in many of their parents as well. The women of Ryovni wore weapons on their backs and smiles on their faces. And though Ryovnian women rarely looked even the tiniest bit elfin, the sight made him homesick for Laesi like nothing else he'd experienced since his exile.

They reached Pemerec just past nightfall. Tash insisted upon seeing the patient. The man was staying in a small cottage; the image carved into the rough wooden door, of a flower growing out of a cupped human hand, identified it as the home of the village healer. The man who opened the door had a neatly trimmed beard flecked with gray, and wore simple but neatly pressed clothes. His eyes lingered on Tash before he introduced himself as Dr. Lasceli.

The doctor waved them through the house and into the back garden without even offering a pot of tea; he seemed quite aware of the urgency of the situation.

Tash and Cliope inhaled sharply at the scene that greeted them.

The sidhe lay on his stomach in the soft grass with a thin blanket draped over his buttocks and back. His features were illuminated by the moons, and he was—

He was lovely: long dark hair and full pink lips; skin pale but warm-hued, smooth as marble; sweet, lean muscles. The boy—man, he *was* a man, but he couldn't have been one for long—was as perfect as a sculpture. Tash could barely breathe at the sight of him.

"Well," Cliope whispered on an exhale. "That—that is a good-looking man."

Tash laughed softly and looked to Dr. Lasceli, who nodded his assent for Tash to approach the other sidhe.

Tash walked to the unconscious elf and bent down beside him. He knew nothing about the man; he could be friend, foe, or someone to whom Tash would be indifferent if they'd met under different circumstances. But he was sidhe and he was in need of assistance, and Tash—

Well. Tash was different now. At least he was trying to be.

Tash settled cross-legged in the damp grass beside the other elf and took the man's cool, limp hand in his own. Up close, the man was even more striking. He looked younger than Tash, perhaps by fifty years or even a century, and his dark hair was a glossy near-black. His eyelashes were equally black, sweeping to dramatic lengths against his fine cheekbones. His long, slender ears were dotted with small hoops and cuffs of copper and silver all the way up to their points. Some of the earrings were connected to one another with tangled chains.

Tash closed his eyes and inhaled deeply. He could feast upon the other man's beauty like the greedy, touch-starved celibate he was, or he could do what he could to save the man's life.

Centering his own power, Tash released the man's hand and checked the four points of his body.

His midsection gave no response, which didn't surprise Tash. If the man wielded water, being submerged would probably have revived him, even if he had lost consciousness before falling into the water. His forehead pulsed warm but not hot—probably low-grade compulsion, healing, or telekinesis, but not the center of his power, unless he wielded an even weaker expression of the Common caste than Tash himself. If this was the man's only point of power, his chances of survival were slim.

Tash moved his hands to the tops of the other man's feet and felt warmth again, which was a relief—two points of power made his survival that much more likely, after all.

Tash wet his lips nervously before proceeding to the final point. He hadn't dared to hope that the one way in which he was most likely to help would be available to him, but as he gently lifted the man's shoulder so that he could slip his hand below the sidhe's chest and hold it over his heart, Tash's entire body gave a jolt and he gasped. His eyes slipped closed at the heat that shot up his arm and into his own heart.

Fire. The true center of this man's power was, in fact, the only power Tash could truly understand. The man drew a deep breath at the contact, and his entire body shuddered.

Tash exhaled in relief as he pulled his hand away from the other man's chest lest the man's greedy and depleted power center drain Tash into unconsciousness as well.

Tash looked up at Cliope and Dr. Lasceli. "I think I can save him. I'll need to stay with him for at least a day or two, possibly more, and I'll need access to outdoor space, someplace where I can safely set up a fire."

"My family has a holiday cottage nearby," Cliope said. "We can use the gardens there. Perhaps the good doctor could spare a carriage?"

"Of course, my lady," Dr. Lasceli assured her in his deep, quiet voice. "I do have a carriage and I would be happy to drive our guest to Marble Point."

"There is no need for that, Dr. Lasceli," Tash responded, rising to his feet. The doctor smiled at him, but his eyes remained nervous. "You have done more than enough, and I assure you that if this man does survive he will owe it in part to your attentions. But it is late, and you should sleep. I can carry him on horseback. The life force from the horse and me will be better for him than a carriage."

"Life force, hmmm?" Cliope murmured quietly as Tash bent to lift the other sidhe into his arms. "Is that what it's called?"

Tash rolled his eyes. "I suppose you don't think this might be an inappropriate situation for vulgarity?"

"I suppose that you don't think I noticed the way you looked at him like he was the main dish at the Feast of Spring?" she shot back. Tash stood up and wrapped the blanket completely around the other elf. The man wasn't light, but he was a bit smaller than Tash, and his whole body shifted to press against the warmth of Tash's chest.

Tash didn't know who this man was or why he was here. But that didn't matter. Not yet.

All that mattered to Tash, as he rode through the darkened streets with the stranger's warm body pressed against his own, was that he was going to keep him safe. He had to.

He didn't know why, but it seemed it might be one of the most important things he would ever do.

CHAPTER TWO

"*Y*OU AREN'T HONESTLY PROPOSING THAT YOU CROSS *THE BORDER* alone, *Firae. That would be madness.*"

"*Well, what else do you recommend? I certainly can't cross with a legion of guards. The point is to* remove *the influence, not to enhance it.*"

Firae blinked his eyes open. His vision instantly went fuzzy from the throbbing in his skull. "What—" Wincing, he stopped himself cold. That horrible croak surely couldn't be his voice?

"Shhhh…" The voice was calm, soft, mellow. "Don't push. Just take your time." He felt a cool hand on his forehead.

Firae sighed softly and let himself slip back into his dream.

"*Villalu is my responsibility. It has always been the concern of the Eastern Border Lands. I can bypass the mess along the border cities if I travel by boat. It is the only solution.*"

Firae looked around the room at the Council. The queens of Laesi, and a few kings like himself, watched him impassively. He had never been so acutely aware of his youth, of the fact that he was younger, by centuries, than all other heads of state assembled in the hall. He squared his shoulders and met each and every eye in the room. They had reason enough to doubt him. He would not give them further cause.

"*And if you don't return?*"

Firae swallowed; his throat went dry. He did not let his voice or his eyes falter. "*Then you shall do what is necessary,*" *he said.*

Firae curled his fingers into the… grass? Yes, that did seem to be grass beneath him. The cool hand returned to his face, and he leaned into the touch, but winced at the slight movement of his head.

And suddenly he realized that he should have left for Villalu days ago. Why hadn't Runa woken him? Was it too late already? Had the Council—

Firae gave a sharp cry of pain as he attempted to sit up; his arms managed just enough shaky leverage to lift him up and then allow him to crash to earth again. "The ship—" he croaked, trying to remember.

The mellow voice he couldn't place said something about a broken ship, but the words seemed buried beneath a layer of earth. He concentrated, trying to understand, and found himself utterly exhausted by the effort.

"Ready the ship," Firae whispered, drifting out of consciousness.

"What are those?"

"Seed loaves. Brieden made them. They're quite delicious, and they keep for a long while if you would rather not stop to eat."

Firae willed himself not to throw the blasted seed loaves to the ground and stomp on them like a petulant child who had missed a nap. Firae was mature. He was understanding. He had told Sehrys to go to Brieden. He had *insisted.*

So why, precisely, did hearing Sehrys speak Brieden's name with such breathy reverence set Firae's blood to an angry boil?

He accepted the loaves. "Thank you, Sehrys."

Sehrys tilted his head, studying Firae. "Are you sure you want to go to the Western Isles alone? That's a long journey to take without any company."

"I will be fine, Sehrys," Firae insisted with a smile; his heart was warmed by the evidence of Sehrys's affection. It might not be the variety of affection he preferred, but it was affection nonetheless. He would take it.

"Sehrys…" He spoke the name so softly he did not even hear himself. He didn't know if he had done more than move his lips to make the sound. Sehrys… Sehrys would have read his letter by now. He would have learned the truth, except… except that didn't make any sense; Firae had not yet left for Villalu.

Had he?

A loud crack and a blast of unnatural lights... something heavy and large tearing through the floor of his ship, flinging him into the cold, roiling sea...

Firae wasn't aware of the sounds he was making until he realized that someone was whispering words of comfort to him: the someone with the sweet, mellow voice; a someone who smelled wonderful and had strong arms wrapped around him; a someone who made it clear that Firae was dry and warm and *safe*.

He slipped back into unconsciousness.

"HERE YOU ARE, MY LOR—" THE WOMAN STOPPED HERSELF AT THE look on Tash's face. "Mister—that is—um—"

"Just Tash is fine," Tash assured her, accepting his freshly bagged purchase. "Mr. Tash if you prefer, I suppose."

She nodded, seeming relieved. "Mr. Tash, then. Thank you for stopping in."

Ryovni may have been a vast improvement on mainland Villalu, but it was still a monarchy and a much different sort of monarchy than the one in which Tash had grown up. Since he was an honored guest of the royal family, few of the tradespeople he had interacted with seemed to feel comfortable addressing him by his first name.

Tash slipped the bag of dried herbs into his satchel as he left the little shop. His stomach constricted when the smell of cooking meat from vendors along the main street assailed his senses.

He was in the heart of Pemerec, a small but bustling community on the southwestern coast of Ryovni. It was crisscrossed with narrow cobblestone streets. The salty tang of the sea was a constant presence in the air; the sound of gulls made a ubiquitous backdrop to the cozy community. It reminded Tash of the feririar in which he had grown up. It was the sort of place where families lived for generations; where choices were restricted but love and support were ample; where packs of children ran about in a manner that might appear wild and unruly to an outside observer while, in reality, every adult they passed had some of their attention on those children.

Tash never thought he would yearn so deeply for a place he had fought so hard to escape.

He hastened down the road, away from the smell of street vendors' crab stew and clamcakes and sausages, from the rows of shops, and the little school with tiny, curious faces popping up at the windows as he passed.

Tash whistled to himself as the buildings thinned around him and the sound of gentle waves replaced that of human voices. He moved to the side of the road to allow a horse-drawn cart to pass him and considered removing his shoes to walk barefoot in the grass beside the road. It would be such a relief—humans clearly did not understand how it felt when one's bare skin pressed against the anchors of the natural world. The fire beneath his skin didn't throb as vehemently as it did in others; his powers were small, and he knew it. But when he let the energy flow through him, it lit up his nerves and brought him to life. It didn't throb, but it did hum.

But—the humans would think him strange, even stranger than they thought him already. And even in Ryovni, where Brissa's rule was accepted absolutely, even here, his association with the Keshells clearly made some people ill at ease. The looks cast his way were more likely to hold fascination than suspicion, but the suspicious looks were there nonetheless. And the last thing Tash wanted to do was make things difficult for the Keshells.

The street sloped downward sharply about an eighth of a mile before the beach, and the already-narrowed road split into two paths that were narrower still. One led directly to the beach, and the other faded from cobblestone to packed earth as it wound along the edge of a cliff that overlooked the ocean.

He rounded the corner and was struck anew by the beauty of the house at the end of the path. Modest by royal standards but lavish by any other, the house—known as Marble Point to the people of Ryovni—was three stories high and built of wood and pale blue polished marble. From nearly every room that faced the sea, balconies jutted over the lip of the cliff, above the crashing waves.

Once past the gate, Tash walked around the house to the little garden beyond the main drawing room. The man was there, sprawled on his stomach in a patch of sunlight. He appeared to have fallen into a peaceful sleep.

"He was a bit agitated earlier, My Lo—Mr. Tash." Eshessa smiled at Tash from the rose bush she was pruning. Eshessa was one of the few year-round house staff who lived at Marble Point tending to the minimal housekeeping needed, but mostly to the gardens, which flourished. Keeping an eye on the mystery sidhe while Tash went into town was hardly an expected addition to her duties, but it had been her idea, since she would be in the garden. Tash had been nervous at first, but when the sidhe awoke he would hardly be in any condition to pose a threat.

"Yelled a little in his sleep. Tried to sit up again," Eshessa continued, pulling off her heavy work gloves and setting them aside as she rose to her feet and approached Tash. She was a short, plump woman of not-quite middle age and always wore her hair pulled back into a tight bun. She was one of the few humans Tash knew who'd seemed almost immediately comfortable in his presence.

Tash patted his satchel. "I picked up some herbs that should quiet his mind while he heals," he said. "Thank you, Eshessa. Would you mind looking after him for just a bit longer while I prepare the tea?"

"My pleasure, Mr. Tash. I need to finish the rose bushes anyhow, so it really is no bother."

Tash thanked her, already beginning to feel his own mind quiet in the simple security of being at that house, away from all the humans who looked at him like a spectacle, back to the man he was tending, the lovely man with the glossy black hair and full, rosy lips, who could be anyone at all, but who would most certainly not look at Tash as anything more or less than a fellow person.

Tash prepared the tea, hoping that the necessary substitutions he'd made wouldn't limit its effectiveness too severely. But lavender shared many properties with *walwasha* blossoms, and sandalwood *should* produce calming effects similar to those of the slatewood bark his mother had always used.

Tash set the tea beside the sleeping sidhe in the grass and pulled leaves from one of the giant bamboos that lined the outer edge of the garden. He sat and pulled the other man into his arms, thus lifting him enough to allow him to eat and drink. The man came to, still at least a good night's sleep away from true presence of mind, and smiled up at Tash. "Your eyes are like his," the man murmured.

Tash smiled. "Like whose?"

The man closed his eyes and hummed. "Sehrys."

Tash considered him. It was the third time he'd mentioned the name, and, though it wasn't a *common* name, it was hardly unique. The chance that the Sehrys this man referred to was the same Sehrys Tash knew was beyond improbable—unless, of course, it was not a matter of probability, but rather one of significance.

Coincidence is nothing less than the Gods whispering in our ears. The echo of his mother's voice was almost audible, it was so strong. Tash had never been particularly religious, but he had experienced things in his own soul-walks that had placed him firmly beyond skepticism.

And… more than that. In the moment—in the *precise* moment that Tash chose to ally himself with Sehrys and Brieden, to help them even when it meant destroying the only protection he'd known since his exile, in that moment, Tash had felt a shift, a clear sense that he had chosen a path that mattered, that if another world existed in which he had chosen differently, that world would end up different at its very core.

But in this life, on this path, he had settled in Lekrypal, unsure what he was going to do, where he could possibly fit, and Cliope had found him. Cliope had found him because Sehrys had sent her. And Cliope, cocky, warm, confusing, hubristic child-warrior that she was, had begged him to help her change the world. She and her twin, barely more than children, were charging headlong into battle against the established ruling family as if it were a thrilling game.

The thing was, it was a game they appeared to be winning. And Tash could not only help them do that, he could help them change the game altogether.

He could help them shatter the cage that enslaved them all.

And if this man knew Sehrys, if that were truly the case, couldn't it be a sign?

The man curled into Tash's lap and coughed softly. His lungs sounded much better already.

"Can you drink this for me?" Tash murmured, holding the cup of lukewarm tea to the man's lips. The man managed a few tentative sips before raising his own hand to tilt the cup farther as he gulped it down.

The man licked his lips, and Tash attempted to feed him some leaves.

"They're bamboo. Tender, easy to digest. If you haven't had them before, they're delicious."

The man ate a few leaves, but he didn't appear to have much of an appetite. Apparently exhausted by his tiny meal, he fell asleep before Tash could convince him to take more.

Tash rose to his feet. If the tea helped as it should, the man should sleep through the night and awake the following day. He would be a bit disoriented, but once he was truly healed that should dissipate. At least Tash could make sure the man had some proper comforts when he awoke.

Tash wasn't sure where this man had been journeying from, but he did know that he was a sidhe, and sidhe are particular about their hair. One's hair is one's pride, after all, even if one has nothing else in the world. And this man's hair was a tangled, salt-encrusted mess.

Tash only needed to ask Rasha, one of the chambermaids, for bathing supplies, and before he knew it he was stumbling beneath the mountain of balms, soaps, lotions, and creams she had pressed on him. The cook and her assistant followed him into the garden with folded towels and two tubs of water, and the whole house seemed strangely aflutter over the simple request. It was clear that Marble Point was not a house that saw much activity, and Tash imagined that the mysterious guest was the most exciting thing that had ever happened here.

Tash washed the man's body, avoiding any direct touch of his private areas out of respect, but flushing hot at his proximity to said areas, especially when the man grew a little hard when Tash ran a wet cloth over his thighs. Tash massaged lotion into the man's skin, then washed the man's hair before working a thick, moisture-rich paste into the tangles. He slowly, gently, painstakingly combed out all the snarls. Tash hummed to himself as he rinsed the comb, thus allowing the paste to do its work, when a strange shape caught his eye. A strand of the man's black hair was arranged in an intricate pattern along the back of his neck. Tash carefully ran his thumb over the area, wiping away the hair paste that covered it.

He gasped even before the pattern was revealed. He knew what it was. No elf born in Laesi could possibly *not* know what it was.

It wasn't hair. It was black ink, directly below the hairline on the back of his neck.

It was a tattoo: a broad, short *lackente* tree whose branches bore the flowers of all ten Queendoms, reaching up until they disappeared into the man's hairline, and which was stacked atop an identical tree. The roots of the upper tree morphed into the branches of the lower tree.

The significance of the tattoo was not lost on Tash.

THE OCEAN WAS NEARLY INVISIBLE BENEATH THE NIGHT SKY, BUT TASH stared at it regardless. What little time he had spent in his assigned bedchamber since arriving in Pemerec had mostly been spent on the balcony, gazing at the sea and listening to the waves crash against the rocks far below. It soothed him, connected him to the world in a way he hadn't experienced for many years.

"How is our guest faring?" Tash started at the voice. He had been far too lost in thought to hear Cliope approach him.

"Better, I think," Tash answered as Cliope joined him at the balcony's railing. "The tea seems to have helped. I imagine he'll be lucid by tomorrow evening if he sleeps well tonight."

"That ship," Cliope began, "I've never seen anything like it. We don't have all the pieces, but those we do—they fused together when we held them side by side. It was as if they were mending themselves."

Tash smiled. "A living boat. He definitely came from Laesi, then. Sidhe don't like dead things standing between us and the lifestream of the world."

"*Dead* things? Such as—"

"Wood, leather, smelted metals." Tash shrugged. "Boots, even. At least the sort of boots one can procure in Villalu."

Cliope shook her head. "Amazing. I should like to see the Faerie Lands before I die. Living boats, and living *boots,* houses made of trees, castles made of flowers, beautiful sidhe men as far as the eye can see—"

Tash laughed. "There are plenty of beautiful human men in Ryovni."

Cliope waved a hand. "I suppose. But they all seem to want wives who will tend their houses and bear them broods of squalling children. I do not get the sense that sidhe men expect such things of their women."

"True. I think very few sidhe men would ever call a lover 'my woman,' in fact."

"Is it because they all prefer men? Or has it just been my tremendous luck to only meet sidhe men of your persuasion so far?" Cliope turned to lean against the railing with the sea at her back and her arms crossed over her chest.

Tash turned to face her. "You really are tremendously lucky. Plenty of sidhe men prefer women, but those of us who prefer men are undeniably handsomer."

Cliope's expression—surprised, but earnestly accepting of what he'd just said—made Tash fight back a laugh. "Really?" she asked, eyes wide.

"No. But—well, I wouldn't say that a strict preference for one's own sex is more common amongst The Sidhe than amongst humans. The majority of sidhe have no strict preference one way or the other, though they may lean a bit toward one type of person. I do wonder if humans are perhaps the same, and that it is only the restrictions you place upon yourselves that make it seem otherwise."

"Perhaps," Cliope said. "It isn't as if Brissa has had any trouble finding lovers, after all."

"That she has not." Tash had rarely known anyone to take as many lovers as Brissa seemed to, though his knowledge of the sexual appetites of queens was very limited.

"So... this sidhe, whatever his persuasion, his powers are like yours?"

"His powers are stronger and more varied than mine, but we both hold fire at our power centers."

"And that means you can blend your powers!" Cliope swung around to face him head-on. She seemed very proud of herself for remembering this particular tidbit from Tash's teachings.

Tash nodded and turned to look out over the sea. "In theory, if he is amenable to doing so, then yes."

"But that's perfect! The door—"

"Yes. The door. If it really is just a matter of needing enough raw power, I believe that he and I could likely get it to open."

Cliope frowned. "You don't sound excited at the prospect."

"It isn't—" Tash looked out over the black sea and considered. "His presence here is good for—for you, for Brissa, for Villalu. But for me— well. I'm not so sure anymore."

"Anymore?"

"He has a tattoo. On the back of his neck."

"All right..."

"Tattoos hold deep significance in sidhe culture. We live for a long time, and objects can wear out or get lost. Tattoos denote something significant that is intended to be permanent. Like... like marriage." Tash's hand went to his chest to touch the scar there, all that remained of just such a tattoo on his own body. "Or one's station in life, if it is of a significant and permanent nature. That man... he has the royal tattoo. I still don't know precisely who he is, but he is royalty, *born* royalty. And the fact that a sidhe royal has crossed into Villalu is unprecedented, especially this far from the shrine of The Mother." Tash lowered the hand that had lain over his marriage scar, and pushed back thoughts of the invisible mark on the back of his own neck, the one that ensured he would never return to Laesi.

Cliope was quiet for a long moment. "This could actually be a good thing. A very good thing. We didn't manage to convince Sehrys to stay, but this could be almost as good."

Tash fought not to flinch. The words weren't meant to be hurtful, but the intent didn't erase the sting. He couldn't deny that she was right, after all; *Tash* couldn't be considered almost as good as Sehrys because he wasn't. He wasn't even close.

"For you, yes. But he will want to know how I came to be here, living amongst you. And if he discovers that I am a criminal in exile, it is likely he will not wish to associate with me." Tash chewed his lip; his stomach sank as he realized the impact that knowledge could have, not just on him but on the Keshells. "Or with you, come to think of it, for allying yourself with someone like me. The last thing I wish to be is a liability. Perhaps it would be better if—"

"Perhaps it would be better if you stopped saying ridiculous things. You are not a liability to us, Tash, and you never will be. And if this man can't see that, royal or not, he can just find all the pieces of his ship and let them meld together and be on his way home."

"His ship will die before he can do that," Tash replied with a shrug, as a tiny smile tugged at the corners of his mouth. "It's been torn up and on dry land for too long. But I appreciate the sentiment."

"Poor ship," Cliope said with a sigh. "But—you do have our loyalty, Tash. I hope you understand that."

Tash frowned. "I understand that it is true, but I can't say I understand why. The things I've done—"

"A man is helpless to influence his past; is it not unfair to judge him by that against which he is helpless? I should find it wiser to judge a man by the progress of his choices, so that he may walk free from the shackles of his

past and shine a light upon the eternal present moment," Cliope recited. Tash tilted his head in silent question, and she smiled. "Kashlet Giroc. A Villaluan poet and philosopher from Delazesh in the Isles of Sheevalu."

"He is very kind," Tash muttered, turning his attention to the invisible sea.

"He is also right. And you don't know that that man in the garden thinks any differently."

Tash turned toward Cliope and raised an eyebrow. "You have clearly never met a sidhe royal."

"Well, how many have you met?"

Tash took a deep inhalation of the crisp ocean air. He curled his left hand into a fist at his side; the invisible mark on his palm pulsed as he remembered the last time he had stood in the presence of sidhe royalty. The mark was not a tattoo in the traditional sense; it held no ink, and its significance was nothing to celebrate. Instead, it was his silent, constant jailer, a thick block of immutable magic that kept him trapped inside The Border, no matter how he might try to escape; it would destroy him if he tried to cross that barrier.

"Just a few," he responded, and moved to retreat into his room. "And that was more than enough."

THE FIRST THINGS FIRAE UNDERSTOOD WERE THE SIMPLEST. THE AIR was warm, and the breeze was cool; the grass was damp and soft; the air smelled of salt; and a lone bird pierced the quiet with a shrill cry.

Firae opened his eyes. It seemed as if it took a century of hard work, but he managed to blink them open entirely, and survey what he could manage to see without moving any other part of his body.

The sun had either just set or was about to rise; he could see the dim blue shape of his own hand sprawled in the grass beside his face and a shrub a few feet beyond that. Firae concentrated on not allowing his eyes to slide closed for more than a blink and on gathering the energy to assess where he was and what had happened.

Of two things he was entirely certain: He was completely naked, and he was someplace he had never been in his entire life.

The sky slowly grew lighter. Firae experimented with moving his fingers. This progressed to his hands, then his arms, and then—in a feat of incredible effort—he managed to roll himself onto his back.

Firae experimented with moving his feet and legs as he rolled his head slowly from side to side. The muscles in his neck and legs screamed in both pain and relief.

By the time he managed to rise to his feet, hobble on shaking legs to the nearest tree, and brace himself against it, the sun was beginning to rise.

Firae leaned back against the tree. His body felt better second by second, and he breathed deeply. He was in a garden, which was adjacent to a strange-looking structure. The structure appeared to have been built by stacking large pieces of stone together; the windows and doors were apparently crafted of dead tree-flesh that had been artificially colored. Strips of dead tree, carved into something like spikes and painted the same unnatural pale blue as the door on the building, were laced together in a circle around the garden.

Firae dug his fingers into the papery bark of the tree behind him, taking slow, measured breaths and willing his heart not to pound. He struggled to clutch the last thing he remembered. He had been planning to leave Laesi, he was *going* to leave Laesi—

"Are you sure you don't want me to come along? I've always wanted to see the human lands. I hear the ladies—"

"No, Jaxis. This isn't a holiday, and there is no need to risk the safety of more people than is necessary." Firae stepped into the little green boat and turned to face Jaxis on the shore. *"What I need for you is to make sure that the Queendom stays in one piece while I am gone."*

Jaxis snorted. "You certainly came up with an interesting choice of leadership in your absence if your wish is that the Queendom remain in one piece."

Firae smiled. "They are going to work beautifully together. Trust me. Just please promise me you will actually deliver the message straightaway this time."

Jaxis promised without so much as a glint in his eye, and then Firae was off. He ran his hand down the stem at the center of the boat. The stem was paper-barked and brown, like an impossibly tall and sturdy sapling, and it shivered before unfurling one enormous leaf, both gossamer-thin and as strong as stone. Its sail in place, the boat knew where it was going. It was compelled to its water-soaked roots to bring him as close as possible to the one who threatened es lemeddison rubrio.

Firae watched the sun rise over Yestralekrezerche as his little boat moved swiftly away; he watched until his lands were vague shapes on the horizon. He gazed back for a long, long time before he finally turned around and faced The Border.

Now the sun rose, and it was wrong.

The sky was muted and opaque, as if filtered through frosted glass. The pinks and purples and oranges of the sunrise were lovely, but they were strange.

Everything about this place was strange.

Seconds before he heard the humans, everything clicked into place: the sky, the dwelling, the dyed tree-flesh, the boat—*I was in that boat for days, I remember*—and it wasn't enough time to get his bearings. It wasn't enough time to *think,* to evaluate who they were and whether or not they appeared hostile. Everything was strange and wrong and painful and overwhelming, so the very second they came into view—two of them at first—Firae acted.

Tash and Cliope were already on their way to the garden when they heard the screams, and both broke into a run.

The entire garden was ringed in fire. The flames were knee-high, and inside the burning circle were Eshessa and her assistant Petine. Eshessa was soaked from head to toe; Petine clutched an empty water bucket in white-knuckled hands. Half of the hair on Eshessa's head seemed to be burnt off, but other than that—at least from Tash's vantage point—she seemed unhurt, though both women looked too pink in the face.

The heat rolled in heavy waves, and not just from the ring of fire along the perimeter of the garden. A column of fire, standing taller than the house, was wrapped around the fig tree at the center of the garden. Tash didn't need to guess who was inside.

"Fill a bucket from the well," Tash yelled over his shoulder to Cliope as he charged toward the outer ring of flames. "And hurry!"

Cliope was halfway to the well by the time Tash ran through the flames to Petine and Eshessa.

Tash pulled one of Petine's hands from her empty bucket and held it tight. She looked up at him with wide gray eyes, an unnatural expression for the teenager whose loud laugh frequently boomed across the garden.

"I need you to hold on to me very tightly," Tash said, taking Eshessa's hand as well. Eshessa nodded, but didn't speak, and squeezed Tash's hand so tightly he winced.

"Now, when I give you the word, close your eyes, hold on tight, and run as fast as you can. Do you understand?"

"Yes," Eshessa whispered. Petine nodded.

It was a tiny eternity before Cliope returned with her pail of water. When she did, Tash took a deep breath, pulling every bit of power he could from the earth below his bare feet, even pulling in a bit of the other sidhe's power—it was everywhere, thrumming, nearly impossible to avoid.

"When we get close, Cliope, throw the water on the flames right in front of you!" He yelled. "Now, Petine and Eshessa, GO!"

"What the—lovely warning, Tash, really!" Cliope yelled as Tash barreled forward, clutching both the women's hands in his own as tightly as he could and pulling all the strength he could into his heart.

Cliope threw the water over the patch of flames in front of her, and Tash used that very moment to let his power surge forth through the power center of his heart and ahead of his body to merge with the flames and push them aside. His power wasn't as strong as the other sidhe's, but together the water and Tash's focus on and proximity to that particular section of flame gave them a window. A gap appeared in the flame-wall, as if a chunk of solid fire had been sliced away with copper wire.

Without sparing a moment's thought for delicacy, he all but threw the two humans through the gap. They stumbled and fell into the grass beyond, but they got through before the hole closed.

"Get everyone inside the house," Tash called to Cliope.

"I'm not leaving!" she called back, as she helped Eshessa to her feet.

"Fine! Just keep a safe distance."

Tash was fairly sure she said something else, but he didn't hear her. It didn't matter, because the man, the sidhe, the *person of the royal court* Tash had been caring for... he was here. And he was amazing.

CHAPTER THREE

B RIEDEN SMILED INTO HIS PILLOW AT THE FEELING OF WARM,
soft lips on the back of his neck.

"Don't move," Sehrys whispered when Brieden stirred. "Stay just like
that. The morning sun looks incredible against your skin."

Brieden hummed and let himself melt into the bed. "You're home."

"I'm home," Sehrys confirmed between kisses.

"Mmm, let me look at you." Brieden rolled onto his back and blinked
his eyes open. He smiled into the kiss that followed.

Sehrys sat up and looked at him, his hand trailing down Brieden's
bare chest. "I'm not the only one who looks beautiful in the morning
light," Brieden said, tucking one hand behind his head. It was true;
the translucent golden-white leaves that covered the windows created a
gorgeous and slightly dappled effect over the entire room and painted
lovely patterns on Sehrys's pale skin.

Brieden was still getting used to the room—*their* room. The house was
still growing and wouldn't be complete for several months, but they had
a bedroom and a kitchen and their own hot spring in the back garden.
Every day, when Brieden saw a new piece of their home weave itself into
being, he could see their life together, growing into something strong
and sustainable and permanent.

The bed was the most comfortable thing he had ever experienced,
and he wasn't sure what it *was*. Four slender but sturdy *elcei* trees grew
from the floor and comprised bedposts, and stretched between them

was a tightly woven network of vines covered by a thick layer of soft, dense moss. The sheets were woven from *posselke*, the impossibly soft and silky inner lining of a large milkweed-like plant that grew just about everywhere in Khryslee, and their blankets…

Well, they had to keep *something* from their tent. Sehrys hadn't even tried to protest.

Like all elfin dwellings, this one blurred the outdoors with the indoors, from the walls made of leaves, flowers, and vines to the silken-soft grass that carpeted the floor.

Sehrys gave a soft laugh at the frustrated chatter that came from the window. A tiny blue arm reached through from the outside for just a moment before the leaves covering the window tightened and pushed it back out. "I see the pixies haven't stopped trying to get in."

Brieden frowned. "I feel sorry for them, actually. What harm would it do to let them come inside?"

"I am half tempted to let the fool thing inside so that you can see for yourself." Sehrys smiled. "They get into everything, especially food stores, and steal anything shiny that is light enough for them to carry. Sometimes they become territorial. They might try to drive us out, which would entail a lot of very painful biting."

"But—Sanya keeps her windows open all the time—"

"Sanya's house is complete. When ours is finished, the growers will lace it with *verlokinlee*, but adding it now would interfere with the growing process. The *verlokinlee* repels them completely."

"But—"

"You can still visit with your pixie friends in the garden, sweetheart," Sehrys said, his eyes impossibly fond.

Brieden smiled. Perhaps it was silly, but he had a soft spot for the little creatures.

He settled his hands on Sehrys's hips and refocused his attention upon his fiancé. It had been nearly a year since they had arrived in Khryslee, and he still had trouble believing that his life was real. True, Sehrys traveled for work far more than Brieden would have preferred, but Brieden loved Khryslee. He loved his job on Sanya's farm; he loved the sweet-smelling valley where their home was growing into existence; he loved their community. He even loved the monthly community meetings and hadn't missed one.

But most of all, he loved waking up warm and safe with Sehrys in bed beside him.

Sehrys ran his fingers over Brieden's promise pendant. *Soon,* Brieden thought. *Soon it will be so much more than just a promise.*

"Please tell me you will be home for more than just a few days this time," Brieden murmured.

Sehrys bit his lip. "I—Firae and I are scheduled to meet with the heads of some of the northeastern feririars later in the week. I thought I had mentioned it."

Brieden sighed, but mustered the discipline not to roll his eyes. "I don't believe you did. But I have today and tomorrow off from the farm, so can I at least request the attention of our great ambassador for the next couple of days?"

Sehrys grinned, moved his hands from Brieden's chest, and ran them up his arms until they slid into Brieden's hands. He pulled Brieden's hands from beneath his head and laced their fingers together to hold him in place as Sehrys lowered himself onto of Brieden's body.

"You have his full, undivided attention," Sehrys murmured into Brieden's ear, before gently nipping at the lobe.

Brieden gasped at the perfect weight of Sehrys: his smooth bare chest and strong thighs and the undeniable hard bulge of his cock beneath his breeches.

"You were gone for so long," Brieden whined, lifting his head to meet Sehrys in a hard, wet kiss.

"Too long," Sehrys murmured, releasing Brieden's hands and moving to slide Brieden's undershorts down his legs before getting to work on his own breeches. "I missed you so much. Your voice, your laugh, your eyes, your skin—"

"Yes," Brieden rasped as Sehrys settled on top of him: hard naked flesh against hard naked flesh. He wrapped his hands around his lover and ran the rough callouses on his palms over the silken skin of Sehrys's back and buttocks. "Everything about you; love you so much—"

The conversation trailed off into little more than noises as they kissed and touched and moved together, slow and careless, just reveling in being so close after being so far apart, in letting their scents mingle and their bodies unravel.

"Please, Sehrys," Brieden whispered, his voice barely audible even to himself; the strength of his need nearly choked him.

He lived in paradise with the man he loved, he enjoyed his work, and he was looking at a life expectancy that he still couldn't fathom.

But he hadn't thought it would be like this.

He had thought that he and Sehrys would spend more time together, that their day to day lives would involve one another more. He had thought that Sehrys would spend most of his nights tangled up with Brieden in their little flower-mound near the pink sand shores of Merkhryslin Lake.

He understood the necessity for Sehrys's near-constant travel. He was proud of him, and it was a small price to pay, in the end, if it meant that he could be with Sehrys in any capacity. But he also couldn't deny that it was making him desperate.

He *craved* Sehrys when they weren't close. He writhed in their bed on his nights alone, spread *hubia rija* flower oil across his own skin, and let his mind run wild, as if it were boiling with fever.

"Please, Sehrys," he whispered. He couldn't bear to spend another moment without deep and complete connection, but he was too overwhelmed to do anything more than plead.

Sehrys drew up onto his knees and plucked a red *hubia rija* flower from the thick vine that grew, heavy with blossoms, on the wall behind the head of the bed. He twisted it open with practiced ease. "What do you need?" he asked.

He looked like a fertility God from the forbidden religious texts that had been passed around the academy when Brieden was a boy. Sehrys's hair was still tangled from the long flight; the points of his ears poked out of the violet-red mess. His strong, lean body was dappled with golden light, and the muscles in his thighs seemed to be thicker than when he had last been home. His lips were red and swollen from Brieden kissing and nipping at them, and the flower was cupped perfectly in one slender hand. A bit of oil was already dribbling out and running down his wrist.

Brieden whimpered and twisted beneath him, rolled onto his belly and hiked onto his knees, and spread his legs wide to present himself in the most essential way he could.

"Gods," Sehrys murmured, running a hand across the hot skin of Brieden's cheeks, then rubbing a gentle finger between them and making him shiver. "You are breathtaking."

Brieden closed his eyes and sighed as Sehrys touched him, as he worked Brieden open with slick fingers and made pleasure ripple through his body.

But the pleasure of stimulation was nothing compared to the relief when Sehrys was inside him, with his chest pressed tight to Brieden's back and his arms wrapped around Brieden's torso, holding him close.

Brieden braced himself on bent arms. His head dropped between his elbows as he allowed Sehrys to guide their bodies, to consume him completely. Sehrys dropped erratic kisses on the back of Brieden's neck as his hips sped up and pleasure jolted through Brieden's body with each perfectly angled thrust.

Brieden was too overwhelmed to speak, and Sehrys fared only slightly better. He panted ragged endearments into Brieden's hair.

Brieden came first, which was no surprise—the only surprise lay in how long he was able to hold out—and Sehrys followed close behind as his hands slid down to tightly grip Brieden's hips while he buried himself to the hilt and let out a long, deep groan.

It was easy to roll onto their sides and lie spooned together after Sehrys pulled out, and they reveled in their closeness as the sweat cooled on their overheated skin.

"Am I to take this blessed silence as evidence that the two of you are finished?" came a voice, loud, sharp, and unwelcome, from the other side of their bedroom door.

Sehrys went stiff. "Please tell me that I've fallen asleep and did not just hear that," he muttered.

Brieden sighed. "If so, we appear to be sharing a dream. I heard it too."

Sehrys swore under his breath and rolled away from Brieden; he crossed the room to fetch a robe for himself before throwing one to Brieden.

Brieden had barely finished fastening the sash on his robe when Sehrys threw the door open to reveal Sree, Firae's closest advisor, standing in their half-finished sitting room, where the ceiling and one wall were still open to the sky save for a skeletal network of roots and vines. "What in the name of the Gods are you doing here?" Sehrys demanded by way of greeting.

When they had first settled themselves in Khryslee, Sehrys had named a lack of proximity to Sree as one of his favorite features of their new home, better than the sparkling waterfalls of Merkhryslin or the Rijamiknauvriog with its singing flower-trees, which emitted a haunting melody each evening at sunset to attract grimchins to pollinate them. Brieden knew that much of the acrimony between Sehrys and Sree was due to Firae and Sehrys's former betrothal, and Sree's vocal opposition to the union, but the fact that there would be no such union had done little to ease the tension.

Sree and Sehrys found themselves on opposing sides of most issues and seemed to be in constant battle for greater access to the king's ear, but Brieden had always had the sense that the rift went far deeper than he knew.

"It is lovely to see you as well, Sehrys," she said, stepping around him to let herself into the bedroom. Her ice-blue eyes skimmed over Brieden as if he were furniture, and the fact that Brieden was sitting made her height more imposing than usual. "I would have preferred to have this conversation without waiting for you to finish with your pet—ah, your partner—first, but the Gods appear to have willed it otherwise."

"Fiancé," Sehrys corrected through gritted teeth. "I'm surprised The Gatekeeper let you into Khryslee, given your limited tolerance for humans."

"The Gatekeeper knew I had critical business," she responded, as she settled herself in a plush chair by the window and ignored Brieden. If Brieden hadn't been wary of her, he might have told her how lovely she looked: the long waves of her peach, rose, gold, and coral hair were tied back in a loose knot, making the beautiful but sharp contours of her face appear softer, and her pale blue shift matched the color of her eyes to near perfection. Her deep blue boots matched the stones of the bracelet around her wrist to *actual* perfection, and the golden light brought out the warm peach hues in her pale skin.

Sree gave Sehrys one of the most unpleasant smiles Brieden had ever seen. "I'm afraid I've had to cancel your meeting with the northeastern feririar chiefs."

"You *what?*"

"Sit down, Sehrys. This is serious. Perhaps your human can prepare us some tea."

Sehrys's lips constricted into a tight line and his eyes flashed. Brieden couldn't help the sharp laugh that escaped him; everything about this situation—and Sree—was ridiculous.

His laughter seemed to calm Sehrys enough so he didn't hurt Sree, but held her eye in a hard stare and said, "Brieden is not my servant. He is my partner. Anything you wish to discuss with me will involve him. Now speak." Brieden smiled at Sehrys's restraint and rose from the bed to stand beside him and rub a soothing hand along his back.

"Very well," she said, her tone laced with irritation. "Firae is gone."

"Gone?" Sehrys asked. He sounded more concerned than Brieden liked.

"Gone. He set sail for Villalu alone over a week ago, on behalf of the Council."

Sehrys blinked once. Brieden quietly led him over to the bed, and Sehrys allowed himself to be guided, as if in a daze. "Wh-why on all of Ullavise would the Council send him into Villalu? I—we—we have spoken to them of the dangers, of what happened to me there. How could they do that to him?" As Sehrys's fear edged toward anger, Brieden gave his hand a gentle squeeze. Sehrys squeezed back so hard that Brieden yelped.

Sree shrugged. "It needed to be a royal. They are the only ones allowed by The Border spell to bring a criminal branded with an exile mark back through. Apparently he volunteered, insisted that he be the one to undertake the mission."

"The *mission?* What mission could possibly demand such a thing?" Sehrys demanded, his volume raising with each syllable. "He is a *king* of Laesi. He is needed here. And he barely speaks three words of Villaluan. He has no sense of how things truly work in Villalu, despite what he's heard me say. He—Gods, what if someone—what if he—"

Sree sighed and pulled a pale green scroll from a pouch on her belt. "He left a letter. I'm meant to ensure that you read it," she said, and handed it to Sehrys.

Sehrys jumped up to snatch the scroll, and unrolled and read it immediately. His eyes grew wider and wider as he read. After a few moments he stopped and looked up. He turned to Brieden, seeming lost and overwhelmed, and then looked at Sree.

"He says—he wants me to run the Queendom in his absence?" Brieden gasped at the news. "But that's—I barely know the first thing about—"

"Keep reading." Sree sighed. Her voice was still edged with irritation, but smugness was emerging as well. Brieden narrowed his eyes at her. *What—*

"*What?*" Sehrys whipped his head up from the scroll to gape at Sree. "What—he—has he gone completely mad?"

"It would appear so," she responded dryly.

Brieden furrowed his brow. "What—what does it say?"

Sehrys turned to him, eyes still wide with shock. "It says that Firae wants Sree and I to run the Queendom together."

Chapter Four

Tash approached the column of fire at the heart of the garden slowly. He was fairly certain that the man was acting defensively, but fear could be dangerous, especially in a sidhe powerful enough to belong to the Royal caste. And as comfortable as Tash may have been amongst the flames, he was not impervious to harm.

It was difficult to hurt Tash with fire because fire was at the center of his own power. He was not hot or uncomfortable where he stood, and walking through a wall of flame registered as little more than a warm flush. But if the man wished to do harm, if there was focused intent, Tash could be burned to death just as easily as any other creature on the planet.

Tash touched the ring of flame and flinched in pain at the message. *No.* It was so clear he practically heard it spoken out loud.

Tash closed his eyes and reached out again, slower, concentrating. When his fingertips made contact with the flames, he pushed through some of his own power, softly, with almost no force. *I mean you no harm. I wish to help.*

The sting that shot through him in response was mild: inquisitive but suspicious. He flinched, but kept his hand outstretched and his fingers dipped into the flames as he repeated his message and made his request.

May I enter?

Tash tensed, ready to pull back if the response was hostile. But he felt a searching ripple of warmth course through him.

He was at this man's mercy, and would be even more so if he entered the ring of flame. But then again, the man would be vulnerable to him. To let another person touch the heart of one's power like that, to let them *in*—allowing Tash inside a protective ring of magic that emanated from the man's power center would put Tash in a position to bleed the man of essence, to destroy him with the force of the man's own power.

Suddenly, the flames softened, and Tash smiled at the invitation before stepping inside.

The beautiful man whom Tash had been nursing back to health stood with his back pressed to the fig tree. His flesh glowed in the light cast by the fire all around them; his eyes were the colors of deep red wine and sweet dark plums, and they sparkled with magic. He cast his eyes upon Tash, and Tash felt as if the breath had been knocked from his lungs with the force of the other elf's stare.

And stare he did, shamelessly and thoroughly. His expression was unreadable and intense. "Who are you?" the man asked after several moments. The trembling in his voice was subtle but clear. This man was afraid, but he was desperate not to appear afraid, which made him especially dangerous.

Tash held his arms out, palms up, to convey his peaceful intentions. "My *nomkin* is Tash. I live amongst the humans here. They wish you no harm."

The man narrowed his eyes. "Are you a slave?" the man demanded, letting his eyes sweep over Tash.

Tash gave a surprised bark of laughter. "No. Nothing of the sort." The ring of fire around them thinned, growing translucent.

"Where are we?" the man asked, his voice a bit steadier.

"Ryovni."

"Ryovni." The man sighed. "I suppose that should mean something to me, but I can't say that it does. I have no understanding of Villaluan geography east of the border cities. At least I—" The man frowned. "I should know it, but I cannot recall why."

"It is an island state off the southern coast. May I ask where you were headed, if you are unfamiliar with the islands of Villalu?"

The man chuckled, raising his hands and looking at his own naked body. "I had a stone with me that was supposed to guide my way once the ship brought me as far as it could. My only plan was to assume I would reach land safely, but as you can see, even that did not go in my favor."

Tash gave him a rueful smile. "We do have a few of your things, though I am afraid your ship has perished. I don't recall seeing a stone. I can send for what we did recover if you would like, though."

The man raised an eyebrow. "You can send for them, can you? Precisely who are you to these humans?"

Tash shrugged, trying to ignore the squirming in his belly. "We have a mutually beneficial arrangement. Ryovni isn't Frilauan; they have no hatred for me here. They give me some measure of safety, and I give them the same in return."

"But you are Common caste."

Tash blinked. "Y-yes, that's true."

"When you sought passage through my fire," the man explained, "I could feel it, how much weaker you are."

Tash had absolutely no idea how to respond to *that*. He had spent time in the border cities and grown up in a remote, low-power feririar. Challenges and displays of dominance were nothing new to him, but the way this man spoke—this man stood naked and stranded in a strange land, yet still regarded Tash, who only offered to *help* him, as utterly beneath him. Tash had never felt so dismissed and diminished, except at the trial that had sealed his fate years ago in Laesi, the trial before all those *royals*.

Tash took a deep breath, then squared his shoulders and folded his arms across his chest. "I may be weaker than you magically speaking, but you will probably need my help to return home, complete your quest, or whatever else you choose to do, unless sitting inside a ring of magic fire until you collapse from exhaustion is your only plan. In which case, by all means, allow me to leave you to it."

And with that, Tash turned and walked away. The wall of fire instantly thickened, burning hotter and stronger, attempting to seal him in. But Tash had no patience for it. He didn't even slow down. He might be *weaker* than this man, but it wasn't as if he were facing an avalanche or a tsunami. This was fire. This was the element that surged through Tash's own veins. The power that, though weak, filled him with a sense of strength. It might be a bit uncomfortable walking through these flames in the face of the other man's resistance, but it was hardly a feat.

Once outside the ring of flames, he turned and waited. It wasn't long before the flames thinned and then dissolved into nothing. The flames surrounding the garden remained, but Tash counted victories where he could.

"I don't know if I should trust you," the man said, leaning back against the unharmed fig tree. "I know how humans are—"

"You know what you've *heard* about how humans are. And even if much of what you've heard is true, it doesn't speak of all humans. It only speaks of the world upheld by those in power. Besides that, I don't know if I should trust you either. You haven't told me who you are or why you've come here."

"I've met humans. Well, one of them," the man muttered. "I suppose he wasn't that bad." The admission came as if it pained him to say it. "But I got the impression that he wasn't... usual amongst his kind."

"His kind is more varied than you realize. Most of the humans here in Ryovni... there are quite a lot of good people here. I imagine you will find yourself surprised."

"My *nomkin* is Firae."

Tash blinked. He hadn't expected to gain that level of trust so easily. "Well, Firae, it is a pleasure to meet you. And though it is no hardship to look upon you and it is true the day is warm, I wonder if you might like some clothing. And perhaps something to eat?"

Firae arched an eyebrow; his eyes went darker as his lips tilted into a half-smile. "I am happy to hear that it's been no hardship, especially since I imagine you have been looking upon me for several days now."

Tash tried to fight away the heat in his cheeks, but the way Firae's eyes danced let him know that his blush was just as visible as he feared. "Yes, well, I." Tash cleared his throat and looked away.

"Thank you," Firae added, his voice softened. "I know you probably saved my life, and I did not greet you graciously."

Tash looked back at him. His shoulders relaxed when he saw that the playful glint in Firae's eye had been replaced with something much softer. "You were confused. And frightened," Tash offered.

Firae gave a small laugh. "Yes. Well, I suppose I'm still both of those things, but much less so. Did you mention something about food?"

"This house is *dead,*" Firae said, his nose wrinkling as he walked across the floor as if it were covered in sharp spikes.

"Humans don't have the means to sustain a living house," Tash reminded him, but Firae continued to treat the wood as if it were repulsive. He kept his arms close to his sides and away from the banisters as they ascended the stairs. Tash remembered having a similar reaction all those decades ago when he was first banished to Villalu, but he had forgotten how viscerally *wrong* it could feel, having those thick, sickly layers of death between himself and the life force of the earth.

Tash showed Firae to the vacant room they had reserved for him and offered him some clothing options. Firae frowned at the bundle of woven fabric that Tash handed to him, but took it into the room while Tash went to the kitchen and its many glorious window boxes full of fresh herbs and salads.

"These garments are strange," Firae grumbled, picking at the fabric he was wearing when Tash returned. "What is this substance?"

Firae was dressed like Tash, in close-fitting breeches and a loose tunic of pale gray, belted with a royal blue sash.

"You probably don't want to know," Tash replied, motioning for Firae to follow him to the balcony.

Firae sighed. "It's dead, isn't it?"

"If you are going to spend any time in Villalu, you will need to get accustomed to that. Death is a part of life, after all."

"Death is a *distinct* part of life," Firae argued. "Death is dressed in death. Life is dressed in life. We wrap corpses in dead fabric, not living bodies."

"Humans live in closer proximity to death. They are fragile, and their lives are short."

Firae smiled at Tash as he settled into a chair and accepted a large cup of water and a bowl of salad greens. "You make very good points, but I can't say that I like it."

"I do not imagine you will ever like it, but you will most likely grow to tolerate it. I rarely think about it anymore."

Firae swallowed a mouthful of greens. "How long have you been here?" he asked before popping another couple of leaves into his mouth.

"Fifty years, perhaps? Something like that." Tash knew *exactly* how long he had been in Villalu, but he couldn't bring himself to admit that he still counted the days, that he would probably never stop counting.

Firae chewed, and Tash could see the curiosity brewing, could sense the question that would come next, the one question he wasn't quite sure how to answer—not until he knew why Firae was here.

"You are royalty," Tash blurted. Firae blinked. "Your name. It means 'A Victory Blessed by the Gods.' That name is reserved for the Royal caste."

There was no reason for Firae to learn that Tash had come upon a certain tree design while washing his hair as he lay unconscious in the garden.

Firae nodded. "I am. But I am not here as a royal, I am here as an envoy."

Tash furrowed his brow. "An envoy? But *es lemeddison rubrio—*"

"Excellent, you are familiar with it." Firae sounded as if he were praising a child for making a daisy chain, and it hit Tash like a jolt to the chest.

"Of course I have heard of it. It may surprise you to learn that the strength of my magic is not related to the strength of my mind," Tash responded crisply. *Honestly! Did Firae think those of the Common caste were little more than mindless pixies?*

Firae frowned. "I did not mean—I simply didn't know how much schooling you may have received while you were in Laesi. I didn't want to presume anything."

"Firae, every child in Laesi learns the tale of the Great Change and the Non-Interference Doctrine even before our powers have settled. If I had received no more than the most rudimentary education, I would know."

"I apologize. I keep offending you." Firae sighed.

"This is why people of our castes rarely spend time together." Tash hoped his tone was light enough to move them from the strained atmosphere that had developed. He shot Firae a quick wink—something that would have been beyond unacceptable in Laesi—and, sure enough, the other man gave him a hint of a smile.

"My mission concerns the Doctrine," Firae explained. "I was sent to Laesi by the Council of Nations because the Doctrine has been compromised. There is a sidhe criminal interfering with matters of human governance."

"I see. Do—do you know who this criminal is?" Tash curled his left hand into a fist to conceal his palm. The mark of exile—the mark that kept him trapped in Villalu for the remainder of his days—was invisible, but he swore he could feel Firae's eyes boring into it, and it *throbbed*.

Firae frowned. "No. The sphinx who guards The Border brought the news to the Council when it happened." He sighed and ran a hand through his hair, mindlessly working his fingers through the tangles he encountered. "The spell that created The Border—it was never meant to be undone. There is a fail-safe, of course, which will allow The Border to collapse without causing an implosion. Any spell of this magnitude needs a fail-safe, but this sphinx—she calls herself The Watcher—she is riddle-bound. So all I have to work with to find the fail-safe are some cryptic words, some educated guesses, and a guide-stone that is probably at the bottom of the ocean. My only alternative is to find the criminal who is interfering."

Tash took a sip of water and willed his racing mind to slow down. "And if you find this criminal?" he asked carefully. "What is to be their fate?"

"That is undecided. She must be stopped, that much is clear. The Non-Interference Doctrine—"

"It is an immutable doctrine," Tash murmured, nodding.

"Precisely. It is tied to The Border itself, to the stability of the spell. If the problem is not addressed soon, The Border will weaken beyond repair."

"Is—" Tash took a deep breath. He was stepping into dangerous territory, but it couldn't be helped. "Would that necessarily be such a terrible thing? The Border has caused such great suffering, and if it were to be eliminated—"

Firae shook his head. "You don't understand. The Border wouldn't disappear or dissolve or even explode. It would *implode*. It would destroy all of Villalu and everyone inside it in the blink of an eye, and then it would most likely destroy the rest of Ullavise as well."

Tash stared at him. "Are you sure about that?"

Firae nodded, picking a deep purple leaf from his bowl and twirling its stem between his fingers. "The Council wants to destroy Villalu before the weakening of the spell destroys the world. I convinced them to let me try to resolve the problem first. There are tens of thousands of people in Villalu. And though humans are flawed, I cannot allow us to stoop to genocide, even in the name of self-preservation. It..." Firae swallowed; his eyes were bright. He looked out over the sea, beyond the railing of the balcony. "I couldn't live with myself. Not if there is something I can do about it." Firae popped the leaf into his mouth and continued to watch the sea.

Tash clutched the arms of his chair and breathed in and out slowly, methodically.

"There is something you can do about it," Tash said, his voice quieter than intended. Firae looked at him, head tilted in question.

Tash cleared his throat and sat straighter in his chair. "There is something you can do about it, because I am it. I am the criminal you are looking for."

CHAPTER FIVE

"FIRAE. PLEASE."

Firae looked ahead and refused to react to Tash or to the people gathered along the side of the road, who murmured and pointed to the two sidhe in the middle of the royal procession. Though Tash assumed the man had never ridden a horse, he managed to look graceful and regal as he rode with his back straight as a fencepost and his hands resting lightly on his thighs. When a groom had brought him the chestnut stallion, Firae had stroked the animal's muzzle and whispered to him in the old language of land beasts, and then insisted that the horse's bridle and saddle be removed before he would climb on his back.

"His name is Acorn," the groom had said nervously, twisting his hands, and Firae had looked at Tash, silently demanding a translation, which Tash had given him.

Firae had scoffed. "I certainly doubt that. How could that child possibly know this creature's name? I can't imagine they share a language."

Those had been the last words Firae had spoken to him since they left Pemerec.

Once Tash had revealed himself, Firae had gone cold, demanding to know who Tash worked for and then demanding an audience with Brissa and refusing to answer any additional questions. When Tash had tried to explain, Firae had simply walked away.

"Please," Tash repeated. "I know you're upset with me, but if you'd allow me to explain, I believe you may be sympathetic to our cause. You see—"

"I will allow the human queen to explain," Firae said abruptly, his eyes remaining fixed on the front of the procession. "And you may consider yourself under arrest without liberty to speak."

"I—with all due respect, you have no jurisdiction over me, Firae."

"I beg to differ."

"It doesn't matter if you b—" Firae finally turned his head and looked Tash square in the eye. Tash closed his mouth. Perhaps he should hold his tongue and wait for Firae to speak to the queen. In fact, Tash couldn't imagine what he could say. It was best if he remained silent until—

"How *dare* you!" Tash spat, pushing out the words with all the force he could muster. "You must have known that wouldn't work, I'm not *human.*"

Firae turned his attention to the road ahead. "It was worth a try," he said with a small shrug.

"If you try to compel the queen, I swear to you, you will not make it back to Laesi alive," Tash snapped as his heart thrummed from the effort of pushing the intrusion from his mind.

"Your queen shall come to no harm," Firae told him, "but I cannot make the same promise to you. So unless you would like to incriminate yourself further, I suggest holding your tongue until I have spoken to this queen."

Tash sighed. The last thing he wanted to do was comply, especially after Firae had tried to *force* him to stop speaking, but the man did have a point. Tash still didn't know who Firae was or how much influence he held with the Council of Nations. Firae was more powerful than he— much more powerful—and Tash had no doubt that he could force him back across The Border to meet his death. And as many times as Tash had thought that death would be a kinder fate than expulsion, the truth was that he did not want to die. He was not as young as Firae, but he was hardly old. He had centuries before him, and he was just starting to feel as though he was finally part of something meaningful.

Tash took a deep breath and fixed his own eyes straight ahead.

The journey back to Okoskeshell was long, and most of it was spent in silence.

Firae tried not to reveal how impressed he was when Keshell castle came into view.

He had no idea what to expect from this human queen; though he had for the most part refused to engage the criminal once he knew who he was, he hadn't been able to ignore the information Tash had pressed upon him, nor what little he knew from Sehrys's time in Villalu.

He knew that the queen was new; that she had overthrown the regime that was responsible for Sehrys's enslavement. He knew that she was barely a woman; only twenty-two or twenty-three years of age, which to him signified an *actual* child, but which apparently was a human equivalent to Sehrys's age of sixty-three. Firae himself was only ninety-seven, and when he had been Sehrys's age—

Well, when he had been only a bit younger than Sehrys, his mother had been murdered; shot down by Redcaps while flying over the Iron Mountains. Firae had roused from his carefree slumber, ready to spend another day climbing trees and frustrating his tutors, to find that the future of Yestralekrezerche was in his hands.

But this woman was barely grown, had spent only twenty-two years on the planet, and she had not merely accepted the throne, she had actively pursued it.

Firae was just a bit frightened.

He could have spoken to the queen's sister before leaving Pemerec, but he was all too aware how vulnerable his position was. These humans still didn't know who he was, and he was too woefully uneducated as to the rituals and expectations of human royalty to risk speaking with anyone of lesser status than the queen herself.

The criminal could have helped him, he was sure, but he refused to rely on that man for anything. He couldn't trust him and he couldn't show him any sympathy, no matter how his heart pleaded with him to do so.

He wasn't shocked to learn that Tash was a criminal. The man spoke Elfin with a slight but unmistakable accent of the Pelzershes. And there was no other likely reason for him to be living amongst humans in Villalu. But to learn that he was *the* criminal, that he was the one influencing the Villaluan government…

Firae had assumed that the family of Sehrys's former captor was still in power. He had assumed that any elf who sought to help King Dronyen's regime had evil in their heart—after all, the Doctrine had specified that any interference with human government by force or under duress would have no effect on the stability of the spell. Whoever was helping the human government was doing so as a matter of unencumbered choice.

His feelings had been so much clearer when he believed the Panlochs were receiving a sidhe's help. Firae couldn't kill the Panlochs without violating the Doctrine himself—at least not unless he was forced to do so in self-defense, and he had held out more than a little hope that he would be required to do just that—but he could destroy the criminal who threatened the stability of their very world.

Except… except that absolutely none of what Firae had been expecting had come to pass.

"Beautiful, isn't it?" Tash asked, eyes fixed on the castle.

"It looks dead." Firae dismissed, unable to disagree.

Tash chuckled. "Well, this is made of stone rather than wood, which makes it no more dead than the sands that carpet the world."

Firae ignored that, letting his eyes drink in every new detail of the palace that came into focus as they drew nearer.

The entire building seemed to be tinted shell pink, though that may have been the emerging sunset. It was incredibly tall, bringing to mind the treetop Halls preferred by some sidhe queens and kings. Various shapes rose from its sprawling mass: window-lined towers with pointed tips and grooved patterns along the broader sections of roof. The body of the palace was dotted with many large windows and dozens of wide balconies. The castle did indeed seem to be built largely or even entirely from stone, but much of the stone was obscured by thick green vines.

"Humans grew this without magic?" Firae couldn't help but ask, taking in the ornate copper gates that glinted in the setting sun.

"Built, yes. They're actually quite remarkable creatures."

Once the gates were thrown open, Firae couldn't fight back a tiny smile; the broad cobblestone road that led to the castle was flanked by gardens so lush they reminded him of the grounds outside the Great Hall in Alovur Drovuru. There were trees laden with fruit, some of which he had never seen, bushes with flowers of every color, and many small flower gardens. There were also quite a few objects made of stone, and he found, to his surprise, that he quite liked the way they looked, stark and anchoring, nestled amongst all that vibrant, colorful life. There were fountains, birdbaths, and statues of animals and humans. One particular likeness made his jaw drop.

"But that looks like—"

"The Blessed Guardian, yes. That is precisely who it is," Tash confirmed.

"But how—how?" Firae furrowed his brow. "I was under the impression that humans follow their own religion, something involving dragons and slavery and the celebration of cruelty?"

Tash snorted. "You are referring to two different religions, only one of which actually celebrates slavery and cruelty. But some humans follow the old sidhe Gods. If you had let me explain what Brissa and I—"

"No." Firae arranged his face into as impassive a mask as he could manage. "I cannot rely on the word of a convicted criminal in exile. I will need you to serve as an interpreter between myself and the queen, so I shall reserve what little trust I have in you for that interaction. You may interpret my words for the queen, but if there is any indication at all that you are being less than truthful—"

"I promise I will speak only the truth," Tash said quietly, his gaze heavy on Firae. Firae forced himself to look straight ahead.

At the castle's entrance, a small crowd had gathered, the members of which sprang into action as soon as the horses came to a halt and the riders began to dismount. Firae stayed on the horse he had ridden, looking around in the hope of spotting the queen. But all he saw were attendants in plain, simple garments, no one who could be mistaken for royalty. A few people looked as if they were going to approach Firae, but Cliope quickly swooped in, murmuring sternly and leading them away.

Tash spoke with the princess in soft murmurs before walking to Firae and holding out a hand to help him dismount. Firae ignored the offer and dismounted on his own, just slightly more clumsily than he would have preferred. "Where is the queen?" he demanded, refusing to look at Tash lest he see a trace of laughter in the other man's face.

"She is in the throne room. We are going to escort you there straightaway."

Firae frowned. "Throne room?"

"It is a human custom. Their rulers sit upon ornate thrones that signify their status."

"And they dedicate entire rooms to these thrones?"

Tash nodded. "They do. And when you enter it is customary to bow. Like so." In one fluid movement, Tash leaned his torso forward, the lower half of his body remaining immobile, before moving back to a standing position.

Firae frowned. "Does such a gesture suggest subservience?"

"Not subservience, precisely, but deference," Tash said, as he followed Cliope toward the castle. Firae fell into step beside him. "She… she is the *queen,* after all, human or not," he added, casting a slightly nervous glance toward Firae.

"And I will respect her position. But I am a king of Laesi. I shall greet her as an equal."

Tash stumbled slightly and his eyes went wide. Firae couldn't help but smirk at the response. "You knew I was royalty." He did not look at Tash.

"I knew you were of the Royal caste. That is hardly the same as knowing that you are a *king.*"

Firae glanced around as they walked. The corridor was wide, with high ceilings and tall, narrow windows flanking them to their left. The walls seemed to be made of pale blue polished stone, and the floor was a different sort of stone, white and flecked with bits of something that sparkled in the sunlight. The wall to their right was lined with gorgeous sunwashed tapestries, some of them depicting brown-skinned humans at work on beaches and in fields, on ships, and upon thrones, and others of silver-skinned muirdannoch beneath the sea, tending to coral reefs and building cities of seaweed and shell.

They walked in silence. Tash led him up a broad staircase lined with blue-green carpet. Sunlight poured through a large skylight.

"You… are young. To be a king," Tash said in a cool tone as they reached the top of the staircase and continued on their way.

"I suppose so." Firae glanced at Tash, and did his best to ignore the frown he saw on the other man's face; he squared his shoulders and lifted his chin.

Tash called Cliope to walk alongside them, and Firae could understand a bit of their rapid Villaluan conversation. He heard Tash use the Villaluan word for "king," and he did not miss the way Cliope's eyes went wide. She asked a question, and Tash turned to Firae.

"What… it would be helpful to know your full title. So that we may announce you to the queen properly."

Firae nodded. "I am *Rigday Firae efa es Alovur Drovuru Feririar, Silerth Valusidhe efa Ferban Gira efa es Alovur Drovuru Feririar ala es Fervishlaea efa es Yestralekrezershe.*"

Tash nodded and did not look at him.

One of the guards provided Tash with a scroll upon which to write Firae's name and title. The guard darted into the room and closed the door behind her. Mere seconds later, the doors were thrown open, and he heard a somewhat mangled and mispronounced version of his name called out in Villaluan.

Firae walked into the room. It was difficult not to stare, but he had long years of practiced impassivity to rely on, and so he only allowed himself a cursory glance around the enormous, airy room. There were several floor-to-ceiling windows to the left, and the gauzy, translucent blue drapes that covered them danced in the breeze to reveal an outdoor space beyond. The walls were covered in mosaics; much like the tapestries in the corridors, they depicted humans and muirdannoch alike. Though he did not allow himself to look up, Firae had the distinct impression that the artwork continued on the ceiling.

In the center of the room was a dais of polished white stone. And upon the dais was a large silver throne with deep blue and green cushions. And upon the throne sat a woman.

She was undoubtedly a woman rather than a girl. Though she was young, her eyes were shrewd and confident. They weren't lacking in warmth, but she was clearly guarded.

Firae was perhaps no judge of human beauty, but this woman was clearly beautiful. Her hair was long and as black as Firae's and fell across her shoulders and down her back in thick, glossy ringlets. Her lips were full and plum-colored; her eyes were wide and dark. She had the darkest skin Firae had ever seen, and it contrasted gorgeously with her gown, which was palest pink. She was slender and long limbed, and, as she stood it was clear that she was tall, perhaps even as tall as himself.

"*Mikrigday,*" she said. Her voice was slow and careful; her pronunciation was a bit off. Holding the edges of her gown, she dipped slightly before rising to her full height. "*Esilog supanauvo nau'at ul zersheog esilog filameton wa peristorn nau'at telfidan nauefa feririar.*"

Firae stared at her. He had never heard a human attempt to speak Elfin, and though her face remained impassive, he could tell how some of the words strained her throat, possibly to the point of pain. He wondered how long she had practiced them. But more than that, he wondered how she knew them at all. "*We welcome you to the lands that we guard and invite you to treat them as your home."* It was the traditional greeting throughout Laesi when welcoming another royal into one's realm.

Unsure if he was doing it right or whether the timing strictly called for it, Firae took a chance and leaned forward at the waist briefly just as Tash had shown him.

"Your Majesty," he replied to her in Villaluan. "I thank you for your…" Firae glanced at Tash and spoke the word in Elfin in order to procure a translation.

"Hospitality," Tash said, his voice cool and flat, and Firae repeated the word.

The queen smiled and descended from the dais, gesturing for Tash and Firae to follow her to the balcony. Once outside, she gestured for both men to sit at a round stone table beneath a rose-dotted trellis, and she turned and closed the doors firmly behind her.

In the center of the table was a platter of fresh fruits and leaves and a tall glass container of what appeared to be water and mint leaves.

Tash fixed plates and poured water for the three of them as Brissa sat facing him. She began speaking in Villaluan, and Tash focused intently and then turned to translate for Firae.

"The queen asks that you speak in your natural language so that you may express yourself fully, and allow me to interpret."

Firae considered the young woman. "Tell her I accept and that I appreciate any assistance she may provide in bringing home the elfin criminal with whom she has been associating." Firae took a deep breath and looked Tash square in the eye. "And tell her that I am willing to compensate her for the loss of your services."

Tash looked back at Firae with a neutral expression before returning his gaze to Brissa and speaking what Firae hoped was a correct translation of the words he had just spoken.

Brissa's eyes went wide; she looked incredulous at the words Tash spoke, and then the two began conversing in rapid Villaluan as if Firae weren't there. Firae took a sip of water and tried to pick up what words he could.

He heard his own name and the human word for The Border, but most of the other words were spoken too fast. Tash finally turned back to Firae and took a deep breath.

"Her Highness knows ⟨ ～～～ ⟩, but she did not know that her rule had become established enough to enact a response. She apologizes for the circumstances of your arrival, but she invites you to reconsider your mission. She has in her possession an *Imervish* scroll. It is a map to the Undoing Spell for The Border itself."

Firae's eyes darted to Tash and Firae as if he could somehow make sense of what he was hearing by looking at either of them intensely enough. "What good is the map if the spell is not here?"

"That is precisely it. The spell *is* here."

"In Villalu?"

"Yes!" The coolness dropped from Tash's voice, and he sounded nearly gleeful in his excitement. "Yes, precisely, *in* Villalu! It was a brilliant place to keep it if you think about it—no human can get to it, and no sidhe would think to look for it here. We even found the door that will lead us to it, but—but I'm not strong enough to open it on my own. But perhaps you and I together—"

Firae glanced at the queen, who gave him a slight smile and chewed on a piece of pale orange fruit, seemingly content to observe the two men while they conversed in Elfin.

"Why on all of Ullavise would I help you with such a thing?" Firae demanded of Tash.

"Because you could help us to destroy The Border without killing everyone inside. Don't you understand? This is the fail-safe spell crafted by those who created The Border. You could—"

"I could also take you back to Laesi, as I have been tasked by the Council. That will save just as many lives. Well, possibly one less, depending upon what the Council elects to do with you."

Tash's eyes flashed and he narrowed them. "With all due respect, Your *Majesty,* this is not about me." Firae startled slightly at the edge of menace in his voice, at the way he nearly spat Firae's title at him as if it were something dirty rather than a sacred gift from the Gods. "For if you choose to do nothing about The Border, you will have the blood of thousands upon your hands, in addition to the blood that is there already. There is a darkness here, a spiritual poison that causes too many humans to live lives of brutal suffering. Not to mention the lives of all the sidhe you have banished here—"

"Criminals," Firae growled. Fire roiled just beneath his skin despite the uncomfortable truth of Tash's words. "Criminals like you who deserve—"

"Criminals like me who do *not* deserve to endure decades or even centuries of torture, slavery, and rape!" Tash shot back, his voice rising to a near-yell.

"Tash," the queen said. Her voice was gentle but firm, and seemed to settle him like a cool bath on a hot day. Tash took a deep breath and a long drink of water and turned away from Firae.

Firae looked at Brissa and considered.

He knew well enough not to dismiss a coincidence such as this one. If Tash spoke the truth… well. He knew that he had come to Villalu for a reason, that he *had* to be the one who made the journey. Beyond all logic, beyond all law, there was the image from his soul-walk of two worlds, two paths: *risk or security, a king or a criminal.*

"Tell her I am listening," Firae said, keeping his eyes fixed squarely on the queen's face.

"TELL ME," CLIOPE SAID, TOSSING HERSELF INTO THE CHAIR WHERE THE sidhe king had been sitting only moments before.

Brissa smiled at her; it was a weak and tired ghost of the smile she had kept plastered on her face for Firae's benefit, but in the language of twins it was a lengthy monologue.

"So he is not going to help us." Cliope sighed, shoulders slumping, and picked up a slice of melon that had been left on Firae's plate.

"No, it isn't as bad as that. He asked for some time alone in his quarters before the feast to consider it, but…" Brissa shook her head. "I don't know that one person has ever made me feel so *young* in my life, Clio, even when I was a child."

Cliope's eyes snapped onto Brissa's at the nickname. "With all due respect, dearest sister, when were you ever a child?"

Brissa rolled her eyes. "I got up to just as much mischief as you did—"

"I rather recall that you accompanied me in my mischief in order to keep an eye on me, lecturing me on my recklessness all the while."

"Well, *some*one needed to keep you from splitting your skull open, and no one else was volunteering for the job." Brissa took a sip of water and placed her hands primly in her lap. "And it was my idea to start exploring the caves."

"Yes, I believe you may have mentioned that once or twice over the years." Cliope rolled her eyes.

Brissa narrowed her eyes at her sister but could not fight off a grin. Cliope returned the smile, and it was only then that Brissa realized how much better she felt than she had just a few moments before.

"So tell me," Cliope urged.

"We have compromised the Non-Interference Doctrine by accepting Tash's help," Brissa started. "It seems—it seems that, for the purposes of the spell at least, we have conquered the Panlochs completely, and I am the one true queen of Villalu."

Cliope dropped the last bite of melon onto the plate in front of her and gasped as her smile spread across her face. "*Fuck,* Brissa. That means—"

"It means that Firae wants to arrest Tash and bring him back to the Elfin Lands to stand trial."

Cliope's smile deflated into a scowl. "So *that* is what crawled up Tash's backside. I knew it was something, but he wouldn't tell me what." She sighed and slouched in her chair. "Well, he can't have him. I will let him drag me through Frilau's Five Hells before I let him bring more suffering into Tash's life."

"Would that you could, Cliope. He—could you not *feel* his power? And the way he looked at me—it was as if someone had dressed up a field mouse in a robe and crown and presented it to him as his equal." Brissa looked at her hands, which were tightly laced together on her lap. "Blue Shell told me that The Border is degrading even faster than before. We shall be lucky if we have even a year before it destroys us. If he won't help us—"

"It shall not destroy us," Cliope interrupted.

At a soft knock on the frame of the open balcony door Brissa looked up to see Elleryi, one of the women training to join Cliope's battalion once they returned to the mainland, standing awkwardly in the doorway. She was young, plump, strong, and lovely, with cropped hair and a bashful smile. Brissa had gone weak the moment she had first beheld that smile, and her response to it now was tempered only by her frustration and melancholy.

"Am I needed, Elleryi?" Cliope asked, rising to her feet.

The girl blushed. "Oh, I... no, forgive me, princess, but I... Her Majesty..."

Brissa offered her a gentle smile of apology. With all that had transpired, she had forgotten she'd promised an afternoon with the girl in her bedchamber.

"I shall be along shortly, Elleryi. Will Cesmi be joining us?"

The girl's blush deepened; her eyes flicked to Cliope. Most of Brissa's lovers were confident and unashamed of the nature of their time spent with the queen, but there was something appealing in Elleryi's eager, flustered inexperience, and Brissa looked forward to teaching her all the things that her body could do when she lost herself in the pleasure of another woman's body.

"I... I believe so," Elleryi replied, fidgeting.

"Why don't you fetch her and go to my chambers. Order some wine from the kitchens and relax. I will not tarry too long with my sister."

"Y-yes, Your Majesty," Elleryi replied. She gave the sisters an aborted curtsy and fled the room.

Cliope snorted and walked around the table to sit beside Brissa.

"I am not keeping you from important matters of governance, am I?" she inquired with a raised eyebrow.

"Yes. Most important. But I suppose I can spare another moment or two." The smile faded from Brissa's face. "You truly believe we shall prevail?"

"Of course I do. You told me yourself that Firae is willing to consider helping us. Have you somehow forgotten the prophecy of the twin-born queen?"

"Prophecies are merely possibilities." Brissa's voice sounded petulant to her own ears.

"Prophecies are possibilities pursued by the Gods." Cliope took Brissa's hands in her own and turned in her chair to face her. "Why do you sound so despondent? You have always been sure of this, Brissa. You *know* it is your destiny to free Villalu and rule alongside The Sidhe."

Brissa clutched her sister's hands. Yes, she had known. At the age of ten, she had learned the prophecy of the twin-born queen, and though she had not known whether it would be Cliope or herself who wore the crown, she knew it would be *them*. As they had grown older, it became clear that Cliope's strength lay in the sword and the bow, while Brissa had mastered a more subtle set of skills: She could read people easily and persuade them almost effortlessly. She had an innate sense of when to speak the plain truth and when—and how much—to hold back. Her temperament ran cool, and her passions ran hot. When one added her preference for lace dresses over muddy knees and needlepoint over archery, it became clear that she was the natural choice to accept the crown, much to Cliope's relief.

Her doubt had rarely wavered while she and her family hatched the plan, nor when she and her ladies did the slow and painstaking work of winning loyalty from Dronyen's guards and palace staff under his very nose. She had held fast to her conviction while Cliope silently assisted Brieden and Sehrys on their journey to The Border and their killing of Dronyen. Even when she had lain in Dronyen's bed, subjected to his sadism, her faith in their ultimate victory had not wavered. She still woke up in a cold sweat every now and then, convinced he had risen from the dead and was coming back for her, but she knew: her job, her fate, her *purpose* was to save Villalu. Not just from hatred and prejudice and the spread of a religion that celebrated both, but from the isolation of The Border itself.

But Firae… Firae made her question every bit of that.

"I feel as though I have met a person of royal blood for the first time in my life. As though the rest of us have been playacting, and I am indulging in the fantasy that I can save a dying world."

"*We* can save this dying world," Cliope corrected her. "If I recall, a very wise sister of mine once said to me, 'It is never a matter of *me*, but always a matter of *we*. There is no other way to defeat the Panlochs.'"

Brissa chuckled. "She does sound rather wise."

"She is, but don't tell her. She's arrogant enough as it is. And, she keeps stealing my best warriors away to her bedchambers and wearing them out." Cliope tightened her grip on Brissa's hands so that she couldn't smack her twin as she would have liked. "Brissa, the *we* that you always speak of—we are expanding. There are so many of us that even The Border is affected—your rule has already penetrated the ancient magics that keep us trapped in this world. Do not assume the king will not join us just because you cannot charm him as easily as you've charmed everyone else."

Brissa swallowed an unexpected lump in her throat. "Perhaps you should have been queen after all," she said softly.

Cliope smiled. "I am," she said. "Because you are."

FIRAE ROSE FROM HIS SEAT ON THE BED AND PACED THE LENGTH OF THE large room he had been given while reflecting on his conversation with the young queen. There was to be a feast that night to welcome Firae to Ryovni, and he had told the queen that he would come to a decision before the celebration began.

The sea breeze that danced into the room from the balcony had grown crisp, and the stone floor beneath his bare feet was cooler than it had been only an hour before. The first whispers of sunset announced themselves from the room's many windows, and Firae still couldn't decide what he was going to do.

Returning to a cold and detached tone after his momentary burst of temper, Tash had dutifully translated over an hour's conversation between the human queen and the elfin king. Firae had learned that the Ryovnians still worshipped elfin Gods, that they revered The Sidhe and wished to steer human culture back toward its ancient roots from before The Border had isolated them from the wisdom of The Sidhe. He had learned that the tapestries that lined the palace walls told the story of Ryovni's history, and that their alliance with a nearby Muirdannoch feririar went back generations.

But as fascinating as all that was, it was not what had led Firae to sit on the high bed in his room and stare out the window.

He had also learned that Brissa was largely responsible for seeing Sehrys safely home, that Brissa had spent years planning to depose the House of Panloch, had married Sehrys's tormentor in order to do so, and had facilitated Sehrys's and Brieden's escape. And now the House of Keshell was at war with the House of Panloch.

Risk or security. A king or a criminal.

If he helped Brissa, he would not only fail in his mission, he would betray the Non-Interference Doctrine himself. He could be stripped of his crown. And if he, Tash, and Brissa were not successful in enacting the Undoing spell, he could be banished to Villalu as it crumbled and folded in on itself and disappeared into nothing. He could lose everything, including his life.

At the same time, if they *were* successful, he could save thousands of lives. He could help secure the power of a queen who would change the human world. And perhaps, *perhaps* the Council would understand.

Firae walked to the door of his room. A servant sat in the corridor on a plush chair. Regarding him with nervous eyes, she rose and performed what Firae had learned was a *curtsy*.

"Send for the queen," Firae said in slow, careful Villaluan. "And tell her that I have decided to help her cause."

The palace courtyard glowed with the light of a thousand lanterns, dotting the trees like pixies during mating season. Dozens of tables held more food than Firae had ever seen in one place, as well as beverages of every color. A group of humans playing strange musical instruments were placed to one side of the dais upon which sat Firae, Brissa, Cliope, Tash, and a handsome man and woman with lined faces who were introduced to him as Brissa's parents. Brissa's younger siblings ran about the courtyard with the other children, shrieking and laughing and nearly knocking over the servants who carried more food from the castle kitchens.

The celebration was in Firae's honor, and he allowed himself to relax into the good cheer that surrounded him. He accepted more than a few cups of what tasted like the fermented juice of a fruit and sampled every dish that did not feature the carcass of a formerly living creature.

Tash had grown increasingly reserved over the course of the feast, and excused himself far earlier than would have been acceptable at any respectable sidhe gathering. This left Firae without a translator for much of the evening, but with each cup he drained, that fact mattered less and less, and he eventually permitted Brissa to lead him from the dais to dance upon the soft, cool grass amongst dozens of lively humans.

Rather than attempting to emulate the strange human dances, Firae slipped, loose-limbed and smiling, into The Dance of Clouds. He closed his eyes and lost himself to the movements, fluid and undulating, following the pulse of the power in his veins. *Imagine it is the sky that anchors you, and not the ground below,* his dance instructor had told him so many years ago, when he was no more than a boy. *Imagine that you are free of any force that binds you to the solid world.* Joy surged in Firae's chest; he had not danced with such abandon in years. He had lost far too much time to heartbreak and isolation; he had spent too many years without the pleasure of movement for its own sake, or revelry without the weight of responsibility.

When he opened his eyes, the humans had formed a circle around Brissa and himself and the queen was emulating his dance to the best of her ability. Firae hesitated for only a moment before taking her hand and guiding her through some of the more complex movements, while the others clapped and cheered them along.

Firae's heart ached even as it brimmed with the sweetness of the celebration; alone, The Dance of Clouds was about surrender, balance, and connection. When performed with a partner, it was most commonly a wedding dance.

AFTER THE LAST OF THE FOOD AND DRINK HAD BEEN CONSUMED, AFTER the musicians had packed up their instruments and even the servants had gone to bed, Firae wandered through the darkened courtyard and watched the last of the small lanterns in the trees flicker and fall into darkness. The courtyard was empty save for himself, and the castle was almost entirely dark.

He had consumed far too many human libations. The effect was both like and unlike that of the fermented nectars he was familiar with; his body was weightless and tingling and his mind was soft-edged and unencumbered. Desire thrummed beneath his skin, and he couldn't help but think of Sehrys, of his lean body and milky skin and piercing green eyes.

Firae looked up at the castle. Soft light came from the window Tash had pointed out as his own—Tash, with his golden skin and muscular body, his lovely face, and his bright green eyes.

It had been far too long since Firae had sought comfort in another man's body. He knew that Tash found him attractive; that had been plain from their very first interaction.

He did not think any further. He simply went.

Tash blinked in surprise when he opened the door to find Firae. Firae allowed his eyes to drag the length of the other man's body before returning to his face.

"Let me in."

Tash appeared to tighten his grip on the door frame, but otherwise did not move a muscle. "You are drunk," he said.

"Yes. And I am not tired in the slightest. Let me in."

"And why would I do any such thing?"

"Because I am king of Yestralekrezerche and I have commanded it." Firae stepped closer to Tash, whose eyes were bright even in the dim lamplight shining in from the corridor. "And also because I have seen the way you look at me. I can't imagine you would find my company in your bed to be a hardship."

"You are not my king." Tash's tone was so full of ice that a shiver rippled through Firae's body. "I owe you nothing. And no matter how I may have looked upon you before I learned the truth, I could never willingly find pleasure in the touch of *Ferban* Gira's heir."

Firae narrowed his eyes at the other man as heat rose beneath his skin. "And what precisely does my mother have to do with this?"

"Who do you suppose banished me to Villalu, *Firae?*" Tash demanded, spitting Firae's familiar name, title free, with such vehemence that Firae took a step backward. "For half a century I have been trapped in hell. I have been captured by slave traders twice, subjected to things I can't even begin to talk about, done things that…" Tash swallowed; his eyes flashed with pain. "I have done horrible things to keep myself safe. My life… until I met the Keshells, my life was *nothing.*"

Firae gave a mirthless laugh. "And now you beg for pity instead of forgiveness. You would not have been banished had your crime not been atrocious, if you had not caused suffering worthy of such a punishment."

Tash threw the door to his room wide and stepped into the hall, so close to Firae that their noses nearly brushed. Firae forced himself to stand firm, and did not back up so much as a single inch.

"My *crime* should have been punishable by half a century or less of labor in the Iron Mountains," Tash hissed. "*Ferban* Alqii of the Lower Midlands had a personal vendetta, and your mother chose not to question it."

"Even if you speak the truth, I am not my mother. Would you blame me for her mistakes?"

Tash backed up and crossed his arms over his chest. "It is not a matter of her mistakes. *You* chose not to question *her*. Your mother may have sentenced me to exile, but I was banished under your rule, *Rigday* Firae."

Firae froze. "It was not my place to question my mother's decisions," he finally managed to respond, keeping his voice cool and steady by sheer force of will, as he did his best to force away the grip of guilt in the center of his chest. "Carrying out the sentences she had handed down was little more than a formality once I was crowned."

Tash snorted. "So you were merely following the precedents set by your mother without bothering to examine her choices. You truly are your mother's son. And even if I were to set aside the matter of my banishment, I still would not allow you in my bed. You treat me as a bit of filth on the bottom of your heel rather than as a trusted advisor to your new ally, the queen. And despite this, you seem to believe that appearing at my bedchamber entitles you to my body and my attention."

Firae smirked slightly. "It appears that your attention is mine already. And your body... are you truly going to deny how much you would enjoy sharing your bed with me?"

Tash looked away. "It does not matter."

Emboldened, Firae stepped closer. "It does. Let me in."

"I am going to tell you something I imagine you have not often heard before, Firae." Tash looked him square in the eye. "*No.*"

And with that he closed the door in Firae's outraged and bewildered face.

CHAPTER SIX

SHORTLY AFTER BREAKFAST, TASH ACCOMPANIED BRISSA, Cliope, and Firae to the cave where they had found the door.

Finding the door had not been difficult; Tash had known what to look for, and Brissa and Cliope had known that the cave was special when they had discovered it as children. The trouble had come in prying the door open.

"We thought we would need a Spiral caste sidhe even to read the scroll," Brissa explained to Firae, with some help from Tash, as they rode toward Keshemerk Lake. "But as Tash was able to read and understand the scroll completely, we are hoping that if the two of you combine your power, it might be enough to open the door."

Firae frowned. "How do you know of such things? I was under the impression that the humans of Villalu had grown ignorant of sidhe social structures."

Brissa smiled. "We are not Villaluans, we are Ryovnians. Our island is special. Our caves are full of writings of The Sidhe, and a Muirdannoch feririar lives just beyond the lake. We are friendly with them. Your written language is similar to theirs."

"It is our belief that the writings were left for us intentionally by Queen Tyzva herself," Cliope added. "There are scrolls that speak of an alliance between Tyzva and our ancestors."

Firae nodded, but the uncertainty in his eyes was clear. Tash understood; no such alliance on the part of Tyzva the Liberator was recorded in sidhe historical texts, nor did it make sense—why would such a shrewd and celebrated leader risk leaving such unstable magics amongst humans in Villalu?

Tash chose not to enlighten Firae any further without being asked directly. Perhaps it was childish of him, but he preferred to see Firae struggle with confusion and discomfort, to realize that all he sought to have and to understand would not be presented to him upon a platter.

Of course, the truth of the matter was that Tash was not altogether opposed to the concept of offering *himself* to Firae on a platter, and that was what annoyed him the most. He kept his gaze trained straight ahead, half afraid that Firae would be able to tell the effect he had on Tash, would somehow *know* that Tash had wrapped his hand around his cock almost the moment that he had shut the door in the king's face, with those eyes—heated and confident and dripping with equal parts lust and entitlement—burned into his mind as he found his release and then found it again upon waking with the sun.

The ride took little more than a quarter of an hour, and the morning sun shone warm, but not too hot, upon them as they rounded the northern shore of the lake. When the trail grew rocky and uneven, they tethered the horses in the shade of a *tochet* tree.

Even Brissa was dressed for the task at hand in a sleeveless pale blue tunic, close-fitting breeches, and sturdy boots, her hair arranged in a knot at the back of her neck. She led the way without hesitation, managing to look graceful even as she navigated the rocky terrain. Tash nearly laughed at the way she was juxtaposed with her twin. Cliope scrambled behind her on equally deft feet, but without sparing a thought for appearing regal; instead she leapt from rock to rock like an energetic child.

Both sisters paused once they reached the cave's darkened entryway so that Tash might light the torches that lined the walls.

Bringing up the rear, Firae stared at the walls, patches of which were covered in etched writings and drawings, some in standard Elfin, and some in the high language of the spellmakers. The floor of the cave was flat, smooth rock, curved to accommodate a small pool of water where the lake flowed into the cave.

"There are at least half a dozen caves like this one on Ryovni," Tash said, coming to stand beside him, "though this one is the most ornate by far." He did his best not to appear excited at the prospect of finally getting to share this with another sidhe. "And there may be even more that remain undiscovered."

"Can you decipher any of this?" Firae asked, touching some writing in the old script.

"Yes," Tash answered. "It speaks of the coven that created The Border. It's quite fascinating. I believe this story may be lost to Laesi's own history texts."

Firae tilted his head, continuing to study the etching. "One doesn't often hear of those of the Common caste reading fluent High Elfin."

"When one lives in a great royal hall and all information about those of the Common caste is received third or fourth hand, it is unsurprising that one would not have any idea what Common caste sidhe do." Tash was careful to keep his voice even.

Firae glanced at him sidelong. "So it is not uncommon, then?"

Tash sighed. "No," he grumbled, "I suppose it is a *bit* uncommon. I simply have an interest in and an aptitude for learning languages, and my father was a repairer of old texts when I was growing up. They were strewn all about his workspace, and I learned to read quickly, before they were due back to their owners."

Firae turned to face Tash. "You must be very clever."

Tash's cheeks went a bit warm. "If only cleverness were enough," he murmured.

"*Boys!* Stop flirting and come light the rest of the torches!" Cliope yelled from deep within the cave. Firae's jaw fell open at her audacity in addressing him so. Tash could do nothing but laugh.

TASH TOOK ONE SIDE OF THE CAVE AND FIRAE TOOK THE OTHER, LIGHTING torches dotted along the wall as they retreated farther and farther into the belly of the cave. The etchings on the walls grew sparser and fainter as the air around them grew cool and still. Brissa and Cliope trailed behind Tash, whispering, their voices drowned out by the echoing clack of their boots upon the stone floor.

Firae and Tash met at the back of the cave. Each lit a lamp on one side of a patch of wall that appeared to be blank except for two complementary handprints pressed deep into the stone.

"This is the door," Tash said, his voice barely louder than a whisper. "I still don't know that this will work. The spell is intended for a Spiral sidhe—"

"I know of only one way to find out." Firae's voice was more confident than he felt as he held out his hand.

Tash glanced at Brissa, who offered him a smile of encouragement. "We know what to do. Don't spare us a thought," she said, and gave his arm a quick, friendly squeeze.

Tash took Firae's hand, and then each man pressed his free hand into the handprint-shaped indentations in the wall.

The shock was instantaneous. Firae gasped and squeezed Tash's hand as searing heat ripped through them like a lightning bolt. Firae closed his eyes, remembered Tash's instructions, and breathed deeply. He remained as still as possible and gathered energy in his heart, whence he drew his command of fire, and then carefully reached out with his power to join the current of… *something* that was racing through his body and making him want to itch and shudder and move away. He touched the current with his power and then quickly jumped back at the sting.

This was going to hurt.

Clutching Tash's hand even harder, Firae pushed his other hand deeper into the stone, and then focused on directing an enormous fireball directly into the stone itself.

Firae gritted his teeth at the effort. His power pushed against the current whipping through him. He felt as if he were trudging upstream in knee-high water after a heavy rain.

His power moved at a sluggish pace, but move it did. He did not know how well Tash was faring, but he could hear Tash's heavy panting beside him and feel the weight and flavor of the other man's power beginning to mix with his own.

"A-are you close?" Tash gritted out, his voice rough and breathless and *wrecked*, and Firae's throat went dry.

"I… I think so… it feels… almost there…" Firae managed, as the heat of his own—of *their* own—fire reached his wrist.

"Me too. Tell me when—"

Firae took another deep breath and pushed with all his might. He kept his eyes closed lest he lose concentration, until the fire crept into his fingertips and finally, *finally*, shot through the tips of his fingers and into the stone, drawing his hand impossibly deeper into the wall.

"Now! *Gods!*" Firae gasped at the intensity.

"All right, hold it, Firae. Hold it steady and don't let go."

Firae gritted his teeth. The stone around his hand was already red-hot, hot enough to blister and burn anyone who could not wield fire as he could.

Tash gave a sudden shout, and Firae's eyes flew open as the current was replaced with a stream of pure fire, which radiated from the blazing hot press of their joined hands and into the wall before them.

Tash inhaled sharply, then recited in High Elfin. His voice echoed and the wall glowed orange as he spoke: *By the Gods of all elfin races, by the Mother and the Guardians of all worlds, we swear that this spell must be undone, for the good of all, in the name of Queen Tyzva the Liberator. Accept our offering of fire, of warmth and creation, of transformation and destruction. Accept our offering in exchange for truth. Blessed Be.*

When he finished speaking, the wall cracked and bright light poured from whatever lay on the other side, until the patch of wall between the two torches crumbled into a glowing pile of embers to reveal a hallway.

Tash and Firae moved the larger embers out of the way so that Brissa and Cliope could step through the doorway with them.

They traveled along a corridor that was only wide enough for them to walk single file. Tash walked at the front of the group, and Firae brought up the rear, providing a magical buffer to protect Brissa and Cliope.

The corridor seemed to be lamplit, though no lamps were visible. They walked in silence for several moments before coming upon a shallow, ancient-looking stone staircase. They climbed the stairs and found themselves in a sumptuous room.

The room was enormous, but it felt cozy and warm. They saw a stone hearth with a fire and several large, dark wooden chests of drawers, and felt soft carpets of red and plum and rust beneath their feet. The floor was littered with dozens of plump cushions in various sizes and colors. At its center sat an enormous purple velvet pillow, upon which lay a sleeping sphinx.

She was curled into a ball, and as her guests entered the room she raised her head and blinked her large yellow eyes at them, stretched like a cat, and came to stand before them.

Somehow managing to capture and hold all four pairs of eyes at once, the sphinx nodded her head. "It is time," she said.

CHAPTER SEVEN

SEHRYS GRUMBLED TO HIMSELF AS HE OPENED HIS SATCHEL AND threw his gear onto the bed of the guest quarters he had been assigned. In the week since he had discovered what Firae had done, he had stopped his angry muttering for perhaps an hour's time. When—if—*no, not if, I refuse to contemplate the possibility of if*—when he saw Firae again, he was going to punch him square in the face. And then hug him as hard as possible.

Firae had gone to Villalu alone. Sehrys didn't want to think about what that could mean for his dear friend.

Even more frustrating was that Sehrys was certain Firae had gone in search of Tash. There was every likelihood Tash was helping Brissa and Cliope; Sehrys himself had orchestrated it.

Sehrys sighed and sank onto the bed of soft moss. He was staying at the Great Hall in Carzet Vrel, the queen's feririar in the heart of the Upper Midlands. His reception had been lovely, and he was being treated with all the respect a proxy for a king could expect. But he had no patience for any of it; everything was a mess, and he was partially to blame.

Sehrys rose to answer the knock on his door and opened it to reveal Sree; her near-constant look of smug disdain was fixed. Sehrys forced himself not to scowl.

"Is it time?" he asked.

"It is. Is that truly what you plan to wear?"

Sehrys ignored her. "Let's go," he said, leaving the room and striding to the meeting room where the most of the members of the Council of Nations were assembled.

The room was enormous, with a high ceiling of translucent blossoms that allowed sunlight to filter in and a window nearly the entire length of the northern wall that displayed the lush, rolling valleys below. Queen Bralashe's Hall was built from a dense canopy at the very top of eight strong *srechelee* flower-trees, and the view was spectacular.

Along the western wall of the room was a long table, behind which sat seven queens and two kings. A palace aide guided Sree and Sehrys toward a smaller table facing the large one. Both remained standing.

Queen Nitrae of the World River Valley rose from her seat at the center of the table. "*Sehrys Silerth Valusidhe efa Naisdhe efa es Zulla Maletog Feririar ala es Fervishlaea efa es Vestramezershe* and *Sree Silerth Banvalusidhe efa Seledhe efa es Alovur Drovuru Feririar ala es Fervishlaea efa es Yestralekrezershe*. We welcome you to the Council of Nations. We receive you as guests and shall regard you as royalty."

"We are humbled by your attentions and thank the Gods for the creation of the Royal caste," Sree and Sehrys recited in unison. Nitrae nodded and waved a hand in their direction.

"You may sit. I believe the two of you have come to discuss your king's journey to the human realm."

Sehrys did not bother to correct Nitrae that Firae was not *his* king precisely—as a citizen of Khryslee, he had no queen or king—but merely nodded.

"Your Majesties, it has come to our attention—"

"We believe that if Firae does not return within—"

Sehrys and Sree stopped mid-sentence and glared at one another. Sehrys cleared his throat and charged ahead.

"Forgive me, but it has come to our attention that Firae has been given six months to complete his task. We would like to request clarification as to what will happen should he not meet that deadline."

Nitrae glanced about at the others seated around her. "The Council remains split on that topic. We are hoping that Firae will return quickly and that it will not be necessary to decide."

"I would not say we are *split*, precisely," piped up Dariet, king of the Forest Islands. "While it is true that a few of our number are in favor of granting Firae additional time, the Council is leaning toward removing the threat if we have not heard word in six months."

Sehrys felt as if his blood had turned to ice in his veins.

"You... surely you cannot truly be considering just letting Firae *die?*" Sree demanded. "He is of your caste. A king of Laesi. A descendent of Tyzva the Liberator!"

"He is one man," Dariet replied.

"He may be one man, but Villalu is teeming with tens of thousands of women and men! Would you truly commit genocide so freely?" Sehrys asked. His capacity for appropriate decorum was ebbing rapidly.

"The death of tens of thousands is a tragedy, but if we allow The Border to implode, it will certainly destroy the entire planet and everyone on it. If we must settle for a lesser tragedy, then we must," Bralashe said gently.

"And I suppose you would give up just as easily if it were tens of thousands of sidhe inside that border? We put the humans inside. We owe it to them—"

"We owe the humans nothing."

Sehrys stopped short at the icy voice of Alqii, queen of the Lower Midlands. "We would have been well within our rights to put them all out of their misery fifty thousand years ago. Terrible, nasty creatures."

"I agree, Your Majesty," Sree cut in quickly before Sehrys could respond. "The fate of the humans and the criminals inside The Border are of little concern. But I implore you not to leave Firae to perish with them."

"Humans are *people*," Sehrys snapped, doing his best to contain his volume. "Do none of you understand that?"

"If you love humans so dearly, Sehrys, perhaps you should lead a search party into Villalu to find Firae."

Sehrys froze. The silence in the room seemed to last for an eternity.

"I am sure we all recall Sehrys's testimony as to the atrocities he suffered in Villalu," Nitrae finally said, her voice gentle. "To suggest he return to such a place shows little regard for his need to heal."

"Fine, then," Sree said, apparently unperturbed by her own inappropriateness. "I propose that Sehrys's human lead the search party. From what I understand, the king will be just *thrilled* to see him again."

Sree screeched as her chair legs, which grew directly from the floor, shot several feet into the air and then tilted sharply, throwing her to the ground.

"That will be enough, Sehrys," Nitrae said. Sehrys took a deep breath. He'd barely been aware that he'd done it, or that his knuckles had gone white from clenching his fists on the table in front of him.

"Of course," he said sweetly. "My apologies."

He left the chair where it was, and Sree, forced to remain standing, crossed her arms over her chest and glared at him. "Were we not before the Council right now, Sehrys, I swear to the Gods—" she hissed.

Sehrys laughed. "What? You would cause a book to hurl itself at me? Perhaps spray me to death with water? If you could even manage a full spray. Your power is so weak that you—"

"*Enough!*" roared Nitrae, her eyes flashing blue as the entire room trembled. "I cannot imagine why Firae saw fit to leave the two of you in charge *together,* but if this is how you plan to run the Queendom in his absence, I would say that Villalu is the least of his worries."

Abashed, Sehrys looked at his hands and shrunk Sree's chair to its former height and angle.

"This is a serious issue, and the Council appreciates the concern that you have both expressed. But I would advise you to work things out between yourselves before you come before us again. The Council of Nations has little time and no patience for squabbling children."

Based upon some of Firae's descriptions of other Council meetings, Sehrys wasn't entirely sure that was true, but he knew that Nitrae was right. As much as he loathed Sree, he must at least attempt to find some common ground with the vile woman.

"Yes, Your Majesty. I beg your forgiveness," Sehrys said.

"As do I," said Sree. To Sehrys's surprise, she sounded contrite.

They were dismissed, and Sehrys returned to his quarters without sparing Sree so much as a word or a look. They would be traveling back east by grimchin in the morning, and another long trip beside her was more than he wanted to think about.

So instead he thought of Brieden: of Brieden's clear brown eyes and the way they lit up with joy whenever Sehrys returned from a trip; of the way Brieden smelled, of calendula and woodsmoke and sometimes honeysuckle; of Brieden sleeping, sweet and gorgeous, as the morning light played across his skin.

Sehrys did not want to think about Villalu. He had fallen in love with his fiancé in that horrid place, but he could not stand the idea of going back—or of *Brieden* going back.

Sehrys sank into the moss bed in his room and wrapped his arms around himself. He took slow, measured breaths and longed for freedom from the fear and panic that thoughts of Villalu still inspired. He longed for the strength and patience to somehow work with Sree, and for even the smallest bit of information about the safety and whereabouts of Firae and Tash and the Keshells. But more than anything else, he longed for Khryslee and the safety of Brieden's arms.

CHAPTER EIGHT

OR AS LONG AS THE SIDHE HAD RECORDED THEIR HISTORY ON the planet of Ullavise, The Sphinx had guarded their biggest and strongest spells: the spells that altered the fabric of reality in some significant way; the spells that even The Sidhe could not be trusted to guard without falling prey to their own whims, vendettas, or egos.

As far as Firae knew, no one amongst The Sidhe understood where The Sphinx came from. All that was known was that they did not seem subject to such constrictions as life and death and they took their duties very, very seriously.

Firae respected The Sphinx. He deferred to their judgment. He knew that they were creatures of unfathomable wisdom.

And yet, when they were riddle-bound, he wanted nothing more than to shake them and demand that they speak the plain truth.

"I am The Truthkeeper," the sphinx spoke—the language was difficult to pinpoint, though all understood her with perfect clarity—when Brissa, Cliope, Firae, and Tash walked into her chamber. "I keep not what you seek, but only what you are destined to discover. Come. Sit."

"Madame Truthkeeper, if I may—" Brissa began in Villaluan.

"Sit," The Truthkeeper repeated.

"I have been sent by the C—" Firae interjected in Elfin.

"Sit." The Truthkeeper's face remained placid; her voice betrayed no irritation.

"The lady said sit." Cliope hurled herself onto a plump gold cushion. Only Tash remained silent. They all found cushions and made themselves comfortable.

"She of the gold heart," the sphinx said, winding around Cliope's pillow and letting her tail drag across the princess's lap. "Your path is not what you believe it to be. Learn to decipher the truth wherever you may find it." Cliope raised her eyebrows at the creature and lifted her arm as if to stroke the sphinx's tail, but then appeared to think better of it.

"She of the blue heart," the sphinx continued, circling Brissa on her sky-blue cushion. "You shall be tested. Never forget that a queen stands alone, even in a crowded room. Keep your gaze to the sea and never forget that your trust must always remain a precious and finite commodity."

The sphinx rounded Firae's pillow next. "He of the scarlet heart," the sphinx said, "descendant of Tyzva the Liberator. Your fire is your strength, but it is also your weakness. If you do not learn to tell one from the other, the flames shall consume you alive."

Firae shivered at the pronouncement; the sphinx's deep, smooth voice seemed to penetrate his very lungs. She moved on.

"He of the violet heart," she said, circling Tash. She came to a stop before him and looked directly into his eyes. Tash went very still and stared back, eyes wide.

"Do not be afraid," she said. Tash swallowed audibly.

The Truthkeeper walked to her own pillow at the center of the room and settled upon it with her paws stretched out in front of her and her shoulders squared.

"There are eight; you are four. The world breathes, and does not know when it shall perish. The universe expands, and does not know when it shall grow thin and tear. You are each of you but specks of sand."

Cliope and Brissa exchanged glances. "Um," Cliope said, appearing to search her mind for the suitable way to respond.

"She is riddle-bound," Tash interjected. "She cannot speak the direct truth to us, at least with regard to the spell."

"The spell you seek to undo is the most significant in the history of The Sidhe on this world," the sphinx said, nodding. "Riddles protect the truth and are not meant to be easily solved."

"All right, so I need to stop thinking I know everything, Brissa needs to listen to her gut even if other people argue, Firae needs to calm down, and Tash needs to grow a spine. But it doesn't matter, because we're all just insignificant specks and the universe is enormous and we're all going to die eventually anyway. There, I solved it. It's hopeless." Cliope moved to stand up, but the Sphinx was back in front of her in an instant, urging her back into a sitting position with an enormous but gentle paw.

"You must stop thinking that you know everything," The Truthkeeper said. Cliope opened her mouth to argue, but then snorted and rolled her eyes.

"Fine. I see your point," she said, and crossed her arms over her chest.

"Prophecy lives in the shadowed pathways that we do not see or dare not travel. The truth exists. The future is eternal. But you must choose. The path is too long to walk alone."

"So… we should walk the path together, then?" Tash asked.

"There are eight; you are four."

"There are four others we must find?" Brissa ventured.

"There are eight; you are four."

Brissa closed her eyes and took two deep breaths, clearly fighting her frustration.

"What *are* you able to tell us?" Cliope asked.

"What are you able to ask?"

Firae wanted to pull the creature's tail.

"There is a prophecy," Tash said, "and we are a part of it."

The sphinx met his eye and said nothing.

"I cannot ask what you cannot tell," Tash continued, studying the creature. The sphinx nodded. "Is there anyone who *can* tell us what we need to know?"

"Quiet are the *La'ekynog*, those that stayed behind," the sphinx answered. "When the journey is long enough, one always ends precisely where one began."

"I am certainly feeling the futility of the journey," Cliope grumbled.

"The *La'ekynog*," Firae repeated back to the sphinx. "In sidhe mythology, they are the Blessed Guardian's most trusted helpers and companions," he explained, turning to look at Brissa and Cliope. "They tend to the small things so that the Guardian may keep his focus upon matters of the divine."

"Oh," Brissa said, excited. "Yes, they exist in our religious texts as well, but we call them the Lekianoche."

Firae smiled at her. "Your Majesty, I do not mean to switch topics, but I wonder how it is that we understand one another right now. I am speaking Elfin, and I assume you have not become fluent overnight."

Brissa blinked. "I—I am speaking Villaluan."

The sphinx made a brief kneading motion on the floor. "This chamber neutralizes all barriers to linguistic communication. I speak only my own language, and if you were to hear it directly rather than filtered through your own, your hearts would explode."

"Charming," said Cliope dryly.

The Truthkeeper laughed, low and rich.

"If there is a prophecy," Tash began, his face screwed up in concentration, "that means there is a way, a path to victory for us. That means it is not too late."

"There is a path," The Truthkeeper confirmed. Firae blinked, switching his focus from the queen to the sphinx. "It is a narrow path, grown over with thorns and nettles, but it is navigable with the correct tools."

"How do we know if we have found the correct tools?" Brissa asked.

"There are eight; you are four."

Cliope groaned.

The Truthkeeper stalked back to her velvet pillow in the center of the room, kneaded the fabric, and circled twice before curling into a ball. She lowered her head, but kept her eyes open.

"I have spoken all I shall speak on it this day," she said. "You may remain in my chamber for as long as you like." And with that she closed her eyes.

"And I thought trying to get the door open was frustrating," Cliope grumbled, rising to her feet. "I feel the need for a bit of sword practice to settle my nerves. Tash, would you care to join me? You could use the practice."

Firae bit his lip at the glare Tash shot toward Cliope. He resolved not to tell Tash how adorable he looked when he got aggravated, at least not for now.

Tash did seem to pick up on Cliope's intent to give the king and queen some privacy to talk, however, and he left with a bow to Brissa and a stiff nod to Firae.

"Do you mind staying here?" Brissa asked. "I would so enjoy the opportunity to speak without need of a translator."

"I welcome the opportunity," Firae confirmed, smiling at her.

"I hardly know where to begin," Brissa said with a nervous chuckle. "You—The Truthkeeper said that you were a descendent of Tyzva the Liberator."

Firae nodded. "Tyzva was queen of the Eastern Border Lands many generations ago. Well, it was the Eastern Sea Lands when she began her rule, until the easternmost part of the land was sacrificed to create The Border."

"It seems significant that you are a part of the prophecy."

Firae shrugged. "I suppose so. But it is difficult to discern what matters are significant to the prophecy when we know so little. It could be little more than a coincidence."

Brissa appeared unconvinced. "Coincidence is nothing less than—" she began.

"—the Gods whispering in our ears," Firae finished. "My mother used to say that to me. It is an old tenet of those who worship the earthbound Gods."

"Well, it made its way to Ryovni as well, and I happen to believe it."

Firae considered her. "You truly do revere the old Gods, don't you?"

"I do. I want you to understand, Your Majesty, that I am very serious about cultivating a Queendom that will fit into the fabric of Laesi. When The Border is gone, I will not implore The Sidhe of Laesi to leave the human realm alone. The prophecy guarded by The Truthkeeper is not the only prophecy we have found in the caves of Ryovni. It is also prophesied that a twin-born Ryovnian queen shall lead the people of Villalu out of darkness. I believe I am that queen, and I wish to demonstrate how worthy I am to rule alongside the queens and kings of Laesi. I wish to earn a seat on the Royal Council of Sidhe Nations."

"And as surprised as I am to admit it, I believe that perhaps you shall. But I will not lie, Your Majesty, I am wary of sharing lands with humans. Surely many of them will not be persuaded to peacefully coexist with those they believe to be worthy of enslavement?"

"Surely not. Just as surely as many sidhe will have no interest in treating humans as anything close to equals. But I do believe that I can change a good deal of hearts and minds in Villalu. I have to believe that."

"And if you cannot?"

Brissa laced her fingers together in her lap and sat up straighter on her pillow. "If I cannot, then I will do what must be done."

"Even if it means bloodshed."

"I have a large collection of very fine gowns," Brissa said. "I prefer not to stain them with blood. But blood will wash out of even the finest silk with cold water and good soap. So yes, I shall do what must be done for the greater good of my people and yours, Your Majesty, no matter what that means."

The fire in the young queen's eyes made Firae's chest throb.

"Perhaps we should do away with the titles. We are equals in our stations, after all," Firae said.

Brissa's face lit up. "Are—do you truly mean that?" It was the youngest he had heard her sound.

"I do, Brissa, if you agree."

"Of course, I agree." Brissa squeezed Firae's hand. "Thank you, Firae."

CHAPTER NINE

Tash's eyes snapped open and he gasped, immediately pulling himself to an upright position as he pressed his hand to his heart.

A strange sensation bloomed in his chest, almost a throb, but more like a *pull*. He did not understand it and did not try. Instead he pushed back the covers on the bed and stepped onto the cool stone floor.

The sky was pitch black, the stars hazy beyond the filter of The Border above. The greater moon was completely dark; the dwarf moon was little more than a sliver. Tash held his arm out and produced a palmful of fire to light his way through the castle.

The palace was silent around him, and the slap of his bare feet against the floors echoed softly as he made his way to the front gate. He wasn't sure where the pull in his chest was leading him, but he had some idea.

He didn't bother fetching a horse; the cave was less than an hour from the castle even on foot, and the thought of a detour to the stables made the pull strengthen and squeeze his heart almost to the point of pain.

When he heard footsteps behind him, he didn't stop, but he did slow his pace. When Firae, also using a fire-filled palm to light his way, fell into step beside him, Tash wasn't the least bit surprised.

"You feel it too," the king murmured.

"I do."

"What do you suppose it means?"

"I imagine The Truthkeeper has something she wishes to say to us," Tash said, standing aside to allow Firae to navigate the rocky area that led to the cave's entrance.

When they entered the cave, Firae waved a hand, and all the torches along the wall sprang to life.

Tash raised an eyebrow. "You couldn't have done that the last time we were here?"

Firae looked abashed. "I thought the lighting of the lanterns may have been part of the ritual," he said, but seemed to realize how implausible that sounded as soon as he said it. He shrugged and looked away. "And we were getting along quite well. I did not wish to chance ruining it by showing off."

Tash gave in to a small smile. "Well. Thank you for showing off," he said, and made his way to the door.

He was not surprised to see that the door had rebuilt itself, and he and Firae approached it and joined hands without discussion.

Opening the door was easier this time, almost alarmingly easy. Tash gasped when the glowing embers crumbled to the floor, revealing The Truthkeeper standing directly in the entranceway with her tail twitching and her eyes fever-bright.

"Time bleeds away too fast. Possible outcomes are narrowing," she said, before turning to lead them to her room.

The room looked and felt different; though the pillows remained, most of them seemed threadbare. The room smelled of mildew, the fire in the hearth was low, and the air was cold. Strange shadows danced on the walls and made Tash uneasy, though he could not say why.

"What do you mean?" Tash asked her, eyeing a patch of mold on the cushion he had sat upon mere days before, and hoping she would not demand that he sit again.

"There are eight; you are two," she said, pacing around the room as agitation rolled from her in palpable waves.

Tash closed his eyes, took a deep breath, and willed the energy in the room to ebb away from him so that he could focus. They could glean more from the creature, if only they asked the right questions. She would not have summoned them if that were not the case.

"There are eight," Tash said slowly. "Tell me about the eight. Eight of what, precisely?"

"Eight keys," The Truthkeeper answered. Tash blinked at the straightforward response.

"Eight keys," Firae murmured. "The Border. The spellmakers anchored it in eight ways, is that right?"

The sphinx continued to pace, but her steps slowed. "There are eight; you are two," she said, and it sounded like an affirmation.

"Who—" Tash began, and then stopped himself. "What I mean to ask is, *what* are the eight keys?"

"No," Tash added quickly, just as The Truthkeeper was about to respond. "No, I know you won't be able to answer that. What... can you tell me what each key requires?"

The Truthkeeper came to a stop before him and let her tail curl around her paws.

"Each key requires each lock," she said.

"And what does each lock require?" Tash asked.

The Truthkeeper blinked at him; the corners of her mouth tugged into a near-smile.

"There are eight; you are two." The Truthkeeper sounded almost *relieved*. "The violet heart requires freedom. You must not hide from the mirror of your soul."

Tash choked on his own breath, but disguised his shock with a gentle cough.

"The scarlet heart," she added, circling Firae, "requires naked courage. When your ancestors whisper into your ear, you must listen."

Firae swallowed, looking just as shaken as Tash had.

"And what of the six remaining keys?" Tash asked. "What do they require?"

'Two require sacrifice. One requires love, another faith. One requires strength, and the last requires strife. With the purest heart tethered to the greatest power, each key shall unlock the prison of the human realm."

Her voice had slowed; her eyes were growing heavy. "Time bleeds away too fast into the darkness. Possible outcomes are narrowing."

"There will be time," Firae said, his voice fierce. "There must be."

The sphinx plodded to her enormous purple pillow in the center of the room.

"Now you must go," she said, "before it is too late." She climbed onto the pillow and circled twice before curling up. She lay her head down and blinked at them.

"Where must we go?" Firae asked.

"Quiet are the *La'ekynog*, those that stayed behind," she said. "When the journey is long enough, one always ends precisely where one began." She closed her eyes and settled in for a sleep.

"Come," Tash said, gesturing toward the door, before Firae could ask any questions. "She has gone dormant, and for all we know the room could seal us in if we don't move quickly."

"We know too little," Firae said with a loud sigh as they made their way through the cave. "Even given that Brissa and Cliope are also keys, there are four others that we must find, and they could be anywhere in the world."

"Prophecies are designed to work," Tash countered. "We will find them. We just need to pay attention. And at least we know—" Tash came to an abrupt stop and tried to make sense of what he saw in the distance. It looked almost like—

"Fire," Firae whispered. Tash used both hands to climb to the top of the cave's hill and pushed bursts of flame into the rocks below to create a glowing pathway. Firae followed without a word.

At the top of the hill, Tash faced the direction of Keshell castle, hoping desperately that his fears would not be confirmed. But luck had turned her back on him this night, at least as far as Okoskeshell was concerned.

The castle itself did not appear to be aflame, though it was illuminated by the many buildings around it that were. Tash listened with all his capacity, tuning toward the palace with the excellent hearing that nearly all sidhe possessed. He could hear screams in the distance, and a sudden loud crack followed by a brilliant explosion which knocked half a turret into pieces. The dark shapes of human figures fell to the ground along with broken chunks of stone.

Firae gasped and seemed to go unsteady on his feet for the briefest of moments. Tash grabbed him by his shoulders and turned to find the king's face ashen and his eyes wide with fear.

"That—I thought it must have been lightning, that there must have been a storm. But it didn't seem right, and—" Firae swallowed, closing his eyes as he clutched Tash's arms. "Whatever that was, the thing that caused that noise and that violent burst of light—that was the thing that destroyed my ship. I'm certain of it."

"We need to go," Tash said. Firae clutched his arms harder. "We need to—dear Gods, *Brissa!*"

Brissa's name seemed to strengthen Firae. He let go of Tash's arms and nodded before barreling down the rocky cave wall and toward the commotion.

OKOSKESHELL WAS IN CHAOS, AND BRISSA WAS NOT PREPARED.

She should have been prepared; Lord Pyke had been cagey for far too long, insisting that Brissa visit the Isles of Sheevalu on her own, without her guards or even her sister, to discuss a potential alliance against the House of Panloch.

Even so, the Pykes and the Keshells had always remained on good terms—fellow island folks who participated in friendly trade—and Brissa had never foreseen an attack from their neighbors to the east. But Ryovnians were warriors, all of them, and protecting their island was something each and every one of them had been trained to do since childhood.

Brissa had been roused from her bed before she heard the first cannons fire. The ships had come quietly, taking advantage of the dark night and the friendly history between the two territories. When the Ryovnian sentries had seen the fleet of ships traveling through the Nosfin Channel that lay between the Vrali peninsula on mainland Villalu and the eastern coast of Ryovni, they were not concerned, though they had sent word to the other coastal sentries, as was protocol.

"It is most likely nothing, Your Highness, they appear to be headed north to the Muirdannoch coast, but it looks to be quite a lot of ships for their usual trade," Gejene had apologized when she woke Brissa from her slumber.

Shrugging on a thin robe over her nightdress, Brissa had frowned. "It is strange indeed, particularly since we have heard no word of it. The Pykes usually send word when they are delivering a large shipment to the mainland so that we may join in the trade." Hesitating, Brissa weighed the unlikelihood of trouble against the gnawing feeling in her gut.

"Fetch my boots and my sword. And wake Cliope. Tell her to ready the palace guard and that I will fill her in on the particulars within the hour. Send word to Coral Mountain as well, just to be safe. Let us pray that I am overreacting, Gejene, but something simply doesn't feel right about this."

Standing at the battlements atop her castle and watching her village burn, Brissa was grateful that she had listened to her instincts; there was nothing right about this at all.

"Your Majesty." Cesmi panted as she ran toward Brissa. One of only two members of the Queen's Council who had accompanied Brissa to Ryovni, Cesmi was usually the very picture of cool composure, but that appearance had slipped since the Pyke ships had attacked. The woman's small frame was covered in sweat, grime, and blood, and the long braid she wore down her back had been sliced neatly in half in the battle. Its frayed edges clung to her sweaty neck.

"What news, Cesmi?" Brissa asked. She watched as a fifth cannon was wheeled across the roof and another was fired at the three enemy ships that remained in the water. The other two had managed to come ashore.

"I am afraid that Tash and Firae are still nowhere to be found, Your Majesty," Cesmi said. Brissa nodded, breathing deeply to tamp down the knot of fear in her chest.

"Thank you for informing me. I can only hope that they have found someplace safe, and that the enemy is not armed with iron or verbena."

"There… I am afraid that iron swords are amongst their weaponry, Your Majesty," Cesmi said, wiping her forehead with her sleeve and managing to do little more than smear the dirt.

"Pray the Guardian guides them safely," Brissa responded. "But keep looking. We cannot lose either of them."

"Yes, Your Majesty."

"Have you news of my parents and the children? Have they found their way to safety?"

"Your father and the children of the castle have made it safely to the escape tunnels," Cesmi said. "Your mother insists on joining the battle. She is on the ground with Cliope as we speak."

Brissa bit her lip against a fond smile. "I imagine she is. It was a fool's wish to hope that she would be sensible and go to the tunnels. What about the others in the village?"

"Gejene is doing her best to see all who cannot fight to safety, beginning with the young and the elderly," Cesmi said. "So far I have not heard of any harm coming to those who are not joining in the fight, but—"

"Let us not worry about that just yet," Brissa interrupted. "All we can do now is fight to win and avoid as many losses as possible. Are reinforcements arriving?"

Cesmi nodded. "We have sent riders to alert all the villages and gather those who wish to join the fight. But there—there are many of them, Your Majesty, and their weapons are fine."

Brissa sighed. "Of course they are. There is no doubt in my mind that Thieren Panloch has seen to that personally."

A deafening crash sounded as an enemy cannon landed a direct hit to one of the northern battlements, and the warriors who had been stationed there didn't have time to scream before they and the cannon they were firing went hurtling to the ground along with a large chunk of the castle wall.

Cesmi gasped as Brissa pulled her to the floor. "That—that was Ilyiope. She—"

"I know," Brissa whispered, swallowing hard and running a soothing hand across the other woman's back. "I know she was your friend. And we shall mourn her and honor her sacrifice. But I need you to remain in this battle and protect our people. Can you do that?"

Cesmi blinked the tears from her eyes and nodded. "Of course I can, Your Majesty."

"Thank you," Brissa said as her hand flexed on the hilt of her sword. "Hold the castle. Keep it safe. I shall see you when we claim victory over these cowards who prostrate themselves before Frilau and Thieren Panloch."

"B-but where are you going, Your Majesty?" Cesmi asked, her voice edged in desperation as Brissa strode toward the narrow stairway that would take her to the lower floors of the castle. "It isn't safe—"

"If it is safe enough for our people on the ground, it is safe enough for me." Brissa cupped Cesmi's cheek and placed a whisper-soft kiss on her lips. "We shall see each other again, Cesmi, I promise you that we shall. But right now I need to show Wilkyen Pyke what happens to those who make enemies of Ryovni."

Brissa did not look back at the other woman's frightened and heartbroken face as she slipped through the tower door and toward the melee below.

CHAPTER TEN

IT WAS NOT CLEAR TO FIRAE WHO AMONG THOSE FIGHTING WERE the enemy, and who were their allies against the invasion.

"Look for green tunics with yellow sashes. The enemy will all be men; their women do not fight," Tash advised in a harsh, urgent whisper as they crouched behind a thicket of sourbrush bushes and watched the battle.

Firae blinked in surprise. "*None* of their women wish to become warriors?"

"I don't know that it is a matter of what their women *wish*, but—this really is a discussion for another time."

Firae nodded. "Green tunics, yellow sashes, no women." He moved to stand. Tash pulled him down by his arm.

Firae swallowed a yelp and glared at Tash. "What in the name of the Sacred Whore—"

"Do *not* rush into this battle," Tash hissed, grasping Firae's shoulders and turning him so that their eyes met dead-on. Firae's eyes flashed, and he opened his mouth to retort, but Tash pressed on: "Listen to me first. *Please,* Firae. I know that you have spent many years commanding your own warriors, but the humans are different. If they capture you, you will be weakened beyond any capacity to fight back or escape."

Firae scoffed. Tash gritted his teeth and gripped Firae's shoulders tighter. "We are in no position to accommodate your ego, Your *Majesty,*" he snapped. "These men have iron swords, Firae. Iron chains. Possibly arrows soaked in verbena tincture. We do not know whether or not they know there are sidhe here, but there is every chance that they may be prepared for us."

Firae sighed and rolled his eyes. "Very well, then, I shall be careful. Is that all?"

"Nearly. If you see chains, melt them. If you see swords, melt them. Any metal at all—do not hesitate to destroy it, and assume all of it has the ability to render us powerless. You are able to compel?"

Firae looked as if he very much wanted to chastise Tash for his impertinence, but he nodded. "Yes, but it is one of my weaker powers; I cannot compel more than one mind at a time, possibly two."

"That is still enough to constitute a threat. Use it. Use everything at your disposal. If the House of Keshell loses this battle—"

"They shall not lose," Firae said. His eyes blazed with fire the color of dark wine. "*We* shall not lose, Tash."

"No, we shall not." Tash agreed and felt his own power stir at the thought of battle, felt the flash and glow of fire in his own eyes. A jolt of shared power shot through them, and Tash gasped at the sensation and quickly released Firae's arms.

Quiet as cats, the two sidhe crept through the forest along the edge of the path that lead back to the village. They emerged from the woods at the edge of the village. The heat from a burning cottage gave off enough heat to make the air ripple like water around them.

Tash walked toward the fire, breathing slow and deep and letting the heat and crackle of the fire seep into his skin, his bones, the very core of his physical self. He knew that Firae was doing the same just behind him. The air around them cooled as they absorbed the energy. His nerves were on edge at the saturation of power flowing into him.

No sidhe would be foolish enough to cause a fire in the heat of battle, but fortunately for Tash and Firae, these humans knew no better. The fire of violence, of willful destruction, of attack had a specific flavor and power. It was not the same as drawing energy from a hearth or from a celebratory bonfire or even from an accidental forest fire. The presence of violent fire only strengthened the power of fire-wielding sidhe. When Tash turned to catch Firae's eyes, they blazed so brightly that they would have been visible in the blackness of a moonless night.

They didn't need words. The energy thrummed through them and guided them as if laying out a visible path.

Take us to the queen, Tash commanded silently; his heart throbbed with heat. *Guide us in battle against the enemy.*

The fire listened.

Into the night they ran, dodging the sounds of battle around them, weaving their way through the damp grass toward the palace gates.

Tash had known warrior women throughout his life. There was no novelty, not even the slightest sense of shock.

But nothing could have prepared him for the sight of Brissa, her hair knotted tightly behind her head and wearing a thin sleeveless nightdress tied up around her waist, lace-trimmed bloomers, and heavy leather boots. Her cream-colored garments were stained dark in several places, and blood dripped from several gashes on her arms and legs. She carried a heavy sword nearly as long as she was tall, and the tight muscles in her slender biceps rippled as she swung it. A shower of blood rained upon her as she severed the head of a green-clad opponent in one smooth stroke. Tash and Firae drew closer to the thick of the battle at the palace gates.

A knot of Pyke soldiers surrounded her, and though her own warriors were holding most of them off, the Ryovnians were clearly outnumbered.

"All right," Tash whispered to Firae, as they crouched amongst the thick branches of an unburnt hazel tree. "I think we are best off coordinating a diversion so that—*Firae!*"

But the king did not so much as spare Tash a backward glance. He ran straight for the melee with his black hair whipping behind him like a broken-off piece of the night.

Swearing under his breath, Tash ran after him.

And by the time Tash caught up, the screams had already begun.

They were not the usual screams one might hear in battle, but rather roars of pain, bursting forth from the throats of more than a dozen Pyke men all at once. Green and yellow-clad men fell to their knees; their weapons hit the ground as they clutched their hearts.

Firae *snarled* as he stalked toward them. The night air was thick with the strength of his power, and his skin glowed gold as he gave over to it completely.

Once it became clear that Firae was the one causing their compatriots to fall, the Pyke men began to run, but Firae's energy curled around each of them as they attempted escape, and brought them howling to their knees as they tried to break free.

Firae walked a straight, cleared path toward the queen. Men screamed all around him as wisps of smoke wafted from their skins, and their clothing began to blacken and sizzle. The few Pyke soldiers who escaped the king's wrath attempted to retreat, but the Ryovnians redoubled their efforts and managed to topple them all.

Tash could only stare as skins crackled and blistered, as more and more smoke escaped from their bodies when their flesh split, as black-red flames licked from within while their blood boiled from the cracks in their skin.

By the time the flames consumed them, the men were all well past dead.

Brissa stared at the men on the ground, then up at Firae, and then back at the men.

"You... you two are all right," she said. "I was worried."

"We were summoned to the cave," Tash said. Firae was silent. Embers still burned in his eyes.

Tash glanced to the north, where he could hear Pyke reinforcements headed their way. "But I fear we have more pressing matters to discuss at the moment."

Brissa nodded as another cannon crashed. "Listen, all of you. We haven't much time."

LIQUID FIRE RACED THROUGH FIRAE'S VEINS AND BROUGHT THE WORLD around him into sharp, clear relief. It was as if everything and everyone around him were moving just half a beat too slowly, while his own movements were fast and fluid and driven by instinct.

Around him, swords clashed with shrieking metal voices, though they were not loud enough to drown out the squelch of pierced organs or the snap and crunch of breaking bones and crushed skulls. His ears tingled as they perked up, taking in everything from the loudest battle scream to the smallest death whimper.

The rational remnant of his brain, intact only due to years of training for battle, told him not to use his power as he yearned to. His skin itched with the desire to wave a hand and cause all the hundreds of invaders to burst into flame, to bring them to their knees, howling, as their flesh sizzled and their lives were snuffed out like candles.

But he resisted the itch; he knew that on such a scale power lacked precision, at least for him. He would kill some of Brissa's warriors along with the enemy. And he would exhaust himself, leave himself sleepy and helpless and slow, and at the mercy of any survivors.

But most of all, he had to conserve power if he and Tash were going to execute Brissa's plan.

So he focused, sharp and clear and half a beat faster than everyone around him. He kept some of his focus on Brissa at all times—when he couldn't see her, he focused on the sound of her boots on the packed earth or the weight of her panting breaths and grunts of exertion as she buried her sword in one man after another—and another piece on Tash.

The other elf's energy pulled at him, almost as if they were bound together by invisible rope, and Firae couldn't ignore him.

Tash also moved with heightened speed and grace, his ears perked to full alertness. He formed small fireballs and hurled them at any opponent who came too close; when the balls hit them and exploded, flames splattered across their bodies and caught in a network of flames that connected and consumed the Pyke men.

Firae sensed the moment when the battle shifted, when the Pyke men were no longer charging but retreated, running toward the North Shore and their ships.

The queen's forces followed.

Brissa slowed to a walk. She was panting heavily, and her arms shook as she forced her blood-caked sword into its scabbard.

"We… we mustn't…" Clearly trying to speak through rasping breaths, Brissa braced her hands just above her knees.

"Shhh." Tash soothed and fell into step beside her. "Breathe." Firae joined them on Brissa's opposite side, took Tash's words to heart, slowed his breath and tried to settle his thirst for battle.

"You need to rest—" Tash began, but Brissa shook her head violently. Her warriors slowed to a stop around her, but Brissa waved them onward. The woman who seemed to be highest ranking took the lead, calling for the others to follow her to the North Shore.

Tash touched Brissa's arm and gave it a squeeze. "I know we cannot stop. I am not suggesting that. Just that you slow down, and perhaps…" Tash looked pensive and a bit hesitant. "I don't know if it would be considered inappropriate, but sidhe don't tire as easily as humans. And as time is of the essence… I could easily quicken our pace if you were not averse to allowing me to… um… carry you…" Tash swallowed, looking nervous, but before he could say anything else, Brissa grabbed his hand.

"What are… you… w-waiting… for?" She wheezed. "Firae, could— could you g-give me a b-boost?"

Firae barked a laugh at Tash's shocked expression as Brissa strode behind him and grasped his shoulders. Firae boosted her onto Tash's back, and the three of them jogged off.

Brissa managed to look regal astride Tash's back; she kept her back rigid as a pole and her eyes fixed squarely on the jostle of noise and fire-bright activity ahead.

When Tash's pace slowed, Firae offered his back, which seemed to surprise both Tash and Brissa. But Firae had been raised on stories of fallen Gods whose pride had cost them everything. Perhaps pride was unavoidable amongst those of his caste, as his mother had always said, but even he could see when it was necessary to lay it aside: to win a battle, to change the world, to willingly release the man he loved into the arms of another.

They moved as quickly as they could into a thick expanse of trees between the castle and the island's North Shore. Tash found a walking stick and lit a small fire at its tip—the fire was tied to his will rather than to the object, so it remained self-contained and burned only the topmost section of the stick. The light was dimmer than they would have preferred, but anything brighter would have drawn attention as they crept through the forest. Firae kept his ears pricked and his senses attuned. The energy of the earth itself wound its way up through the soles of his feet as always. It could tell him things when he paid attention; now it told him that the rustle he heard in the distance was a small quadrupedal animal and not Pyke soldiers lying in wait. It told him they were moving toward a ley line, thick with cool, wet power, and that Brissa's plan just might work.

He was still carrying Brissa, who had her knees hooked through his elbows, when the forest thinned, the sounds of active battle grew audible, and the smell of salt water offset the smell of blood and burning flesh.

"Set me down," Brissa commanded softly, once the beach came into view. Two Pyke ships were ashore, and three more remained in the harbor. One of the beached ships was burning; the fire cast light on the battle raging around the ships.

Firae set her down, and she turned to face them. "Blue Shell and her people are just beyond those rocks," she said, pointing eastward, where the sandy beach gave way to a rocky shore. "Do you think you will be able to find them on your own?"

"Of course," Tash nodded. "I can feel the pull of their magic already. It is very… specific."

Firae nodded. The pull felt cold, wet, salty, and somehow weightless. He had not beheld a muirdannoch in many years, but there was no other source of such power.

"All right. Thank you. I am going to find Cliope. If… if this works, meet me at this very spot."

Both men nodded, but Tash looked concerned. "Are you certain that you are recovered enough for battle, Your Majesty?" he asked.

Brissa spared them a tired smile. "Of course. Good as new, thanks to the two of you," she said, trying to conceal a wince as she drew her sword. "Truly. I have pushed through worse just sparring with Cliope. Now go. They'll try to retreat soon and we mustn't… we must send a message." Her face was set, stony and sure. "And if it takes widowing half the women of the Sheevalus to do it, then that is what we must do."

Brissa squared her shoulders and strode toward the beach; the exhaustion and unsteadiness she had just displayed seemed to diminish with each step.

"She is a child," Firae whispered. "How can a child speak of such overwhelming things with such conviction?"

"If I am not mistaken, you were once called the Child King," Tash reminded him.

Firae scowled. "Some continue to refer to me using that title," he grumbled, as the smug faces of his least favorite elder Council members pushed themselves into his mind. He blinked and turned his focus to Brissa's retreating form. "But I was never… never like *her*. My youth made me arrogant and unwise at times. But she—"

"She is still arrogant and unwise at times, I assure you," Tash said with a gentle laugh. "But it is also different for her. There is so much at stake."

Tash turned to look at the other man, who said, "I wish I had known what was truly at stake when I—I have made some terrible mistakes, especially when I was very young."

Tash's face was unreadable. "We all make mistakes, Firae. But we don't all get second chances."

"No," Firae agreed, "we don't." He didn't understand the knot that had lodged itself in his chest at the wistful tone in Tash's voice.

"Come," Firae said and took Tash's hand without thinking.

Tash did not reject the gesture. He held tight as they ran toward the rocky area where the sea-magic was thickest.

ON THE FAR SIDE OF THE ROCKS WAS A SMALL SUNKEN AREA, WHICH THE high tide had filled to create a pool. In the pool were four muirdannoch.

Firae tried not to stare.

The group consisted of three women and one man, and the pool had been lit from within by some or all of them to create an intensely bright little spot that would have been easily visible were it not so well concealed by the large rocks surrounding it. All four were plump, as the muirdannoch tended to be, with long hair that glistened like wet seaweed in shades of yellow, brown, blue, and green. Their eyes were all the same pale silver, and their skin was silver as well, though in varying shades. Their lips were the color of graphite. Their flesh was decorated with small living barnacles and colorful tattoos, and their hair, arms, necks, and chests were adorned with strings of shells, smooth bits of glass, and glittery rocks.

One muirdannoch was clearly the chieftainess Brissa had spoken of. She exuded a natural aura of power and influence, but there were other indications of her status as well: She was clearly the oldest of the group, on the ripe side of middle-aged if Firae were to hazard a guess, and she was also the plumpest, which, he remembered from his studies, indicated status amongst The Muirdannoch. Her hair was bright blue, and her skin was the color of polished hematite. Intricate patterns of bright white barnacles bloomed across her arms, shoulders, and breasts in much greater detail than on her companions. She was more heavily tattooed than the others; most of her tattoos seemed to depict sea creatures. She was also the only muirdannoch wearing a necklace; it was short, thick, and intricate, crafted from vivid blue shells edged in shining metals. Brissa had said that the chieftainess was named Blue Shell—that was the closest translation the queen could manage. Beneath the water, Blue Shell's tail seemed the same bright blue as her hair and her neckpiece.

The group regarded Tash and Firae silently, but with smiles.

Firae opened his mouth, but frowned when he remembered that they did not practice a spoken language above the sea. The Muirdannoch had a layered language; its simplest form, the form used by children, consisted of hand gestures, while their rich and complex higher language included underwater sounds.

Firae turned to Tash to find that the other man was crouched with his eyes on Blue Shell and his hands moving rapidly.

Of *course* Tash would know how to communicate with The Muirdannoch. Even the simplest form of their language was complicated, and Firae could count on one hand the number of sidhe he knew who could converse in it, but it shouldn't have surprised him that Tash was among their number. The man was too smart for his own good, too smart for the Common caste, which was probably what got him into trouble in Laesi.

Blue Shell moved her hands in response, and Tash did his best to translate, though it clearly took some concentration for him to converse and translate at once.

"This is Blue Shell. She is chieftainess of the Coral Mountain feririar and friend to the House of Keshell," Tash said, settling into a sitting position and lowering his feet into the pool. He gasped as a very faint glow spread up through his legs and across his skin. "She asks me to extend her warmest greetings to you, as a king of Laesi and a partner in the destruction of the cage that is killing the world. She also invited us to sit and draw energy from their magics so that we might feel the power of the sea."

Firae sat and smiled at her. He dipped his feet into the water and immediately understood Tash's reaction; the power was unlike any he had felt, and nothing like that of water-wielding sidhe. It was cool and calming, like a replenishing tonic for his own powers, which, while still strong, had been worn from opening the door in The Truthkeeper's cave and engaging in battle on the same night. He let out a sigh of pleasure and relief as the energy spread all the way up to the crown of his head.

"Please tell her it is an honor," he told Tash. "And tell her I... I apologize if I was staring. I have not interacted with her kind since I was a child, and I had forgotten how beautiful they are. It was not my intention to be rude."

Tash shared another series of gestures with Blue Shell, and she gestured back at Tash and burst into a squeaking sound, which Firae was reasonably sure amounted to laughter. The other three joined in as she gestured some more. Firae glanced askance at Tash, who grinned. "Yes, she was laughing at you. She said she finds you cute. And, um, that she would grow legs for one as handsome as you." Tash's cheeks blushed pink. "That... if I understand correctly, there's actually more to it; it is a lewd expression amongst The Muirdannoch, a phrase they use when they find a land-dweller sexually appealing. She... uh... I believe that her intent is to flirt with you."

Firae laughed at her cheekiness. "Tell her that I would be honored, if what lay between the legs of land-dwelling women were to my taste."

Tash sighed but conveyed the message; his cheeks turned darker pink as he did so.

The muirdannoch all laughed again, and Blue Shell gestured to her male companion, who gestured something back and shot Firae a sly grin and a wink.

"I... imagine you caught the essence of that exchange," Tash said dryly.

"I did indeed." Firae eyed the male muirdannoch. He was stocky and plump, but pleasantly so, with broad shoulders and a smattering of dark hair across his pale silver chest. He had a handsome face, and his dark seaweed-green hair was pulled back into a braid that trailed beneath the water.

"Need I remind you that we are here to carry out Brissa's plan and *not* to find you an exotic bedmate?" Tash snapped, with a surprising bite to his voice.

Firae raised his eyebrows, but couldn't disagree. He also couldn't seem to stop himself from smirking at Tash and saying, "Well, my last attempt at finding a bedmate did not turn out as well as I'd hoped, so you can't blame me for thinking ahead about my options once this battle has been won."

Tash muttered something, but did not otherwise respond, instead continuing to converse with Blue Shell. He was silent for several moments, and it was obvious that their conversation had become more serious. Firae could not see any of the battle on the beach, though he could hear it over the crash of waves. He hoped that Brissa and Cliope were all right, and that neither lost anyone precious to them in this bloody affair.

Firae caught the male muirdannoch's eye, and the man fixed him with a saucy smile as his fingertips played over the tendril-like pattern of barnacles between his collarbones. Firae smiled back and licked his lips. He caught Tash casting him a quick glance and scowling, and responded by offering the male muirdannoch a smoldering look and tracing his own fingertips across his breeches where the material pulled tight across his thighs. The man swam closer and flicked the soft, pointed tip of the fin at the base of his tail against Firae's feet, which were under the water. It tickled, and Firae squirmed and laughed.

"All right," Tash shouted, "the ships are retreating, and we must set to work. Are you able to give your full attention to the task at hand, Your *Majesty?*"

Firae rolled his eyes and didn't pretend that there was no fondness in it. He wasn't sure when Tash's impertinence had grown more amusing than infuriating, but it had. And there was every chance that it wouldn't last, that the man (the *criminal!*) would betray his true nature, and that the betrayal would be too ugly for Firae to forgive. Banishment was just shy of execution and only imposed for serious crimes, after all.

But for now, Firae smiled and enjoyed the other elf's obvious jealousy, which was clear no matter how hard Tash attempted to conceal it.

"Of course," Firae replied. He cast the handsome muirdannoch one last grin and gave his fin a gentle poke with his big toe, mostly to see Tash's scowl deepen, before pulling his feet from the water and turning his head to meet Tash's eye. "You have my full attention. Now tell me what we must do."

BLUE SHELL AND HER ATTENDANTS HAD SUMMONED TWO CREATURES for Tash and Firae to ride.

The creature Tash rode was just slightly smaller than the one carrying Firae. It was about four times as long as Tash was tall and about twice as wide as a horse. Both creatures were covered in tough, glinting, dark green scales; their spiky spines dipped into three deep grooves that were just about the right size for a human or a sidhe to sit in comfortably enough. Their rough, cold, bony backs were certainly less comfortable than the body of a horse or a grimchin.

The creatures didn't have legs—at least not as far as Tash could tell, though their bodies extended deeper into the water than the tips of Tash's toes could reach while he sat astride, and the water was dark, so he couldn't be sure. The crowns of the creatures' heads, along with the knobs of spine between the indents where Tash and Firae sat, were the only parts of their bodies that extended above the surface of the water as they swam. The creatures' eyes were black and shiny as glass on either side of their tapered heads, and whenever their heads bobbed above the water, Tash could see that their mouths were lined with long, fine baleen bristles.

Tash had asked what the animals were called, and Blue Shell had tried to respond, but she used a hand sign that he was not familiar with, and then another, and then dipped her head beneath the water to let out a series of sounds that she seemed to think might help him understand. Not for the first time, Tash wished that he had learned the high language of The Muirdannoch. It was not easy—no less than ten committed water-bearers were required to create the right conditions to begin to learn it—but the School of World Languages in Rasulladrovuru was competitive, and he had made his choice.

He didn't regret the choice he had made—it had never really been a choice at all—but he hated what it had taken from him.

"*To attain freedom, you must not hide from the mirror of your soul,*" the Truth-Keeper had said. But Tash *had* faced it. He had faced it despite the consequences, and he couldn't imagine what more she expected from him. It was the most frustrating thing she had said to him, which was saying quite a lot.

Tash jolted at a hard poke to his hip. He looked down to see Blue Shell and her attendants swimming alongside him. Tash did his best to ignore the fact that the male muirdannoch was ahead of him, swimming next to Firae. He also did his best to ignore the fact that this bothered him.

The others are just ahead, Blue Shell signed to him, referring to the dozens of muirdannoch that were lying in wait below the surface of the water to assist in their attack. *They are on the far side of the third ship.*

The three Pyke ships in the harbor loomed; their shapes were clear in the thinning predawn darkness.

Have they spotted us yet? Tash asked.

I wield the power of the Unseeing, Blue Shell responded. *They will look straight through us.* She laid one hand on the body of the creature that Tash rode and the other on his bare calf beneath the water, and he perceived a shift. He held his hand in front of his face and frowned.

I can still see myself, he signed.

But they cannot see you, she replied. *Not while you are in contact with the ocean. Not while we are close.*

Tash accepted the strange nature of the magic, but his eyes narrowed as he watched Blue Shell's male attendant touch Firae.

Blue Shell let out a shrill squeak of laughter. *You fear that Gold Pebble will take your lover from you,* she signed, and Tash shook his head vehemently.

He is not my lover, he signed back, his fingers clumsy with urgency.

Yet you wish him to be.

Tash shook his head again, but did not protest further. Blue Shell simply smiled and sank beneath the water to swim ahead.

By the time Tash and Firae reached the first ship, it had been rendered utterly still in the water and drawn so close to the other two ships that their transoms were nearly touching, despite a strong wind that should have made their escape from the harbor an easy task. The sound of men's voices, confused and escalating into panic, rang out across the bay; their footsteps thundered as they ran about every level of the ship in search of a solution. Their fear was so thick that it flavored the air around them. It was sour and pungent on Tash's tongue.

Surrounding the ships, invisible to the men, were dozens—possibly even more than a hundred—muirdannoch, bobbing in the water with their eyes glowing and fixed on the ships to hold all three captive in a web of magic.

Firae placed one hand upon the hull of the ship and reached for Tash. Tash bit his lip and looked at Blue Shell, whose eyes glowed a blue so vibrant it was almost painful to behold.

The men were attempting to retreat, to *escape*. They were young, they had families that waited for them—

He looked toward Firae, whose expectant expression was dissolving into impatience.

"What if we… just frightened them?" Tash ventured. "They're trying to leave; they've admitted defeat. We don't need to *kill* them—"

Firae sighed. "If you prefer that I try to do this on my own—"

"No," Tash said. "I just—"

"This is war, Tash," Firae said, "and these are the queen's orders. You know what these men would do to her if they could, what they would do to *us*."

Heat flashed through Tash's veins. Tash knew precisely what men like this were capable of. Dronyen Panloch was not an anomaly, as much as Tash might wish he were, and if Brissa were to carve every bit of poison from the heart of Villalu, she had to be merciless. So did he.

Tash took Firae's hand and slammed his other hand against the hull of the ship, and the rush of heat and power that flew through his body made him gasp.

His vision went dark and then pure white, and he was nothing more or less than a vessel: a vessel for all the power of the muirdannoch who circled the ships and imprisoned the men on board; a vessel for the ancient fires that roared beneath the ocean floor; a vessel for the rage of a thousand murdered sidhe whose ashes were trapped in iron urns, and for the tortured desperation of those who lived their lives in chains.

He surrendered his last bit of resistance, of nervous hesitation and stubborn will that slowed the flow of power through his body and mind and soul. He surrendered completely and could not tell whether the roar of triumph that rang out came from him or from Firae. It didn't matter, because when he opened his eyes, all three ships were engulfed in flames.

Lowering their rowboats into the water was not an option for the men; the fire was moving too rapidly, and the rowboats themselves were already consumed by fire. Survivors hurled themselves into the ocean, but the muirdannoch swarmed and pulled them, struggling and screaming, beneath the waves to their death. Jewel-toned muirdannoch tails glinted against the light of the fire as they dove deep.

Tash dropped his hands; his body was heavier than it had ever felt. He swayed, vision blurring, before the world tilted and he slid into the cool water below.

He heard Firae call out his name before soft, cool arms encircled his waist and the world around him fell into darkness.

CHAPTER ELEVEN

HER LEGS DANGLING, BRISSA SAT ON THE EDGE OF THE CAVE floor. She had lit only a single lantern on the wall after discovering what Firae had predicted: The Truthkeeper's lair was no longer sealed, it was simply gone. The place where the door had been now housed a tall, shallow crevice in the stone, large enough to step into, but only just. Other than that, the cave was as it had always been.

She dropped eight stones at a very specific speed and in a very specific sequence into the dark water. The water that flowed into the cave lapped more steadily against the smooth rock that contained it, and then it slowly began to glow, cool and blue, until she could see her own submerged feet. Within seconds, Blue Shell materialized before her. It was a testament to the somber mood on the island that the muirdannoch did not tickle the bottoms of the queen's feet before revealing herself.

You called for me, Strong Sapling? Blue Shell signed, using the name she had chosen for the young queen; conveying Brissa's actual name through hand signals had proved difficult. *So I did, Blue Shell,* Brissa signed in return. She had learned the summons years ago, in this very cave, when Blue Shell had first sought out the twins to deliver the news that one of them was prophesied to be queen and savior of Villalu.

I am sorry to summon you so soon after the battle, but I require guidance from the secret-keepers of the sea, Brissa continued.

The Muirdannoch of Villalu were trapped within The Border just as the humans were, living mostly undetected throughout the lakes and rivers of Villalu, as well as in the open sea. Many had learned to understand Villaluan by ear, and word travelled fast amongst their kind. They called themselves the secret-keepers of the sea with very good reason; they were privy to more of Villalu's secrets than anyone outside Ryovni could possibly realize.

It was The Muirdannoch, after all, who had first alerted the Keshells to the fact that Dronyen Panloch had taken a Spiral caste sidhe slave. And it was The Muirdannoch who had told them how Dronyen's steward looked at the slave, as if he would lay down not just this life, but his next life as well, to save him.

Blue Shell tilted her head. *You seek secrets so soon after your shores were painted with fire and blood? Sweet Sapling, have you even slept?*

Brissa fought back a bubble of hysterical laughter. How could she sleep when all she could see behind her eyelids was carnage? The burning ships full of men, the crushed body of a child struck by a cannon, a spear through the heart of a woman who had once shared her bed. Her arms ached from swinging her broadsword—from *killing* with her broadsword—and her village was in ruins, with dozens of families left homeless, injured, and grieving.

I fear that sleep is a ways off for me, Blue Shell. There is much to do. My people are in need, and The Border cares not for my comfort.

Blue Shell placed a cool, wet hand on Brissa's knee. *I will help if I may, Strong Sapling. What secrets do you seek?*

Brissa rubbed her arm, and then winced at the gash she had forgotten. *I have not yet had the opportunity to share the prophet's words with you, and now she has departed this cave and left us to our fate.*

Blue Shell nodded, and Brissa did her best to explain The Truthkeeper's words.

I believe I can help you, Sapling, but only if you promise to sleep, Blue Shell signed, and then crossed her arms over her chest to signal that unless Brissa agreed, the conversation was over.

Brissa laughed despite herself. *I promise I shall try. Is that sufficient?*

Blue Shell considered her and then nodded. *Very well, my stubborn Sapling. I believe the secret-keepers can be of some assistance in leading you to a ferriar known as La'ekynog.*

Brissa went a bit dizzy at the helpful news and might have fallen into the water had Blue Shell not held her legs steady.

If I tell you all that I know, you promise you shall rest? Blue Shell demanded.

Yes, I promise, Blue Shell. Please—tell me all you know. Blue Shell croaked a loud laugh; Brissa's hand signals had become less crisp with the combination of exhaustion and excitement, and there was every likelihood that she had inadvertently signed a lewd phrase, of which The Muirdannoch had many.

Very well, Blue Shell replied, still holding Brissa's legs steady, and, without further resistance, she explained.

When Tash awoke, the sun was high. The midday heat warmed the soft, warm sand beneath his body just past the point of comfort. He lay still, attempting to piece together what he could and make sense of where he was.

Voices in the distance spoke in the tones of people engaged in routine tasks. One voice whistled a tune and was soon joined by others. The sea lapped at the sand in the near distance.

Tash sat up, wincing at the stiffness in his muscles, and looked around. The beach was clear, with no lingering signs of bloody battle or burnt ships. Tash looked to the left, but the rocky outcropping where he and Firae had found the muirdannoch was not there. Instead there stood a long, broad wooden pier with a plank at its end that extended into the body of a carrack. The ship was freshly painted in the signature blue and silver-gray colors of the House of Keshell, and the Keshell family crest was emblazoned at its prow. Talking and whistling as they worked, several humans were busy loading the ship. Beyond the pier, the beach curved sharply left and out of his line of vision.

"Oh, good. I was afraid we'd have to load you onto the ship while you were still unconscious, and that you'd panic and burn the whole thing down when you awoke," came a familiar voice from behind him. "I tried to convince Brissa that binding you in iron just this *once* to mitigate the risk would be acceptable, but she acted as if I had suggested turning you into a *slave*."

Tash didn't bother to turn around—he didn't want to test the level of pain in his stiff neck just yet—and waited for Cliope to drop beside him in the sand.

He turned to face her, wincing and rubbing his neck.

"What happened?" His voice came out rough, and Cliope unclipped a canteen of water from her belt and held it out to him. He drank gratefully, barely minding the slight animal taste lent to the water by its leather container.

"We are at Shell Cove. It is Ryovni's northwesternmost point, several hours from the North Shore. I don't blame you for sleeping through the entire journey; it was exhausting after such a long, hard battle."

Tash studied Cliope. She did indeed look exhausted, but also happy. She seemed to be freshly scrubbed, her flesh was bandaged in several places, and a long gash on her left cheek was stitched together with pale thread.

"All right," he said slowly, "but *why?* Are you leaving?"

Cliope beamed. "*You're* leaving. You, Brissa, and Firae. It turns out that our friends from the Coral Mountain feririar were helpful to us in more ways than one. Do you recall what The Truthkeeper said about the Lekianoche? Or the *La'ekynog?* Whatever it is that you call them?"

Tash nodded. "Quiet are the *La'ekynog*, those that stayed behind," he recited.

"Precisely. Well, apparently there is a feririar of sidhe that call themselves the *La'ekynog*. The Muirdannoch don't know precisely where, but they live hidden somewhere in eastern mainland Villalu."

Tash sat up straighter. "That—that is incredible news. But how could they possibly know such a thing?"

"It is incredible what a people can learn when they are only visible to others when they wish to be."

Tash nodded. He shouldn't have been surprised. The longstanding friendship between the House of Keshell and the Coral Mountain feririar had contributed significantly to the successful overthrow of the Panloch regime, and The Muirdannoch had ears throughout the rivers and lakes of mainland Villalu.

"I know it is sudden," Cliope added. "The battle ended barely two days ago, and, though our victory was overwhelming, we did suffer some losses. But time is of the essence if we want to save Villalu, and the queen is needed on the mainland."

Cliope sighed and looked out over the sea. Tash thought he caught the glimmer of a jewel-toned fin whipping out of the water, but he couldn't be sure. "The attack... it was a sorely needed reminder that we are indeed at war, and Bachuc has been sending increasingly urgent messages about the state of things on the mainland. The people need to know that the queen is occupying the throne, that her allegiance is to all of Villalu and not just to her own lands and the people of Ryovni."

Tash ran his fingers through the hot sand. "So you are coming with us, then."

Cliope shook her head. "I cannot."

"But you are commander of the queen's army! And you are among the eight that The Truthkeeper spoke of; I am sure of it."

Cliope hummed. "Vyrope and Tepper are doing a fine job leading the queen's army on the mainland. And while it is true that I am most likely one of the eight, there are four others we must find. And I believe I know where two of them are right now."

Tash stared at her. "You..." He swallowed, his mind racing, trying to come up with an explanation other than the only one he could think of, the one that would be all but impossible for Cliope to pursue on her own.

"Communication is still a bit of a challenge, but Firae's Villaluan is improving," Cliope said, when it was clear that Tash wasn't going to continue. "He told us what the two of you learned on the night of the battle. And 'the purest heart tethered to the greatest power' has *got* to be Brieden and Sehrys, as I'm sure you've realized. Gods, they're nauseating even in *prophecy*, aren't they?"

Tash couldn't summon even a smile in response to Cliope's attempted joke. "You cannot mean to cross into Laesi on your own."

Cliope shrugged. "Not *entirely* on my own. That's what I need you for. I imagine now that you've had a few days to heal and replenish your power, you might have some essence to spare?"

Tash's throat went dry. He took another long pull of water and wrinkled his nose at how warm it had become beneath the beating sun. A cool sea breeze danced across him and blew sandy strands of hair into his face. It wasn't until he pushed back his hair, which was greasy and caked with sand, that he realized how filthy he must be. There was sand *everywhere*, and since he had been laid naked on the beach to heal, it had made its way into less than desirable places.

"You can't cross into Laesi alone, Cliope, not with *my* essence," he said. "It isn't strong enough. You'll grow too tired, you'll get lost within The Border's membrane and end up in some other world altogether—"

"Blue Shell can help with that," Cliope dismissed. She pulled her knees up to her chest and rested her chin on her knees. "She cannot cross herself, but she can help guard me against the exhaustion as long as I have essence."

Tash shook his head. "Even so. Even if you make it across, do you have any idea how dangerous it is for humans there? You don't speak the language, for one—"

"I'll be crossing into the waters just outside Khryslee. I will be safe there."

"The only way to reach that portal is through the Isles of Sheevalu! Whose inhabitants, if you recall, attacked us mere *days* ago!"

"Yes, and the attack crippled them. Besides, Blue Shell will keep me hidden."

Tash forced his hands through his tangled, sandy hair.

"You can't just show up in Khryslee, Cliope. They don't let just anyone through the gates."

"If I announce that I am there to share news of Firae with the Khryslean ambassador, I can't imagine I will be turned away."

"It is dangerous."

"Life is dangerous," Cliope said, her voice softening. She gave Tash's arm a gentle squeeze. "And my life in particular. I would be no safer fighting to defend the crown in Villalu, Tash."

"No," he admitted, "but you would be with us."

Cliope smiled. "I shall miss you, too."

He took her hand and they fell into silence, watching the women and men load the ship that would take him back to the mainland and away from the island paradise that had made him feel almost whole again. He pondered Cliope's plan, searching for any risks she may not have considered.

"Why not ask Firae?" he finally asked. "His essence is stronger. It would give you a better chance."

Cliope pulled her hand free of his and wrapped it around her legs. "Perhaps it would," she said, not meeting his eye, "but I am not sure I can trust him to not tell Brissa."

Tash turned his entire body to face her and barely registered the pain in his muscles at the sudden movement. "You have not told Brissa?"

"No," Cliope said softly, turning herself as well so that they were sitting face to face. "Brissa would try to command me not to go, and I wouldn't put it past her to force me onto that ship to prevent it. Brissa... Brissa understands the risks of battle, but I am her sister, and she worries. Even if she were to agree to the plan, it would only distract her, and she can't afford that right now. Better that she think I am safe at home in Ryovni, helping my parents rebuild Okoskeshell from the damage suffered by the attack."

"Perhaps you should," Tash said.

Cliope shook her head. "My parents are not old yet. They will manage just fine."

Tash sighed. "Very well. I will need a container. Something natural but airtight, preferably glass."

Cliope pulled a small glass jar from a pocket in her tunic and unscrewed its lid. She handed it to him silently.

"I am still not certain that this is a good idea," Tash said with a sigh, but he summoned a thread of magic and concentrated on shaping it into the strongest piece of power he could fit inside the jar. Cliope watched as the golden-orange essence, laced with a tendril of leaf-green, tumbled from his fingers and into the jar, then curled around itself as it danced and swirled. When he had packed as much power as possible into the jar, he screwed the lid back on and handed it to Cliope.

"Thank you, Tash," she said, tucking the jar into her pocket.

"Yes, well, let us hope your sister doesn't discover what I've done. I wouldn't put it past her to turn that enormous sword of hers on me." He shivered at the memory of the murderous glint in Brissa's eyes as she swung the sword hard enough to slice an enemy soldier's head clean off his body.

Cliope laughed. "Nor would I, so I am counting on you not to tell her a thing."

"Since I have just threatened my own safety to help you with your insane plan, do you think you might see your way to finding me some clothes? And possibly some soap and a freshwater bath?"

Cliope rose to her feet, dusted the sand from her breeches, and held out a hand to help Tash to his feet. He groaned at the protest of his aching muscles. "We have a holiday cottage just up that path. The serving ladies there will be happy to help you, but I warn you that they may be fairly disappointed as well. They have *so* enjoyed the opportunity to gaze upon you these last few days, and I can't imagine they will enjoy seeing you cover up that lovely body of yours." Cliope sighed wistfully. "Truth be told, I can't say I will enjoy it overmuch either."

Tash rolled his eyes and gave her a playful shove before following her up the path toward the blue clapboard cottage that lay just ahead.

CHAPTER TWELVE

Brieden was in the kitchen, his hair still damp from a bath as he assembled an evening meal after a long day on the farm.

He sang softly to himself as he prepared a simple platter of bread, cheese, nuts, raw vegetables, and chilled bean pâté. Though he did not hear the door open, his senses were suddenly assailed by the strong and unmistakable scent of wind, sweat, and grimchin dander.

"Sehrys!" Brieden's heart surged with joy as he turned to behold his fiancé, who looked rumpled and exhausted, and pulled him into his arms.

"No, stop, I'm filthy," Sehrys objected, but nestled into the embrace nonetheless.

"I do not care. I can bathe again. We can bathe *together*. You're home."

Sehrys chuckled. "I am. And a bath sounds wonderful. But perhaps we could eat first?"

Brieden kissed him soundly and gestured for him to sit. "You can start with some of this," he said, placing his own platter on the table. Other than the cheese, it was all food that appealed to him and Sehrys equally. "I will go out to the garden to fetch some fresher things."

"You needn't—" Sehrys began, but Brieden had already pulled the large basket from its hook near the back door and was on his way before Sehrys could complete his protest.

"Sree is impossible," Sehrys muttered, once Brieden had returned with a variety of fresh leaves and fruits. Sehrys helped himself to a handful of tender green sprouts from the basket, which Brieden had set in the center of the table. "The Council is talking about destroying an entire civilization, and all she cares about is Firae."

"You care about Firae too," Brieden offered, his voice mild.

"Of course I do. But I also care about the humans trapped in Villalu."

Brieden bit his tongue, unsure why he felt a spike of annoyance.

"But if Firae hadn't gone..."

Sehrys narrowed his eyes. "Brieden, my job, the very reason I have agreed to spend so much time away from home, is in pursuit of a better world. And a better world does not include acts of genocide, no matter what the justification may be."

"Of course," Brieden conceded, tearing a piece of bread into tiny pieces on his plate. "I just meant that Sree... she cares about Firae. And when you care for someone, it can be difficult to see what could matter more than their safety."

Sehrys nodded, and they lapsed into a silence that tugged at the ends of Brieden's nerves.

"I... was hoping you might join me on my next visit to speak before the Council," Sehrys ventured. "Some of them are too firmly entrenched in their bigotry for it to matter, but some of the queens are uncomfortable with the idea of destroying so many lives. If they could meet you, see the truth in how we love each other, hear firsthand how you risked everything to rescue me from slavery, how good you are, the extent of your *person*hood... most of them have never actually met a human before. I believe it could make all the difference in the world."

The strange agitation that had been dancing around the edges of Brieden's mind melted, and he beamed. "You truly want me to go with you?"

Sehrys smiled back at him and reached across the table to join their hands. "Of course I do."

"When would you need me to go?"

"In two weeks. That should be enough time to notify Sanya, shouldn't it?"

Brieden frowned. "Sehrys, it is calving season. Sanya just lost three of her best farmhands and she cannot spare me right now. Some of the animals would perish without people to help with the births. In another couple of months, I'm sure it will be fine, but—"

Sehrys pulled back his hand and stared at Brieden in shock. "Calving season."

The irritation prickled. "Yes. Calving season. One of the most important times of the year. I believe I have mentioned it to you several times."

"Brieden, this is a matter of life and death. I am sure Sanya can manage to rustle up someone to help her with a few pregnant cows."

Brieden flinched against the sting of Sehrys's dismissiveness.

"My job may seem inconsequential to you, Sehrys, but it matters a great deal to me. I made a commitment, and I don't do such things lightly. I am not willing to let animals die and disregard the promise I have made to my mentor, simply because you have decided my time is yours to play with as you see fit."

The air between them had grown so thick with tension that Brieden backed his chair away from the table without making the conscious decision to do so. Sehrys was sitting back in his own chair with his arms crossed over his chest, his eyes hard and bright, his lips in a thin, tight line.

"Mine to *play* with?" Sehrys very nearly hissed. "Do you hear yourself right now? You may resent Firae, but your family is still in Villalu, Brieden. Tash is still in Villalu. The Keshells—"

"I know. And of course I care, Sehrys, you *know* that I do. I am merely asking for some time. I told you, in two months—possibly even six weeks—I would be more than happy to go with you. The Council has said that they will not make a determination for six months. There is time. This need not happen on *your* schedule."

"But it needs to happen on yours."

Brieden barked out a mirthless laugh. "When you are asking me to sacrifice my own time, then yes!"

Glaring at Brieden, Sehrys stood up from the table. "I cannot believe that you are being so selfish about this."

"Selfish?" It was something about that word, in particular, that finally made Brieden snap. After all he had done, all he had sacrificed, and the first time that he told Sehrys *no...*

"Well, perhaps," Brieden said, slowly rising to his feet as he held Sehrys's gaze, "you should offer to marry one of the queens you wish to persuade. That would likely sway her, and all you'd be losing is me, which you were willing enough to do the last time that I got in the way of your mission to save the world."

Silence hung between them for what felt like years. Sehrys opened his mouth as if to speak, but closed it. His eyes welled with tears.

"Sehrys—" Brieden's voice sounded weak even to his own ears, and he had no idea what he could say, but it did not matter. Before he could grasp what he had said to his fiancé, before he began to feel sick to his stomach over the weight and impact of his words, Sehrys turned, tears streaming down his cheeks, and strode out the door, slamming it behind him.

Brieden didn't follow him.

CHAPTER THIRTEEN

BY THEIR THIRD DAY AT SEA, FIRAE WAS CONVINCED THAT HE would go mad before the journey was through.

The ship's captain had told them that the journey to Merdeshe would take approximately eight days—half a cycle of the dwarf moon—and perhaps even fewer if the wind remained in their favor. It wasn't such a terribly long time, really; he had spent longer sailing from Laesi, before his ship was demolished. But that had been different. That had been aboard a living vessel, not a dead wooden ship, blocked from any direct contact with the life force of the earth or ocean.

To be fair, the human crew aboard the ship, as well as the queen herself, did their best to see to his every comfort. A large structure at the stern of the ship, which looked like a tiny human castle with a flat roof, contained quarters for Brissa, Firae, and Tash, as well as the ship's captain, Larpsa, a gruff old woman with dark leathery skin, wispy gray hair, and a shrewd eye. The rest of the crew slept in the more modest quarters of the forecastle and the lower deck. Firae's room was large, second in size only to Brissa's. It contained two round windows, a soft bed, and a small table and two chairs, as well as chests full of clothes, dried fruits, and scrolls and books that he struggled to understand. All of the furniture was bolted to the floor, and from the low ceiling swung a simple bronze chandelier containing six lanterns, their round glass encasements slightly darkened with soot.

The room was stuffy, but the windows opened slightly, allowing Firae to let in fresh air and an occasional salty spray of ocean water. The roof of the little castle consisted of a split-level deck, the slightly lower one in front holding the whipstaff that allowed the crew to steer the vessel, and a smaller raised deck at the very stern of the boat that housed a leisure area with a partial canopy where Brissa spent most of her time.

Though she remained gracious, the queen had grown melancholy. She had lost people she cared about in the battle. Ryovni was her home; she was happy there. From what Firae could gather, the prospect of returning to her throne in Miknauvripal grave her little pleasure. She spoke little and fell into brooding silences that sometimes lasted for hours.

Firae enjoyed her company regardless, even when Tash wasn't there to translate. With little else to do, Firae struggled with reading some of the simpler texts he found in his cabin and conversed with Brissa to the best of his ability in Villaluan when she seemed receptive to conversation. But he found himself too restless to sit still for long; he was easily distracted and excessively frustrated by tiny inconveniences.

But the real source of Firae's mounting madness, the thing that kept him pacing about the ship like a caged beast, was Tash.

Tash had become cool and distant toward Firae again, and spent most of his days on the lower part of the rear deck, writing in a book of bound parchment using a little pot of dark pigment and the sharpened end of a feather. He conversed with Larpsa every now and again, most likely asking questions, the answers to which he would memorize with maddening ease. He took his meals with Brissa and Firae at the long table beneath the balcony on the aftmost deck, but other than that he was difficult to engage.

"What are you writing?" Firae asked him on the second day of the journey.

"Thoughts," Tash said without looking up. "Theories."

"What sort of theories?" Firae settled beside him.

Tash sighed. "About the prophecy, mostly."

"May I read it?"

"No."

Firae narrowed his eyes. "You frequently seem to forget that I am a king of Lae—"

Tash looked up from his book at that. "We have been through this. When you banished me from the Faerie Lands, you destroyed whatever allegiance I may have had to the Queendoms," Tash said sharply.

"And if you had not committed a grievous crime, you would not have been banished," Firae retorted, though he could not deny the thrill that raced through him at the fire behind Tash's eyes.

"I told you, my crime should never have resulted in banishment."

"How can I know that if you are unwilling to tell me the nature of your crime?"

Tash laughed humorlessly and closed his book. "The fact that you do not remember says more than enough about the way you treat those of my caste."

Firae gritted his teeth and clenched his fists against the blind urge to *grab* Tash, to shake him and make him understand. "You know that was on my mother's orders," Firae bit out, trying to remain as calm as possible. "I simply carried them out after she died. I remember every sidhe that I chose to send into exile, Tash, regardless of how strongly you wish to believe otherwise."

Tash stood up and refused to meet Firae's eye. "I have no interest in repeating this conversation. I will be in my quarters."

Firae had attempted to get Tash to speak again that night, but he received no more than clipped, single-word answers. The next morning at breakfast was more of the same. And so, by their third day at sea, Firae was convinced that he would go mad before the journey was finished.

Without the life force of the world to ground him, the life force that emanated from Tash was nearly irresistible, and the magic that hummed beneath his skin was torturous to perceive. Firae wanted—

Well, Firae knew what he wanted. But Tash had already refused him once, and it seemed unlikely that he would be moved to reconsider.

But beyond his undeniable physical urges, Firae wanted—very nearly *needed*—something from Tash, something more than disinterest. Even if it was annoyance or frustration or rage, he craved energy exchange with the other man so desperately that it made him unsteady, and the small taste he had gotten the day before had only fed the fire of that craving.

It wasn't until the morning meal on the fourth day that Firae discovered the necessary tool with which to prod at the sleeping beast of Tash's focused attention.

"Could you teach me the muirdannoch hand language?" Firae asked Brissa in Villaluan as one of the handmaidens Brissa had brought along served them a meal of nuts, sea vegetables, and preserved fruit as well as some cooked tubers that Firae had never eaten, but now found that he enjoyed.

Brissa smiled. "Of course I can. It may take some time for you to gain proficiency, but we can start simply. I don't know how many muirdannoch we will encounter on the mainland, though. They tend to be a more careful sort and rarely speak to any who are not their own kind. The Coral Mountain feririar is unusual in that regard, and their friendship with my family goes back thousands of years."

Firae repeated those words in Brissa's response with which he was not yet familiar, and Tash translated them in a flat tone without looking up from his plate, as had become his custom.

Firae did his best to commit them to memory. *Careful. Unusual. Thousands.*

"I know. I suppose… when all of this is behind us, I thought I might visit Ryovni once again. I would like to speak with Blue Shell some more, and… she had three others with her. Do you know them?"

Brissa nodded. "I believe I do. She has three apprentices who accompany her most of the time."

"One of the three was male. We tried to communicate, but…" Firae could feel his cheeks heating as he spoke. "He was interesting."

A loud clatter cut into the conversation, and Firae looked across the table to see that Tash had dropped his cutlery. Tash muttered something, a single word so quiet he clearly didn't intend Firae to hear it.

But Firae did. Voice edged in simmering annoyance, Tash had muttered, *"Interesting,"* and a flash of something—subtle but undeniable—zipped between them.

Firae's heartbeat quickened, but he did his best to maintain a neutral expression, to pretend that he was not the least bit aware of what had just happened.

"Do you know his name?" Firae asked.

"Golden Pebble," Brissa said. She raised an eyebrow and tilted her head in a way that made Firae think of Cliope. "He is rather handsome, is he not?"

"*Very* handsome," Firae agreed.

"I would hope so, since you nearly sabotaged our mission with your *flirting*," Tash grumbled.

Firae grinned. "Oh, we did no such thing. The flirting had no impact on the mission whatsoever." Firae feigned casual dismissal of Tash's complaint.

Brissa laughed out loud. "It seems not, Tash," she said. "The mission was nothing but a success."

"Luckily so," Tash said. "Though while people were *dying,* they were giggling at one another like a couple of drunken juveniles." Tash stood up and wiped his mouth before dropping his napkin onto his plate. "Excuse me." He turned and left the table without another word.

Brissa bit her lip as she watched him leave, then turned back to Firae with a sigh. "Do not mind him." She touched Firae's wrist. "That battle was hard on everyone."

Firae could only smile. "I know," he said. "And I assure you that it does not bother me."

Brissa could not have guessed just how true Firae's statement was.

That night, heart pounding, Firae knocked on Tash's door.

Tash didn't look surprised to see him—there were, after all, only a few people it could possibly be—but he did look suspicious.

"May I help you?" Tash asked, his tone even and cool.

"I believe so," Firae said, squeezing past Tash to walk into the room. Tash may not respect Firae's title, but Firae was a king and he refused to act like anything else.

Tash's room was a slightly smaller version of Firae's quarters; the table was smaller—barely big enough to fit a single plate—and it had only one trunk and one window, but the bed seemed about the same size, and the chandelier was exactly the same.

Firae sat at the little table and held up a book that Brissa had lent him earlier in the day. It depicted various muirdannoch hand signals, but the words were all in Villaluan. Firae could not have asked for a better excuse to connect with Tash.

"My Villaluan is improving, and Brissa has been very helpful, but there is still a language barrier. I was wondering if you could help me with some of this."

Tash closed the door, turned to face Firae, and narrowed his eyes when he read the book's title. "What do you need assistance with specifically?"

"Some words and phrases, but also some information. The Muirdannoch are a curious people, and I have realized that I know too little about them. With a mind like yours, I can only imagine how much more you know than I do." Firae smiled at Tash as innocently as possible.

Tash sighed, leaned back against the door, and crossed his arms over his chest. He was beautiful in the lamplight. He was beautiful in *any* sort of light, but only three of the six little lamps overhead were lit, and the light they cast made the room feel warm, intimate, and inviting; it made Tash's skin look even more golden and his eyes look an even brighter green.

"What would you like to know?" Tash asked. The lack of warmth in his voice disrupted the sense of comfort in the room slightly, but only slightly.

"Could you tell me how they mate?"

Tash's eyes went so wide that Firae had to fight back a laugh. "How they—"

"Mate. I didn't see any reproductive organs on their lower bodies, but they must reproduce somehow."

Tash exhaled, his shoulders dropped, and he nodded. "Normally their sex organs are concealed. They go into heat. A pouch in their tail opens to expose their genitals."

"And are their genitals… like ours? Do they look the same? Do they work the same?"

Tash shrugged. "As far as I know. I've never seen them."

Firae hummed. "Can they control when they go into heat?"

"To some degree. What is truly fascinating is that both their women and their men can control when they are fertile." Tash grew animated, and Firae bit back a smile.

"It isn't like sidhe, wherein only women can choose when they experience pregnancy, or like humans, who are completely at the mercy of their biology. I would truly love to learn more about the way this influences their culture with respect to gender. They are matriarchal for the most part, though not as thoroughly as The Sidhe."

Firae nodded. "That is fascinating. But I suppose I should have been more clear. What I really want to know is whether their men have cocks, and how often they can use them."

Tash's face fell into what he may have believed was a neutral expression, but he could not fool Firae. His jaw went tight and his eyes went stormy, and the energy that rolled off him was raw and unrelenting and delicious.

"I can't help you with that," Tash said flatly.

"I can't imagine that's true. You were just telling me about their *fascinating* mating habits, after all. You must know something about how muirdannoch men copulate with one another. Or with one of us."

"I know what you are trying to do," Tash said, his voice quiet and dangerous.

"I have no idea what you mean." Firae furrowed his brow in a way that was *perhaps* more heavy-handed than necessary.

"Shut up," Tash snarled, sending a violent shiver through Firae's body. "You think talking about how you want to fuck some *fish* is going to make me jealous? Make me want you?"

Firae chuckled. "I think we both know I don't need to do a single thing to make you want me, Tash."

Tash shoved off from the door and yanked it open. "Get out."

Firae crossed one leg over the other and sat back in his chair. "No."

"Get the *fuck* out of my room right now."

"I do not take orders from criminals of the Common caste, whether or not they respect my crown. If you want me to leave this room, you will have to remove me physically."

Tash stared, pupils blown wide and lip curling under. He reached Firae in two long strides and pulled him roughly to his feet by the collar of his tunic.

Before Firae could respond, Tash spun him around and pushed him toward the door, but just as he started to push him through, Firae's arm shot out, grappled for the door, and then slammed it shut behind him. Firae's back hit the closed door, and Tash stumbled. Their bodies collided.

They stared at one another for an endless moment with their bodies pressed together, their eyes wild, their chests heaving, and Tash's half-hard cock pressing into Firae's hip.

And then Tash's mouth was on his.

Firae's head hit the wooden door with a thud; a jolt of pain mixed with the sweet, hot force of Tash's lips claiming his over and over again until they were both dizzy and panting.

"Is this what you want?" Tash rasped, moving to nip Firae's earlobe.

"Yes," Firae panted as his arms wrapped around Tash to clutch at his back and hold him lest he slip away.

Tash grasped Firae's wrists, pushed them up against the door on either side of Firae's face, and pinned him with a strong, unforgiving grip that made Firae *throb*.

"I'm not some servant boy you can call to your bedchamber when the mood strikes you," Tash said, his voice low and rough as he pulled his head back far enough to look Firae in the eye.

"I know," Firae whispered.

"Tell me what you want from me," Tash said, his gaze bright and intense.

"I—"

Firae knew what he wanted: What he had wanted for so long; what he had thought he might finally experience with Sehrys, before that dream had been dashed. Firae had little experience with rejection, but even less experience with *this*, with a man who was unimpressed by Firae's status and unwilling to give Firae complete control.

He knew what he wanted. But to *say* it—

"Do you want me to fuck you?" Tash asked in a voice like dark, rich velvet. "*Take* you? Is that why you've been driving me mad?"

"Yes," Firae groaned, as Tash dipped for another taste and his lips fastened onto Firae's neck and sucked hard.

"Say it," Tash growled, lips brushing Firae's throat as he spoke.

"I want you—" Firae swallowed, his heart thumping so hard he was surprised it didn't sway the entire ship.

Tash tightened his grip on Firae's wrists and kissed his way up Firae's neck before claiming his mouth once more: kissing him, consuming him, causing his every thought to dissolve into a soupy fog.

"I need you to tell me," Tash demanded against his lips.

"Fuck, Tash, do you want me to beg? Take me. Fuck me. *Do* it."

Tash released Firae's arms and stepped back to look him square in the eye. "Your notion of begging sounds like giving orders."

Firae smirked. "You tell me you do not respect my rule, that you hold no loyalty to a king of Laesi. So stop *asking* already and prove it."

Tash's eyes went even darker and he grabbed Firae by the waist and pushed him toward the bed. Firae stumbled and dropped to the mattress, landing on his back. He pushed himself onto his elbows and met Tash's gaze with a challenging glare. Tash looked feral, his eyes wild and ravenous, lips swollen, skin flushed, chest heaving. He looked like a fantasy come to life.

"You don't know what I've done," he said, stalking toward Firae like a beast toward captive prey. "What I'm capable of, what these years of exile have done to me."

"No." Firae stared pointedly at the straining bulge between Tash's thighs. "But I can see quite clearly what *I* have done to you, and I assure you, there is nothing else I need to know right now."

Tash's eyes flashed deep, bright green as he crawled onto the narrow bed and swung one leg over Firae's recumbent body to straddle him. He lowered his weight onto Firae's thighs, and the heat of their bodies as they connected was enough to make Firae gasp and his muscles twitch.

Tash chuckled. "Gods, if the Royal Council of Sidhe Nations could see you now, writhing and desperate for the touch of a common criminal."

Firae scoffed, willing his heartbeat to slow and his skin to cool. "Do you honestly believe the Council would care? Royals fuck commoners so often it's nearly a sport to us."

Tash's eyes turned wicked, and he bent, lips so close to Firae's ear that they brushed the tender skin as he whispered, "Yes. But do royals usually *beg* for it?"

Tash nibbled Firae's earlobe before raising himself to a sitting position while pulling his tunic over his head. Firae could not speak. Tash was right; he was no better than a pixie in heat. Desperate. Shameless. Subordinate.

And he didn't care.

Tash was impossibly beautiful: lean and muscular, with broad shoulders, searching eyes, and a devastating smirk. His thighs were so firm and thick Firae wanted to bite them; his backside—

Well. The truth was that Firae could bite the man all over.

"I don't fucking care what royals usually do," Firae said. "Just tell me you somehow have a stash of *hubia rija presmij.*"

Tash laughed. "In a manner of speaking…" He climbed from the bed and scooped a bit of fire from one of the lamps.

Tash sat next to Firae on the bed and held out his cupped hand. Firae dipped his fingers into the flame and let the energy flow from the tips of his toes, and *oh,* it felt like a deep, necessary stretch after hours astride a grimchin in flight. His anchor may have been a tiny flame, but it was a tiny flame anchored by Tash's magic. He may as well have rolled about in fresh grass after a rainfall, it was that rejuvenating.

Firae savored it, growing the little flower far more slowly than necessary, decorating it with too many leaves, and allowing its bud to grow so fat with oil that it nearly burst.

Tash rolled his eyes. "I believe it is big enough," he said.

Firae plucked the flower from Tash's palm and kissed him. "For now."

Tash's eyes seemed to flash two shades darker, and he wasted no time in ridding them of the rest of their clothes. Tash twisted the flower open and pressed Firae flat onto his back, and he was touching him *everywhere.* His hands, bold and sure and slick with flower oil, ran across Firae's body as if he owned it. He followed his touches with licks and kisses and tiny bites, waking sensations that had been buried beneath Firae's skin for as long as he could remember. Firae choked on air when Tash gave his cock two firm pumps, then quickly worked his way down to Firae's balls and back along the strip that led to his entrance, no touch lingering long enough; Firae's body was a landscape of pleasure in the wake of Tash's teasing touches.

Every other man who had shared his body with Firae had been intent on serving him as their king. Their ultimate goal had been to deliver him pleasure and perhaps to increase their own status in the feririar. All of them had desired Firae, but more than Firae, they had desired the *king.* They had desired what it meant to be chosen to share his bed.

But he'd never allowed another man to *take* him like this. He'd never encouraged another man to simply shove his legs up against his chest and work him open fast and rough, never found himself moaning with such utter abandon as he submitted to unbearable pleasure.

Tash did not respect Firae's authority. Tash did not *want* to want Firae. He wanted Firae because he just couldn't help it, no matter how hard he fought to deny that.

Tash crawled up Firae's body, grasped his hands, and pressed them down on either side of his head before taking his lips in a savage kiss. Oil from the flower made their palms tingle where they pressed together and made Firae's lips so sensitive that he spread his legs even wider and writhed.

"Please," Firae gasped. "For the love of all Gods, *please,* Tash."

"Tell me." Tash's voice was husky and close, and Firae could barely breathe, he was so hard.

"Fuck me. Don't be gentle."

Tash smiled. "I won't."

Tash moved off Firae's body only long enough to grab him by the hips and flip him onto his stomach and then hike his ass into the air. Firae scrambled onto his knees, spread his legs as wide as he could manage on the narrow bed, and, hands slick with sweat and *hubia rija presmij,* grabbed two of the thin wooden slats of the headboard.

Firae didn't care that the wood was dead, that the pulse of the earth's life was blocked from them at a time when it was usually most pronounced. He barely noticed. Instead he was alive to the sparking fire that ran through his body, the essence of which belonged in part to Tash, the way Tash kneaded the flesh of his buttocks and pulled his cheeks apart roughly as his breath went loud and ragged with lust. The weight of his desire for Firae pulsed between them and flavored the fire that raced under his skin. Firae gripped the headboard tighter, arched his back higher, and let out a strangled noise that didn't resemble coherent speech. But it was apparently coherent enough; Tash let out a desperate sound of his own, and then all Firae knew was the gorgeous, blazing hot stretch as Tash entered him, the broad, strong hands tight on his hips, and the sound of Tash gasping and swearing under his breath.

Tash kept his promise. He was not gentle.

He held Firae in place and fucked him hard, moving slightly faster with each thrust and changing his angle until he hit Firae's pleasure spot, driving hard and fast and deep, making Firae sob and bite into the flesh of his own bicep.

Wet, sparking flames raced back and forth between their bodies everywhere they touched, and as they lost themselves to it, the hunger to touch *everywhere* grew too great. Tash pulled out and flipped Firae roughly onto his side, pressed himself to Firae's back, and held him tightly while he fucked him. Firae threw his head back and let Tash bite and kiss his throat. He allowed his arms to slip free from the headboard so he could reach back and feel; he ran his hand along the delicious damp bulge of Tash's bicep, traced the strong curve of his jaw, touched the place where his perfect, thick cock pumped in and out of Firae's body.

When Tash stroked Firae's cock with firm, slow movements, Firae let out a groan that could probably be heard across the ship, and allowed the fire to consume him.

Firae didn't fall asleep afterward, but he did find himself lulled into a somnolent haze, warm and content as his breaths slowed and he found his way back to himself.

He had never been fucked like that before. No one had ever *dared* fuck him like that before.

He turned on to his side to find Tash, flushed and glowing and spent, watching him with soft and heavy-lidded eyes. "You're beautiful," Firae murmured.

Tash chuckled. "Thank you. You're quite stunning yourself."

They studied each other for several long moments, moments that were wholly separate from the reality of their lives, from the reality of what must be done.

It came back to Firae like a cold fist slowly squeezing his heart, so slowly that he didn't realize it was happening until the pain was overwhelming. He swallowed. They couldn't avoid the truth. And he couldn't bear another dishonest moment between them.

"Five months," Firae said.

Tash made an inquisitive noise; his eyes never left Firae's.

"I have five months to complete my mission. I promised to help Brissa, and I intend to keep that promise, but…"

"But we don't know if we will fulfill the prophecy in time," Tash supplied.

"The Doctrine has been compromised. The Border is unstable."

Tash nodded. "I know." His voice had grown very soft.

"If I don't return with the elf responsible…" Firae forced himself to maintain eye contact rather than close his eyes and cower in the face of reality. For, whatever Tash might think, Firae *was* king of Yestralekrezerche, and The Border and its surrounding lands were his responsibility. "I can sacrifice tens of thousands of lives or I can sacrifice you, Tash. I—I don't want to, but—"

Tash closed his eyes. "I know," he said, his voice barely more than a whisper. He swallowed thickly. "I know."

Firae searched for anything else he could say, but everything that came to mind sounded hollow. It was true that the Council *might* show Tash mercy for his pure intent, but the amount of blood and essence they would need from him to restabilize The Border would likely be more than his body could withstand, even if they did wish to spare him. So Firae just watched Tash until he opened his eyes again.

"I know," Tash said one final time, looking at Firae with such resignation that it was painful to witness. And then Tash turned to face the wall with his arms wrapped tightly around himself. Firae moved to fit behind him and wrapped an arm tentatively around Tash's waist.

"I would like you to go back to your own quarters now," Tash said firmly.

"Tash—" Firae began to protest.

"Just go, Firae. Please."

Firae swallowed around a lump that had found its way into his throat and slowly removed his arm. "Of course. I…" There was nothing left to say. "Goodnight, Tash."

Tash didn't say anything.

Chapter Fourteen

"Your Maj?"

Thieren Panloch looked up from his work to see his advisor standing in the open doorway looking uncertain.

"Yes, Ednec, what is it?"

"Your Maj, I apologize if you were studying the scriptures. I know you prefer not to be interrupted—"

Thieren set down his quill, removed his eyeglasses, and massaged the bridge of his nose for a few blissful moments before replacing them. "No, I was merely working on a letter of response to Lord Chrill. Apparently the Jichyns just pledged their loyalty to the queen and the man is in a state of panic."

"The *imposter* queen," Ednec spat, shoulders squared and eyes narrowed.

Thieren chuckled and waved Ednec into his study. Ednec hoisted himself into the chair opposite his king's writing table; the seat was too high for the man's diminutive stature. "I have news from the islands, Your Maj."

Thieren leaned forward in his chair. "Tell me."

Ednec sighed, bringing his hands to rest upon his ample belly. "The Pyke attack was unsuccessful. And not by any slight measure. The savages burned all their ships to the ground. They destroyed near to the entirety of the Pyke army."

Thieren nodded. He couldn't say he was surprised that Lord Pyke's forces had failed. The man was overconfident, just as Thieren's own brother and father had been, and it had cost them not just their lives, but the family's control of Villalu. The man had been so dismissive of the usurper's largely female army, so certain that he could show the Panlochs how war was waged. He had refused to plan properly, he had refused to wait for reinforcements, and now his lands were hobbled; Thieren knew that nearly every able-bodied young man in the Sheevalus had been on those ships.

"But that is not even the worst of it, Your Maj."

Thieren raised an eyebrow. "No?"

"The few who did survive were absolutely certain that there were sidhe on the battlefield."

Thieren fought back the uneasy feeling in his stomach. "I was under the impression that the House of Keshell has only one slave." One slave who was barely a slave at all, Thieren reflected bitterly. From what he had heard, the family treated the creature better than a servant, indulging his every whim as if he were a spoiled pet. Thieren wasn't an idiot; it was clear that Brissa had taken a slave as a political gesture, to gain allegiance from the less pious slave-owning Houses.

"These elves were not slaves, Your Maj," Ednec said. His voice was calm, but it was clear that it was a chore to keep it that way.

Thieren shot up from his seat. "Explain."

"There were two of them, possibly more, and they were using magic. Their eyes were made of fire, and they burned men to death by the dozens, and then they burned the ships and all the survivors they could reach. They... apparently they were *very* protective of the imposter queen."

Thieren closed his eyes and took several long, deep breaths to clear his mind. He knew Brissa Keshell was the Taker of All. He had known that all along, but to have evidence that it was true—he was shocked by his own shock. He did not doubt Word of The All, he did not waver in his faith, but to know, for certain, that demons of the void were seeing to the queen's protection was downright terrifying.

"This is bad, Ednec," Thieren said, opening his eyes.

His advisor nodded. "Very bad, Your Maj. I am sorry to be the bearer of such news. Would you like to instruct me?"

"I must consult the scriptures before I can decide on a course of action. Notify the inner circle that we shall hold an emergency meeting over breakfast. None will be excused, and any who do not attend shall be made examples."

"Yes, Your Maj," Ednec replied, hopping from the chair and moving toward the door.

"And Ednec, I will be very deep in study for the rest of the evening. Please see that I am not disturbed. Tell Madame Treflir that the serving girl can leave a supper tray outside my door."

"Yes, Your Maj." Ednec paused in the doorway. "Your Maj, we will defeat the Taker of All. We have the will of the God of All and the word of Frilau on our side. Evil shall not triumph."

"No," Thieren agreed. "It shall not."

As Thieren locked the door behind Ednec, a tight fist of unease again made itself known in his stomach. The All would not be pleased with this turn of events.

Thieren approached the easternmost wall of the room. Like all the other walls in the large room, it was covered with shelves full of texts and scrolls interspersed with large, solemn portraits of Panloch lords and kings of the past. Thieren gently lifted the portrait of his grandfather Lozeryn and, by feel alone, found the large brass key in the hidden compartment in the back of the frame. He then crossed to the northern wall and pulled a certain book from a shelf. Behind the book, invisible to any who were not searching for it, was a box. Thieren used the key from behind the portrait to open the box. Inside it was a different key, small and silver.

Thieren replaced the silver key with the bronze one, closed the compartment, and replaced the book. On the western wall, Thieren used the silver key to unlock an unassuming, battered book bound in iron and leather, which was, in fact, a strong, heavy box lined in iron.

Inside was yet another key. Wrought iron and half the length of Thieren's palm, its head bore a detailed representation of the Panloch family crest.

Nearly a third of the southern wall was taken up by an enormous portrait of Lord Thetzian, the first Lord of Panloch to communicate with The All, the first man to bring the word of truth to the masses.

Behind his portrait was a door.

The door blended into the wall almost seamlessly, and it was with eager, shaking hands that Thieren unlocked it and pulled it open.

The Ritual of Keys was tedious when he was feeling impatient, but it was important not just for safeguarding the Panloch family's most vital secret, but as preparation for meeting The All. And in his younger years, when Thieren had ignored the ritual and went directly for the iron key, when he had been desperate for communion the way other young men seemed desperate for a glimpse into the chambermaids' dressing rooms, The All could always tell. And Thieren was always punished for his disrespect.

Thieren closed and locked the door and made his way from the tiny landing where he stood to the long, narrow stone staircase, which was lit as always by pale blue light with no identifiable source.

Thieren tucked the key into one of the deep pockets of his fitted crimson tunic and went down the stairs. He was not an impatient boy; he was a man, a king, no matter what the heretics may claim. And he understood. He knew the importance of The Ritual of Keys now, of preserving it for his own sons, and their sons after them: East, North, West, South, the borders of the world, the edges of The All. Beyond the four directions was Void, chaos, and cruelty worse than the Five Hells, ruled by beautiful demons who were desperate for souls of their own, and who would do anything to devour them from their human prey. The demons told stories of a vast paradise beyond The Border and had used their magic to control human minds and bend human wills until those in westernmost Villalu had built walled cities where the demons lived amongst them like men. Thieren's father had let the cities stand in exchange for the enormous tithes paid by the Lottechets to the House of Panloch. Dronyen had shown no concern over the existence of the cities either, but Dronyen had been a fool.

They had all been fools, every one of them who had allowed this to happen.

At the bottom of the staircase, he unlocked yet another compartment hidden in the wall of the landing. Thieren exchanged the iron key for the final key, which was crafted from a material he could not identify. The key was a deep ruby red, and at first glance might have been crafted from gemstones or even colored glass, but for the constant, rapid movement beneath the key's surface of tiny golden threads, which swam as if through liquid rather than within a solid mass. When Thieren took the key into his hand it grew warm, and the golden threads stilled and expanded until the entire key was a glossy, opaque blood-gold.

Growing up, Thieren had been told that if anyone who did not possess Panloch blood were to attempt to use the key, the key would grow painfully cold, freezing their hand until it shattered. Dronyen had been endlessly fascinated by the tale, and had tried to test it. He had gotten as far as bringing a servant boy to the staircase before he'd been caught.

That servant boy was never heard from again.

Thieren opened the door into a cavernous room, the center of which was lit by an orb of the same pale blue light that illuminated the staircase. He shook his head at the memory. Dronyen was first-born, but their father should have known that Dronyen did not have the proper temperament to rule. He had spent his childhood torturing animals and servants and damaging the family slaves, which would not have posed a problem had he not placed his lust for inflicting pain over his duty to God, family and world.

You are indeed my most faithful servant in ten generations, came a familiar voice, smooth and rich, filling the room and Thieren's mind like water. Thieren bowed deeply, then approached the orb at the center of the room and sank to his knees before it.

"I submit to thee, my master. You are The All, Living God and Perfect Guide, He who shelters us from The Void. Please accept my humble servitude, for my soul is yours."

The orb rippled, and within it Thieren could glimpse his master's face, nearly like the face of a man painted with watercolors of muted blue, silver and gray.

I accept your servitude, faithful one, my chosen king of All.

Thieren took a deep breath and placed his palms flat on his thighs. He kept his mind carefully blank.

"Master, there is a problem. It appears that The Taker is consorting with free demons. She does not control them, and yet they protect her and destroy all men that approach her too closely."

The orb went very pale, and Thieren dug his nails into his own legs. He had learned to read the shifts in his master's colors over the years, and this one was clear: rage.

How was this permitted to happen? The All demanded, and Thieren winced against a tightening in his chest. *Do not waste my time with words. Open to me.*

Thieren nodded, willing the panic in his body to quiet and setting aside the involuntary instinct of his mind to resist the invasion. He closed his eyes, took several deep breaths, and surrendered.

He focused on breathing, on remaining conscious, as The Master slid inside. He tamped down the dizziness and nausea that rose when The Master rapidly absorbed all that Thieren knew of the Pyke invasion, their defeat by the Keshells, even Lord Chrill's panic and Thieren's own concern as more and more Houses offered their fealty to the imposter queen.

Thieren gasped as The All released him. His body was shaking; he couldn't help it. The feeling never became less jarring or unpleasant. As always, Thieren knew that it was no less than he deserved. The House of Panloch had let their Master down, and, no matter what he did now, his soul would always bear the weight of his family's failings.

Yes, the master agreed, easily reading him. *You must pay for sins of your fathers, for the failure of your brother. Prices unpaid invite Void into the world.*

Thieren nodded. "Yes, Master."

At times it has occurred to me to let this world perish. Too many humans continue to practice heresy. Too many demons roam free with the price of their sins unpaid by servitude.

Thieren nodded. He had heard this threat before. And one day, he feared, The All would follow through, cast all of Villalu into the void, and create a new world from chaos: a world that Thieren would not be a part of, a world in which he was nothing more than a distant and inconsequential memory in the mind of God.

That day may very well come, The All agreed, *but not on this day. Listen closely, servant, and I shall tell you how to win back the world. But first you must practice penance.*

Thieren did not shudder at the mention of penance. It was nothing less than he deserved.

Please begin with the Prayer of Oath. Ninety-nine recitations.

"Yes, Master. Thank you for your mercy," Thieren said. His knees and back ached from kneeling upon the hard floor for so long, but he did not complain; after he had finished reciting his prayers, he would long for the mere discomfort of kneeling upon a cold stone floor.

Thieren cleared his throat and began his prayers.

"The All, Master, Soul of our World, I offer you my service. I, Thieren Panloch, rightful king of the world, shall be your limbs and your eyes upon the earth. Every word I speak shall be for you, every deed I undertake shall be for your glory."

Thieren stared deep into The All's blue light, at the face within, the mind behind the face. That perfect mind had never lifted a pen, but he had created the Taukhi scrolls using Lord Thetzian's hand to commit them to parchment. He had brought the truth to the world, but the world had never accepted the message. But it would. It must. The kings that came before him had been too weak, but Thieren was strong. He did not intend to give the world a choice any longer.

"I submit my loyalty and the loyalty of all my sons to you forever more," Thieren continued, "Lord God Frilau."

CHAPTER FIFTEEN

TASH LAY IN THE NARROW BED IN HIS LITTLE ROOM AND STARED out the tiny window on the opposite side of the cabin.

He had blown out all the lamps in his chandelier. The dwarf moon was full; its pale light soothed him as he lay in silence and allowed his mind to wander.

It had been two days since the night he had spent with Firae, and Tash had barely set foot outside his cabin.

Tash had absolutely no idea what he was doing.

He had never wanted another man like that, had never felt so powerful and so desired, so in control while in a state of complete surrender. And of course it had to happen with that utterly infuriating *brat* Firae.

Firae, who had taken him apart until he barely even recognized himself, and with terrifyingly little provocation. Firae, who was impulsive and arrogant and foolhardy. Firae, who was distractingly beautiful, from head to toe.

Firae, who had banished him to a life of imprisoned desperation.

Firae, the man who would most likely lead Tash to his death within a matter of months.

Tash sighed and rolled onto his side. They had scant little to go on with respect to the prophecy. Tash had been studying all the scrolls he could understand—and even a few that he couldn't—on the topic, had been rolling The Truthkeeper's words around in his mind, and still, the fulfillment of the prophecy was only a remote possibility. Tash probably had only a precious few months to live. So maybe… maybe allowing himself a bit of pleasure on the long walk to his execution wouldn't be the worst thing in the world.

Tash furrowed his brow at the sound of yelling from the quarterdeck.

Outside his window there was a sudden explosion of light and a loud bang. Tash scrambled to his feet.

He hadn't reached the upper deck by the time the first cannon hit.

Tash nearly crashed into Firae as he ran toward the quarterdeck to see what he could do to help. Brissa was already there, helping to load and light cannons while members of the crew took aim at the enormous, dark shape of an enemy ship before them.

"How can we help?" Firae asked immediately, looking around in desperation.

"Go to the lower deck and help Larpsa ready the lifeboats!" Brissa yelled over the noise of cannons firing and wood splintering. She let out a sudden, sharp scream as the main mast was hit square on. It blasted apart and rained shards of wood and shreds of rope and fabric all around them.

"Lifeboats?" Tash asked. "How——"

"We knew this was a very real possibility. Some muirdannoch from Coral Mountain have been accompanying us. They can hide us, but only if we're closer to the water. They can't do anything to disguise a ship this size."

"But what about——"

"*Tash!*" Tash stopped short at the near-frantic edge in Brissa's voice. "I have a plan. There is a *plan*. But you need to trust me and just go help Larpsa, all right?"

Without waiting for a response, Brissa ran back to help load more cannons.

"Come on," Firae urged, grabbing Tash's hand to pull him along. Tash went, but kept his eyes on Brissa for as long as possible. Something about this plan didn't sit right with him at all.

They found Larpsa easily. Several little boats were already loaded with those crew members not needed on the decks above. Each one seemed to vanish the moment it hit the water. Larpsa pointed them in the direction of the smallest boat of the lot. It looked newer than the others; its hull had a fresh coat of sky-blue paint, and a number of impractical-seeming pillows lined its floor. "Get in," she said roughly. "Marsa will be right along to lower you down."

"But—" Tash protested.

"Get in," Larpsa repeated, as she continued to usher others onto the larger lifeboats.

"I don't believe you understand," Firae said in his slow, heavily accented Villaluan. "The queen—"

Larpsa sighed loudly, wiping her palms off on her breeches and turning to glare at them. "Her Majesty's instructions were very clear, lads. Now put your behinds in that boat before I have to put you there myself. I don't have time to argue with you."

Firae's jaw dropped at her words, and a storm of indignation brewed behind his eyes. Tash would usually have found this quite amusing.

Tash eyed the little boat. He wasn't sure about Brissa's plan, whatever it may be. But he had no better option than to follow it, however blindly, and pray to the Gods to let them all live to see another morning.

He climbed into the boat, dragging Firae behind him. It wasn't until that precise moment that he realized they hadn't let go of one another's hands since they had first run into one another on the upper deck.

"Sending us to safety like children," Firae grumbled as Marsa, a surprisingly strong deckhand given her tiny stature, lowered them gently to the sea. "I am a *king*—"

"A king of Laesi. Yes, Firae, I believe we are all quite aware of that fact. But you are in Villalu now, Your Highness, and I assure you that the slave traders and flesh peddlers are just as happy to profit from kings as from common criminals."

"Other than to demean me, do you have a point?" Firae snapped.

"Only that these humans, no matter their station, understand these lands far better than you do. You will have to get used to deferring to them until you return to Laesi."

Firae opened his mouth to retort, but his words were swallowed by a gasp as their little boat did not float once they had released the rope, but sank, slowly and steadily, as if another rope, this one from far beneath the sea, was pulling them down. Tash attempted to swim free of the boat, but met an invisible barrier.

"What—I—what—" Firae sputtered, running his hands along the inside of the barrier. Tash frowned. They were still perfectly dry; the barrier appeared to be a clear bubble, pliable but not easily breakable, that had sealed itself over the top of the boat. They continued to sink. The water around them grew dark very fast; the sounds from above became more and more muffled until there was silence.

"I certainly hope Brissa knows what she is doing," Tash muttered.

Firae snorted. "What was it you were just saying about trusting the humans?"

Tash smiled, though it was unlikely Firae could see it in the dimness that surrounded him. "That is a fair point."

They sat in silence, just the two of them in their little pod deep below the surface of the sea.

"Are—are we moving differently?" Firae asked. Tash concentrated; his sense of orientation was still thrown off from spending so many days aboard the dead ship, and, though he could sense magic in the bubble around them, they were still disconnected from the life force of the world, which would have enabled him to better answer Firae's question. Still, it did seem as if they had stopped moving down, and were now being pulled in… some other direction. Tash had the distinct impression of being pulled backward.

"I think so. I wish Brissa had thought to tell us about this plan," Tash said, resigning himself to the situation at hand. He settled back on the pillows, lying on his back with his knees bent. His calf brushed against Firae. He could still see the surface, but only dimly. The ships were nowhere to be seen.

"I hope Brissa got out all right," Firae murmured. Tash started slightly as Firae crawled to Tash's end of the boat and lay beside him.

The movement did not do much to jostle the boat, but the innocent and familiar action was not something he was expecting. They had barely spoken since that night, and Tash wasn't sure that he would call the energy that sparkled between them *affection,* precisely. Still, he couldn't say that he minded the feeling of Firae's warm body pressed against his own.

"As do I," Tash agreed. "She is clever, and she seemed to know what she was doing, but that is certainly no guarantee—" Tash paused to sigh. "Thieren Panloch is growing more aggressive. And from what I have heard, he is both ruthless and devout, which is perhaps the most dangerous combination a leader can have."

"I would have to agree," Firae said. He sounded deeply sad and about half a century older than he was. Tash squeezed his hand in the darkness, and, before he knew it, Firae's warm, soft, and perfectly distracting lips were on his.

With no idea how long it would take to reach their destination, of the fates that awaited them there, or of the fates of those they had left behind, Tash couldn't imagine a more suitable way to spend their time.

THE LAST TIME FIRAE HAD AWAKENED FEELING ANYWHERE NEAR THIS disoriented was when he had come to in Pemerec after having nearly drowned. But now the disorientation instilled no panic; he was blanketed in a fuzzy layer of benign confusion; awareness slowly pooled and spread in his mind like warm nectar.

He was in the lifeboat with Tash, though the boat was above the water now, and the bubble that had surrounded them had disappeared. The air was cool, a soft breeze gently rocked the boat, and, in the distance, birds called to one another in the predawn light. Firae and Tash were nestled close, wrapped around one another like old lovers, and something about that made Firae's cheeks heat.

Firae sat up, gently moving the arm that Tash had draped over him. Tash whined in his sleep, but did not stir.

Looking around, Firae saw that they were floating in a small stream, and that something was holding the boat in place. The stream seemed to be in the heart of a small, mossy glen in a heavily wooded area. The sweet song of the world's life force was too great for him to wait a moment longer. Careful not to upset the boat, Firae pulled his clothes off and slipped into the water.

It was the embrace of a long-lost friend, a fresh and nourishing meal, an excellent night of sleep after a long day of physical labor. It was pure, sweet music, a poem written by the fabric of reality. It was life. It was *everything*.

Firae wept. Only when he felt it again did he truly understand the loss. He had no idea how the humans could possibly *bear* it.

The water was cold, so Firae happily pushed just enough fire into the water around him to encase him in warmth; cool currents of water mixed in as he swam around the boat. The stream was shallow; it came up to his midsection when he stood, and its floor was carpeted in gritty sand. Firae wriggled his toes in the sand and gave a prayer of thanks to the Blessed Guardian of the Sands that Carpet the World for seeing himself and Tash to safety.

He climbed onto the sandy shore, and had already made his way past the shoreline and to a copse in search of something to eat when he heard a strange sound behind him—similar to the croak of a bullfrog, but in a much higher pitch. Firae turned away from the unfamiliar bush he'd settled on—it was covered in pale, tender leaves and sour yellow berries that he decided he liked very much—to see a pair of muirdannoch women watching him from the stream. One of them opened her mouth, and the strange sound emerged once again, followed by a series of hand signals.

"I don't speak Muirdannoch," he called, though he knew they would not understand him. He shrugged his shoulders and pointed to Tash to try to get his point across.

One of the women swam to the boat and rocked it gently. When that produced no reaction, she poked her head over the side and made another screeching sound, loud and sharp enough to make Firae wince. And then he fought to suppress his laughter when Tash shot straight up with his eyes wide and wild and his hair a knotted mess.

"What!" Tash all but barked.

Both muirdannoch were laughing—that's what it looked like to Firae. They were making the sort of squeaking sound that Blue Shell had made when she was amused—and he couldn't help but feel sorry for Tash.

"Get out of the boat, Tash," Firae called. "You have no idea how much clearer your mind will be."

Firae knew he was probably imagining the way Tash's shoulders seemed to relax when he turned to look at Firae and the way the confusion and anxiety in his eyes seemed to melt into pure relief, but it made him smile regardless.

Tash hopped from the boat and let out a wanton moan as he sank into the creek's embrace. Firae popped another berry into his mouth, then wrapped his hand around a short, broad branch heavy with fruit and leaves. He closed his eyes and hummed and let his power flow free, let it weave through the tiny fibers of wood until Firae was able to pull the branch away with a slight tug while causing minimal damage to the bush.

Tash was on the shoreline peeling off his wet clothes and laying them out to dry by the time Firae arrived with the branch.

"Thank you," Tash said when Firae offered him the branch, and the two settled on the shoreline, their feet in the water and slowly warming sunlight on their naked skin, to talk to the muirdannoch.

Firae watched the exchanged hand signals quietly, peeled bits of thin, papery bark from the branch, which was also delicious—what *was* this plant, and why did it not grow in Yestralekrezerche?—and tried to identify some of the words from his brief study of Tash's book on the hand signals. He might have been impatient, but the buzz of reconnection with the natural world was making it nearly impossible to feel anything but mellow bliss.

The two muirdannoch looked like sisters to Firae, though that could be due to his ignorance of common muirdannoch physical traits. Both seemed quite young to his untrained eye. Their hair was the same shade of seafoam green; their faces were round and expressive. He began to notice small differences as they spoke with Firae: The one on the left moved her hands faster but a bit more clumsily, and the one on the left seemed to take more frequent pauses.

Tash made an incredulous noise and shook his head. "Those Gods-blasted Keshells," he muttered. "Brissa *told* them to take us far away from everyone else if there was an attack. Apparently word has reached the mainland that there were sidhe helping Ryovni when the Pykes attacked, and Thieren wants us alive."

"He wants to enslave us," Firae deduced.

"Publicly and viciously," Tash agreed, voice as hard as stone.

"But why lead us away from the rest of the crew?" Firae asked, brow furrowed.

"She knew that if the wrong people learned we were aboard that ship, we would be especially vulnerable. On land she trusts us to hold our own in battle, but after days at sea on a wooden ship? She knew we would be too easy to capture, so she decided to make our safety a priority above all others', including her own. She knew we would insist on staying on board and trying to protect her, and she figured the less we knew, the more likely we were to leave." Tash heaved a loud sigh of frustration.

"She's right, though," Firae pointed out, popping a berry into his mouth. "We *would* have insisted. And we *were* weakened by the journey. And barely knowing what was going on *was* the only reason we agreed to go along with her plan. She's very clever."

Tash rolled his eyes but didn't argue and went back to conversing with the muirdannoch.

"She wanted us to wait in the woods for a few days and then meet her at her palace in Miknauvripal. But—"

Tash went pale and dropped his hands. He stared, motionless, as both muirdannoch signed at him with increasing urgency.

"Brissa was taken prisoner," Tash said. His voice was hollow. All traces of mellow bliss were gone.

"What?" Firae whispered, although he knew he hadn't misheard.

"They… most of the crew managed to escape. Brissa even made it off the boat, but apparently they got her on the shore. It—oh." Tash raised his hands and resumed signing with the muirdannoch.

"Oh?" Firae prompted after a few moments of silence.

"I—just give me a minute…" Tash muttered, eyes glued to the womens' hands. All three of them were signing furiously.

Firae tried to read what he could from their expressions; their hands were moving so fast that he couldn't identify a single word.

"The Muirdannoch have been watching from the rivers and lakes. Those who understand human speech have been listening to news the humans share. It seems that there was great care taken to keep Brissa's capture a secret. Other than her captors, only we, The Muirdannoch, and the ship's crew know that she is missing."

Tash turned to look at Firae with something dangerously close to excitement mounting in his eyes. "Thieren wants to force her to marry him. He doesn't merely want to defeat her; he wants to humiliate her. He wants to enslave her. And he wants to reveal this news very strategically."

"Why are you making it sound like those are good things?" Firae asked.

"Because he isn't going to kill her, which means that we can almost definitely rescue her."

Firae stared at him. "Almost definitely."

Tash nodded, his eyes now possessed by the unnerving gleam they got whenever his brain worked very, very fast. "We will need to send word to Brissa's people, make sure they carry on as if everything is normal and let us handle the rescue. It makes more sense on every level—we're stronger, faster, quieter, designed to not only survive in the wilderness but actively thrive. We—we're closer. We're in the Lajec lands and the others are nearly in Miknauvripal already."

Firae frowned. "Two unarmed elves rather than a coordinated military response. This is your plan to 'almost definitely' rescue a contested queen kidnapped by enemy forces."

"Think about it, Firae," Tash said, twisting around to face him. Off to the side, Firae saw the two muirdannoch watching them with the same fascination he had felt watching them sign.

"As far as Thieren Panloch knows, we're still on Ryovni. He will be *looking* for a coordinated military response, and he won't expect anything so fast. He'll never see us coming."

Firae considered this. It was insane, but everything about their situation had come to fit that description.

"All right," Firae said slowly. "I can see how it might work. But I also see one very big problem. The lands between where we are and where Brissa will be held—they aren't *entirely* wilderness, are they?"

"No," Tash agreed, shifting his eyes from Firae.

"So how would you propose we travel through villages and cities? How are we going to communicate with humans?"

"Um." Tash cleared his throat and scratched the back of his neck. He pulled a berry off the branch and chewed it very, very slowly. "The—the people of the Panloch region tend to be lighter-skinned than most other humans," he finally ventured.

Firae narrowed his eyes. "Are you proposing that we pose as *humans,* Tash?"

"No, not—not *we,* exactly." He glanced sidelong at Firae, who realized what Tash *was* proposing.

"No." Firae didn't realize that he'd climbed to his feet until he was staring at Tash with all the rage and authority he could possibly muster. "How *dare* you, you—you—" he could not think of a word serious enough, dark enough, offensive enough to call Tash. It was one thing to pin Firae to a wall and kiss him until his bones melted. It was quite another to suggest something like *this.*

"Your skin is not dark enough," Tash cut in. "You don't speak fluent Villaluan. You don't understand the culture or the customs, and I have lived here for half a century. Your eyes are stunning—*too* stunning—they draw attention and there is no way you could disguise them, because humans simply do not have eyes like that. It would only be in front of humans, only when *necessary*—"

"*Only* in front of humans? You expect me to pretend to be your slave in front of humans? Can you imagine anything *more* degrading?"

"I have done it," Tash pointed out. "I did not enjoy it, but it was a means to an end, and I knew that Brissa and Cliope did not see me as anything less than themselves."

"You are *not* anything less than they are. But I am not your equal, Tash, I am your *superior*. I am a *king*—"

"You are stranded in the middle of Villalu, and without me there is every chance you will end up for sale at the flesh markets before you manage to find your way home," Tash said, his voice laced with ice. He rose to his feet and looked Firae square in the eye.

"It seems you still do not understand the situation you are in, *Your Highness*," Tash said, enunciating each word. He walked closer to Firae, until their breath mingled. "Sehrys was a slave to humans for *six years,* Firae, and he is Spiral. Your caste *does not matter here*. It does not matter if you are a king, a criminal, a priestess, or a layabout. They can catch you, and they can hurt you, and they can suppress you, and they can do *anything they want to you*. If you think the separation you felt on the boat was bad, imagine living your entire life like that, but much worse. Even if you walk outdoors barefoot, you are still blocked. They will inject your veins with verbena, throw you in iron cages, force you to eat the flesh of animals—"

"Enough." Firae barely managed to force out the word. Everything Tash was describing, every bit of it, had happened to Sehrys.

Tash backed up and took a deep breath. The muirdannoch were still watching them with eyes wide and dark and absorbed in the mysterious fight playing out before their eyes.

"You need me," he repeated in a much softer voice. "If I wear a hat to cover my ears, perhaps a pair of eyeglasses—I could pass for one of them, Firae. And wouldn't that be safer, if they thought you *already* belonged to someone? Besides, Thieren's manor is much closer to The Border than Miknauvripal."

Firae closed his eyes. "If I agree, Tash, we will discuss the terms of the arrangement in very specific detail."

Tash grinned.

Chapter Sixteen

It was early evening by the time Green Crab and River Song—the two muirdannoch women tasked with helping them—returned with the items Tash and Firae would need for their journey. Tash had spent most of the afternoon crafting a letter on a strip of bark for Bachuc, Brissa's senior advisor. Tash used the tip of his finger to lightly singe each letter into place; he took care to avoid burning the entire piece of bark. It was delicate work and required such a degree of focus and self-control that the hours slipped by.

While Tash wrote, Firae explored the little valley. He knelt in a bed of moss, pressed his palms to the spongy ground, and allowed himself to absorb the knowledge-rich song of the land around him. *Verbena to the west—this variety smells like citrus. Beware. In the upper canopy of that tree up ahead is a buttery fruit that is especially nourishing for the skin and the hair. The red moss will cause you illness. The blue-green moss is especially nutritious and sweet-tasting.*

Firae tasted the moss and climbed the thick, silver-trunked tree to its upper branches. He found the fruits easily; their tough black skins were a vivid contrast to their creamy white interiors. He communicated with the forest creatures as well as he could; he did not have the gift for it, but neither was he completely unskilled. He saw some creatures that were familiar to him—serpents, small felines, and brightly colored birds—and others that he had never seen. Through the trees raced little silver-furred creatures, chattering and shaking their long, bushy tails.

Other creatures, similar to the tree-dwellers but nearly hairless, popped their heads in and out of holes in the ground and occasionally raced out to snatch a fallen piece of fruit.

He could not remember the last time he had explored a forest like a naked child at play, but, he decided, it had been far too long. It did take some of the sting from preparing to pose as a slave.

He still hated Tash's plan. But the man was right. Brissa did need him. And if Tash did sacrifice his life to restore The Border, Firae would never forgive himself for refusing to submit to this indignity. Even a king knew that the temporary sacrifice of dignity did not hold the same value as a life.

But if they could manage to fulfill the prophecy...

Firae tasted the creamy fruit. It was mild and almost savory, with an earthy, nutty flavor. He wasn't sure whether or not he liked it.

If they could fulfill the prophecy, then The Border would be destroyed and there would be a new Queendom to the east. And what would The Council do with Tash then? Would Brissa be permitted a Council seat? Would the heads of Laesi simply find a new way to sever their ties to humanity? And when it came down to it, where would Firae stand?

When your ancestors whisper, you must listen.

So Firae dropped his fruit to the ground for the little creatures to fight over and closed his eyes and listened.

THEY LEFT THAT NIGHT.

Green Crab and River Song had stolen two large wooden bins full of items from a busy harbor several miles to the south. They had done an excellent job; the clothing was plain and unassuming, suggesting neither poverty nor wealth. Tash was outfitted with a purse on his belt and a small pack on his back, while Firae's pack was much larger.

They brought Tash an absurd assortment of hats of various shapes and colors, some of which Tash was sure he'd seen on the heads of Villaluan ladies, and all of which were slightly damp. He selected a straw hat with a wide brim for the daytime, and a knitted cap for the evening, as well as a pair of eyeglasses that were thick enough to mute the vibrancy of his green eyes. They made the world a bit bleary and gave him a headache, but with luck he would not have to wear them often.

Firae blinked when Tash turned to face him, fully clad in his evening disguise. Most of his hair was tucked up into the hat, and he wore a brown knit tunic and breeches, as well as boots and a jerkin crafted from animal skin. "What do you think?" Tash asked.

"I think… you look disturbingly like a human," Firae said with a frown.

Firae had a similar set of clothes, though without the jerkin or the boots. The omissions would look appropriate to Firae's station as a slave, and Firae would sooner eat verbena than wear leather.

"Well, that is the idea," Tash replied. His note to Bachuc, secure in a corked bottle to be delivered by River Song and Green Crab, sat on the shoreline beside their little boat. The two muirdannoch, eager to see if there was anything to keep for themselves, were rifling through what Tash and Firae had left in the boxes.

They bid their goodbyes with hand signals from Tash and a wave from Firae.

"Please remind me how you plan to avoid getting lost," Firae said as they made their way through the dark forest west of the creek. Their steps were nimble and sure as they moved across the uneven terrain. Tash's boots were slung over his backpack.

"All we need to do is follow the Durstan Star until we reach the Nostra River, then follow that to the Carzet Mountains until we reach Zegripanloch," Tash explained. "It's a fairly easy route, and one that should allow us to remain in mostly wooded areas."

"Have you done this before? You seem to know the land," Firae observed as the trees thinned to reveal the night sky.

"No. Before I met Cliope and Brissa I had never ventured far from the border cities. But I have studied maps. I suppose I just like to accumulate knowledge."

Firae laughed softly and leapt over a tiny stream in their path. "That is not precisely news, Tash."

Tash smiled, hopping over the stream right behind him. "I imagine not."

They walked in comfortable silence for some time, listening to the sounds of the night: birds of prey and choruses of insects calling to one another, the rustle of leaves and snapping of twigs as creatures scurried all around them.

It wasn't until they had reached the Muirdannoch Mountains and were making a slow and steady climb toward cooler winds and thinner air that Tash decided to speak.

"I apologize for losing my temper with you earlier," he said.

Firae stumbled. "Oh."

"I know this isn't easy for you. It can't be. You have been told all your life that you are my better, that you are above the concerns of the common elf, and I threatened to leave you alone in a strange land if you didn't agree to pose as my slave. I should have... I am sorry, Firae."

"Thank you," Firae said, "but I owe you an apology as well. You are right, there is no caste here. As far as the humans in Villalu are concerned, we are nothing more than potential slaves or potential profit. And I do need your help. While we are here, we are equals. I understand that now."

"Equals might be a strong word even by human standards," Tash said, lips curving into a smile. "I imagine you'd fetch a much higher price at the flesh markets than I would. You are younger and impossibly beautiful."

Firae snorted. "That is the worst compliment I have ever received: 'You would fetch a higher price than I at a slave auction.' And it's inaccurate as well. Have you ever looked into a mirror, old man?"

You must not hide from the mirror of your soul.

Despite The Truthkeeper's words, Tash did flinch at Firae's word choice. He couldn't have known, of course, and if their situation had been different, Tash would have preferred to keep the truth of his soul to himself. But the truth was that his very life might depend upon opening himself to the king. They had few clues to use to decipher The Truthkeeper's meaning, and it wouldn't do to protect secrets at the cost of lives.

"This seems like a good place to stop," Tash said, indicating a copse of conifers just ahead. Firae raised his eyebrows, but then shrugged in acquiescence. "We may as well. We aren't likely to find a better spot, and I'm growing a bit hungry."

The space inside the dense cluster of trees was dark as a cave, but for a few stars visible here and there through the thinner branches above, and the ground was carpeted with layers of soft needles. They shed their packs, and Tash lit a fire, separating it from the ground by a thin layer of magic to prevent the dry needles from burning.

"Firae, we need to discuss the prophecy," Tash said, well aware that Firae hadn't even sat down. "I don't want to die, of course, but I was committed to the destruction of The Border even before I understood what my choice to help Brissa could cost me."

Firae nodded slowly, plucking a few needles from a branch overhead and giving them an experimental nibble. "Of course. Have you... learned anything new?"

"Not exactly. But if we are going to try—I think we need to be completely honest with one another."

"All right," Firae said, and waited for Tash to continue.

"My key. Or... the thing that will unlock my key. *You must not hide from the mirror of your soul.* I have been trying to figure out what that means, what it is that I must do."

"I would imagine it has to do with self-reflection," Firae reasoned. "Perhaps you need to complete a soul-walk concerning your own identity, such as the mirror-souled do."

"But that is just it," Tash explained, heart pounding. He took a deep breath. "Firae, *I* am a mirror-soul."

In the silence, Firae's eyes were round and intent upon his own. "*Oh,*" Firae said softly, his voice alight with wonderment.

"I hope this does not cause you to think less of me."

"*Less* of you? Why would I think less of you? You are one of the Wise Children. Mirror-souls are blessings to their families and their feririars."

"Mirror-souled *girls* are a blessing to their families and their feririars," Tash corrected gently. "Mirror-souled boys, on the other hand…" Tash sighed. "In feririars like the one I grew up in, we are considered more a disappointment than a blessing."

"But… why?" Firae sounded bewildered; his voice was earnest and innocent and young. "How could that be?"

Tash shifted, crossed his legs in front of himself, and stared into the fire. He was unable to meet Firae's gaze. It was an enormous relief to know that Firae didn't share the prejudice of Tash's own people, but explaining the realities of the Common caste to a spoiled royal made him tired.

"Amongst the Common caste, a healthy daughter is cause for celebration," Tash began. "A son… a healthy son is worth about half as much. Men aren't allowed to pursue leadership. We follow the old Gods, we deeply revere womb magic, and we teach our children of the brutality and death that occur when men are permitted to hold power. A daughter—particularly a smart and skilled daughter—can often mean an elevation in status. The Coven Schools of the Great Mother always hold a few spots open to train the smartest and most promising girls of the Common and Spirit castes. That opens every opportunity for higher education, and it is an incredible honor to be chosen."

"And… I am guessing that you were chosen."

Tash sighed. "I nearly was. My parents were so proud. I almost just *pretended* so that I could attend, but when the priestess from the school came to interview me, she could tell right away. She could see my true nature, and there was nothing I could do to hide it."

"So what did you do?" Firae asked, continuing to snack on tree-needles.

"I had my soul-walk. The priestess ordered it, as she would for any child she suspected to be of mirror nature, so of course my parents did not argue. It was… It changed everything."

"I can see that," Firae said with a smile. "How old were you at the time?"

"Fourteen."

Firae gasped. "*Fourteen?* But that—you truly were a child! Most children of fourteen can barely run through the forest at night without falling flat on their little faces, let alone learn the proper meditations to undertake a soul-walk."

It was true; a fourteen-year-old sidhe was analogous in age to a human child of perhaps seven or eight. But Tash had been a smart and inquisitive child, and the idea of doing something as grown-up and important as a soul-walk had appealed to him.

"I suppose that is what is so special about the Wise Children, though, is it not?" Firae mused. "You know the truth of yourself in a way none of your peers could."

"I suppose so," Tash agreed, warmed by Firae's enthusiasm.

"Would you—I certainly understand if you would rather not, of course—"

Tash understood. Etiquette dictated that soul-walks were private; the details were to be shared only with closest confidantes, which, by necessity, was exactly what Firae had become.

"The Mirror Rite is different from the Nuptial Rite. It must be performed at a shrine of *L'auvkinlea*, and there are no guides. One must find one's own way."

"To the Heart of All Worlds? As a *child?*"

Tash laughed softly. "It wasn't easy. But those who are mirror-souled always find their way." He watched Firae, who sat with his knees pulled up to his chin, his arms wrapped tight around his calves, and his eyes alight with genuine interest.

And he told him.

Tash told Firae details that he had never shared with anyone else. Not even Lee, the man he had married, not even when he believed his love for Lee burned hot enough to reduce the entire world to cinders.

He told him about eating the hallucinogenic *zula sopor rija* and performing the meditation ritual. About how *L'auvkinlea* had not spoken to him, but had shown Tash Their many faces: a multitude of possibilities woven through infinite realities.

At the age of fourteen, Tash had looked upon the face of God and it was endless.

He told Firae about the tug he had felt, the invisible pull that had led him to a dark forest clearing in the middle of the universe. In the middle of the clearing had stood an enormous *srechelee* tree, and, embedded in the tree, directly in front of Tash, was a mirror.

And in that mirror was a boy.

It had been instantaneous; Tash had known, immediately and completely, that he was seeing his own true reflection. He had looked down at himself and frowned; the body he saw was the same one he had worn when he began the Rite, the same one he had been forced to wear since the day he was born: It was the body of a girl: the body of one who would one day wield womb magic; the body that had been such a blessing to his parents; the body that brought with it a world of possibilities and options that would be closed to him if he accepted what he knew to be true.

He had raised his head, looked at the truth of himself in the mirror once again, and then run, head first, inside.

He had fallen through the mirror and kept falling. He had fallen for an indistinguishable period of time, fallen without any body at all, fallen until he nearly forgot that he had ever done anything else.

And then he had stopped falling, and found himself face to face, once again, with *L'auvkinlea*.

Tash paused. It had been years since he had allowed himself to settle into that particular memory.

"A lot of mirror children don't seek physical change," Tash explained. "Many wait until they have reached adulthood, and some never do, even later in life. But I knew, Firae. Right away I knew. The boy in the mirror was me. From head to toe."

Firae tightened his grip around his calves. "Were you afraid?"

"I… it's difficult to explain. Yes, and no. I was relieved. I thought, no matter what happened, things were starting to make sense. At least I would be able to see myself when I looked in the mirror. But I was scared as well: living as a mirror-souled boy was one thing, but living as a mirror-souled boy who had sacrificed his womb magic for the sake of a changed body?" Tash sighed. "I knew it would make life more difficult. Even at fourteen I knew that."

"But you chose it anyway."

"I did." Because within the face of God, there was yet another mirror. Tash had stood before it, and seen nothing at all reflected back. It hadn't concerned him; he was without a body, so of course he wasn't going to see anything. And then he had understood; there were no words spoken, but the message was clear.

Reveal the truth, and it shall be so.

And so he had. With no more than a ripple and a thought, Tash was looking at himself in the mirror once again. But this time, the boy within the mirror was also standing in front of it.

And when he woke up, naked and hungry and bathed in the afternoon sun, it was still true.

"And that is why I am so confused. I've never hidden from the mirror. I am not ashamed to have traded power for identity. Am I meant to undertake another Mirror Rite, do you suppose?"

Firae appeared to consider this. "Perhaps? Or perhaps the mirror of your soul is meant to represent something else in the context of the prophecy. She is a sphinx, after all. Why should we presume that the message is the slightest bit straightforward?"

That was a very good point.

But it didn't narrow things down quite enough. "Given the state I have allowed my soul to fall into over the last few decades, I am confident that I would rather not glimpse its current reflection," Tash said with a wince. "But neither am I afraid. I know I will answer to the Gods when my time comes."

Firae rolled his eyes. "We shall all answer to the Gods one day, and many of us with much greater burdens weighing on our souls."

Irritation burned white-hot beneath Tash's skin. "Do not presume to know of my burden, Firae," he said through gritted teeth.

"And do not presume to know *mine.*"

Tash decided against saying something that he knew he would regret, and closed his eyes.

"I will apologize first this time," Firae said, forcing a laugh from Tash, "if we can agree to stop talking for a while."

Tash kissed him.

And then Tash waved away the fire in the middle of their little thicket, leaving them to reach for one another in the dark beneath the dappled moonlight.

They didn't talk about what they were doing, or what it meant, or how it was different this time.

They didn't talk at all.

Chapter Seventeen

Brieden always woke with the dawn, even on his days off from the farm. He couldn't help it, no matter how late he may have stayed up the night before.

Sehrys slumbered in his arms, suffering no such affliction. His face was lovely, smooth perfection in the dim morning light. Brieden ran his fingertips across his lover's bare shoulder, eliciting a sweet murmur that made Brieden's heart swell with a confusing combination of pain and affection.

Sehrys was his everything. And that, perhaps, was the crux of the problem.

They had barely resolved their argument of a few weeks before. By the time Sehrys had returned home, both men were beside themselves. They had thrown themselves into one another's arms, whispering words of love and apology until there were no words at all but the gasps of pleasure that carried them through the night.

The following day they had been particularly sweet to one another. The flavor of their interaction reminded Brieden of their earliest days in Khryslee, when everything had been fresh and perfect and simple and indestructible.

But nothing in the world was truly indestructible. Brieden understood that now, because reaching for one another to avoid heated words was becoming a habit. Swallowing his frustration left a bitter taste in his mouth. And some nights when Sehrys slept beside him Brieden felt as lonely as if he hadn't seen him in weeks.

Four hundred years, that is what The Gatekeeper had told them they could expect. Four hundred years together, and Brieden was lost after less than two.

WHEN SEHRYS AWOKE, HE WAS ALONE. THE LATE MORNING LIGHT CREPT through the translucent leaves that fluttered over the window beside the bed, and Brieden whistled in the distance.

Sehrys smiled as he pulled on his robe. It was one of his favorite garments, and often the only one he chose to wear all day if he knew he would not be venturing far from the house. It was crafted from whole petals of *simblini*, a flower-tree of the Western Sea Lands where Sehrys had grown up. The petals were pale gold and cream and as supple as water against his skin. The material was surprisingly tough and impossibly soft, and the robe had been tailored to perfection by some of the region's best earth-weavers and infused with magic that allowed it to mend itself.

It had been a gift from the Council of Khryslee, a gesture of welcome and an acceptance of his citizenship among them. The gesture had warmed his heart, because the message was clear: *You are home now.*

He was home. From the moment he had crossed through the gate to Khryslee, he had known it.

But lately something was off, because home was not simply Khryslee, home was *Brieden.* Home had always been Brieden, in this incarnation and every other.

Sehrys tied the robe's woven belt and went in search of his fiancé.

Outside the bedroom door, the sitting room was nearly complete, and a network of thick, woody vines had begun to create a staircase to what would become the house's upper level. Sehrys passed through the large opening in the far wall, which had not yet narrowed to the size of a door, and found Brieden tilling a patch of earth near what would soon be their front door.

"What are you doing?" Sehrys asked, darting in to press a swift kiss to Brieden's sweaty cheek.

"I got a few pouches of seeds at the market," Brieden said, wiping his brow with his forearm as he stood. "Vegetables from Villalu that I have not seen here. The girl at the stall said they would grow here."

Sehrys knelt to pick up one of the little pouches and shook a few seeds into his palm. "You don't need to do that," he said, nodding toward the earth that Brieden was preparing. "I can grow anything you like as long as I know what it is."

"I know," Brieden said, and took the pouch. "But I want to do it on my own." He plucked each tiny seed from Sehrys's palm and dropped it into the pouch. His eyes never met those of his fiancé. "I have become too dependent on you as it is."

Sehrys frowned as Brieden went back to work. "There is nothing wrong with depending upon one another, Brieden," he said carefully.

"No, but we do not depend upon one another, do we?"

Brieden raked the patch of earth into even rows and dropped seeds from one of the pouches into one of them.

Sehrys furrowed his brow as his chest clenched. "Brieden, will you... will you please look at me?"

Brieden stood up, wiped his palms on his breeches, and looked Sehrys in the eye. Sehrys nearly stumbled backward at what he saw there.

It was not anger. It was not defiance. It was *defeat*.

Sehrys swallowed around a painful lump in his throat. "Please tell me what you mean. If you think I do not need you..." he trailed off, unsure how to complete such a thought.

Brieden took Sehrys's hand, which helped a little, but not nearly enough.

"I know you love me," Brieden said, his voice soft and careful, "but you do not need me. And the trouble is, Sehrys, that I do need you."

Sehrys opened his mouth to protest, but Brieden shook his head. "It takes more than passion and love to make a life with someone," he said softly, dropping his gaze to the ground.

"More than… Brieden, please, you… you cannot be saying—"

It hit Sehrys so violently that this time he *did* stumble. Brieden caught him, and Sehrys sank into his arms; relief at the contact made his eyes sting with tears. "Do not leave me," he whispered into Brieden's neck. "Please."

"I won't leave you," Brieden assured him, "but—"

Sehrys wanted nothing more than to silence that *but*.

"But I don't know if we should—" he pulled back, and his eyes went to the promise pendant at Sehrys's throat. Sehrys gasped; his hand flew to cover the stone as if Brieden had threatened to rip it from his body.

"No," Sehrys said, tears flowing freely.

"It is—everything was happening so fast, before, and we had just escaped Villalu with our lives, and then Firae let us go to Khryslee together, and—and—it was just so *fast*, Sehrys."

"That does not matter," Sehrys said, stepping out of Brieden's arms as a thread of anger shot up through the center of his fear and sorrow. "It does not matter if we were together for a minute or a century, Brieden, this is right."

"But how do you know?"

"Because," Sehrys answered, "it's *us*." What could Brieden not understand about that?

They stared at one another. Sehrys had never seen such distance in Brieden's eyes. How had he missed seeing that? How could he ever *fix* it?

"I… hope we are not interrupting anything."

Sehrys and Brieden whipped around to see Jaxis making his way from their almost-sitting room.

"Speak for yourself," came a second voice. "I don't care if we are interrupting. It's been six hells of a journey, and I left my manners somewhere back near the Sheevalus." Cliope Keshell stepped from behind Jaxis and strode toward them. Her smile was at least twice as bright as the sun. "Gods, is it ever good to see you boys," she said, and pulled them into a fierce hug.

Chapter Eighteen

Tash and Firae spent nearly a week free of human contact in the Darjec Mountains.

There were a few travelers along the narrow, winding roads of packed earth that snaked through the mountain range, but the elves preferred to bypass the roads whenever possible. It was far easier—not to mention more pleasant—to navigate their way across gnarled tree roots and prickled underbrush. The lifestream of the forest around them guided them so naturally that they barely even noticed it.

By the fifth day, they were naked more often than not.

The land was cooler than Ryovni, but not by much, and the dampness that clung to the air all around them made the difference seem less pronounced. There was no pleasure in covering themselves in human clothing while traveling through the soupy heat of the dense forest, so they opted for the simple pleasure of sun and wind and gentle rain across their skins, and the less simple pleasure of stolen moments together free of fumbling with buttons and strings.

Firae sighed with pleasure as he slid the pack off his back for their midday rest. He stepped into the calf-deep stream they had found, bent to fill his water pouch, and then poured the water over his head. He groaned at the feeling of cool water trickling down the hot, chafed skin of his shoulders and back.

"I would give nearly anything to leave these Gods-blasted packs behind," Firae grumbled.

Tash stepped into the stream behind him, filled his own water skin, and poured some of it over Firae's back as well.

"Perhaps we should dress," Tash said, skimming gentle fingers over Firae's abused skin. "We will probably reach Tonathe before nightfall, and we will need to costume ourselves before we reach the edges of human habitation."

"Perhaps." Firae agreed with a sigh. He smiled and closed his eyes as Tash's hands moved from his raw skin to knead the muscles of Firae's neck down to the space between his shoulder blades.

"You've been carrying the heavier pack," Firae added, and turned to face the other man. He tugged on Tash's shoulder until he turned around so that Firae could inspect his back. Firae winced.

"Why did you not say anything? We could have stopped much earlier."

"I imagine it looks worse than it truly is," Tash said, though he flinched when Firae pressed a feather-light touch to a raw, red place where the top layer of Tash's skin had been rubbed clean away.

"Lie down on the bank," Firae instructed. "On your stomach."

Tash looked at Firae. "Firae, you don't have to—"

"Stop it. You were the one who said that caste is meaningless here, were you not?"

Tash looked at him. The apple of his throat bobbed as he swallowed thickly.

Firae understood; it was one thing to share a bed with a royal. It was one thing, even, to argue with a royal. To address a royal without respect. But healing—healing was intimate. It left one vulnerable, for to heal was not simply a matter of restoring another to health. It was also the act of sharing one's power. Some of Firae's power would linger within Tash, and he could use it while it lasted. He could use it as if it were his own.

Tash and Firae had shared power before, of course, but not like this. This was Firae offering to share the power of the Royal caste with a commoner, and it was unheard of. In Laesi, it was so taboo, it may as well have been illegal.

Tash didn't know that Sehrys was the only other person Firae had done this for.

"Lie down," Firae repeated. "You can consider it a command if you are so inclined."

Tash rolled his eyes at that, but he smiled, too. "You'd do this over no more than a few blisters?"

"I would do it because I prefer not to force a friend to suffer unnecessarily."

Tash ducked his head, but Firae didn't miss how his smile broadened.

Firae stepped up onto the soft mossy bank and sat with his legs crossed and tucked up tight to his body. He gestured at the space in front of him, and Tash didn't bother with any further argument.

Firae pressed his palms into the mossy earth on either side of himself as Tash settled in front of him. He inhaled deeply and slowly as he consciously pulled pure tendrils of healing magic from deep within the lifestream of the planet. Firae's gift for healing was not strong; there were those of the Common caste who were much more powerful healers than he, even if that was the only power they possessed. But he could heal Tash's wounds and his own, even if it took a bit of work to do so.

Satisfied that he had done all that he could to strengthen what natural power he had, Firae laid his hands upon Tash's back.

Tash looked at Firae over his shoulder, and there was something new in his eyes. Something soft and amazed seemed to have settled behind his shrewd, piercing gaze.

Firae smiled back, and Tash laid his head upon folded arms and relaxed beneath Firae's touch.

Firae closed his eyes and focused his intent. His hands glowed, flickering green and gold and rose and burgundy as the exchange began. Energy flowed back and forth between them until their bodies were bathed in a deep golden-rust-colored glow.

The healing itself took just a few moments, but the jolt he felt as Tash's essence washed through his body while his own flooded into Tash was enough to make Firae gasp. Tash sucked in a sharp breath, and his skin warmed as his wounds disappeared.

"There," Firae said softly, but rather than remove his hands from Tash's back, he ran them lightly over the warm, bronzed skin.

Tash hummed in pleasure as Firae trailed his lips down Tash's body; the connection forged by the healing still buzzed between them.

"We should not tarry too long," Tash said, but his voice was sleepy and relaxed and lacking in conviction.

"We'll cover more ground if we are properly refreshed." Firae nipped at the firm flesh of Tash's too round and too perfect buttocks.

"Refreshed?" Tash asked, laughter in his voice, and something loosened in Firae's chest at the playful tone. "Is that truly the outcome you are courting right now?"

"Of course." Firae pressed his hand into the soft moss to grow a cluster of *hubia rija*. "First we shall shed all of the tension in our bodies, and then we shall have a short nap. We can be back on our way within an hour. Perhaps two. *Possibly* three."

"Let us aim for one," Tash said, laughing now, "and accept the possibility of two." Firae plucked and opened a flower and drizzled its contents across Tash's buttocks and back. Tash's laughter stopped on a sharp intake of breath, followed by a contented murmur as Firae rubbed the oil into the muscles of the other man's body.

Firae had never done this for anyone. He had been on the receiving end of hundreds of massages, at the hands of both lovers and healers. Such pleasures came with his station. But such pleasure had never been asked *of* him. Though he would not consider himself a selfish lover, massage was the sort of thing a royal reserved for an equal. And Firae had never taken a lover whom he considered to be his equal; that honor had been intended for Sehrys.

But instead, it had gone to Tash. And to his surprise, Firae could not say that the fact bothered him in the least.

There was something immensely satisfying about seeing a man as reserved and controlled as Tash melt into a puddle of loose-limbed pleasure beneath Firae's hands. He used the lingering traces of the healing connection between them to follow the signals of Tash's body to every knot of tension. It was both like and unlike the satisfaction of provoking Tash until he snapped; this seduction was gentle and easy and wholly unnecessary, but it was a seduction nonetheless and every bit as fulfilling as that night they had spent together on the ship.

Firae plucked another flower and drizzled it down the crack between Tash's buttocks. He smiled as Tash spread his legs and arched his back in the sweetest invitation Firae had ever seen.

"I was going to ask if you liked it this way," Firae said, tracing Tash's entrance with his forefinger, "but I think you've given me my answer already."

Tash gasped and spread his thighs even wider. "I certainly have. Now move along; we haven't got all afternoon."

Firae grinned. "We've got plenty of time." He slid a finger inside. Arousal pulsed through him at the tight heat of Tash's body in combination with Tash's deep grunt.

It had been so long since he had been inside another man! Firae gripped his own erection firmly at its base and breathed slow and deep, fighting to stave off the sharp edge of his arousal.

As he worked another finger inside, Firae ran his eyes across the rippling muscles of Tash's back. From the pronounced dimples just above the swell of his buttocks to the delicate jut of his shoulder blades to the quivering strength of his shoulders, the man was nearly too gorgeous to bear, and this wasn't enough.

"Turn over," Firae urged. He pulled his fingers from Tash's body and nudged him gently in the side until Tash gave a soft groan—a seeming mixture of frustration and acquiescence—and rolled onto his back.

Firae swallowed around a thick knot that had risen, unbidden, in his throat at the sight of Tash spread beneath him on the vibrant green moss. On one side of them the little creek sparkled and babbled as it tumbled past, and on the other the stout trunks of trees fuzzy with moss and lichen grew in dense clusters, making the world seem lush and fresh and simple and small. All that existed was Tash: his smooth golden-brown skin aglow with perspiration, his wide green eyes drenched with slowly simmering lust, the golden-orange waves of his hair fanned behind him like a halo of flames. His cock was thick and dark and fully erect, and his legs were spread.

Tash reached for him, and Firae shut his eyes and gritted his teeth against what even Tash's hand wrapping around his forearm could do to him.

"Just… give me a moment," Firae managed to grit out, gripping himself even more firmly around the base of his erection.

"Ah, to be so young again…" Tash murmured, chuckling at Firae's predicament.

Firae opened his eyes, released his grip on himself, cupped Tash's jaw, and kissed him slowly, lingering. "Careful, old man, or I'll wear you right out," he murmured against Tash's lips, parting with a quick nip to the tender skin of his lower lip.

"I am counting on it."

Tash slid his hands over Firae's shoulders as Firae crawled closer, pushing Tash's thighs farther apart and sliding his hands, palms-up, along the mossy earth until he was cupping Tash's tight, round buttocks and lifting him gently. Tash slid one hand over Firae's shoulder and down his chest. His hand scraped lightly over Firae's nipples, circled his belly button, and caught on the wisps of pale golden hair that led from Firae's belly button to the thatch of golden curls that surrounded his cock. Firae shivered at the sensations and groaned deeply when Tash, his grip firm and dry, grabbed hold of his member and traced its head lightly with his thumb.

Firae swore beneath his breath as Tash used his other hand to pluck a second flower from the cluster Firae had grown. Tash twisted the flower open and made quick, messy work of smoothing its oil over Firae's cock so that puddles of excess oil ran down their thighs and across Tash's hips and stomach. Firae used this to his advantage by rubbing the tingling oil into Tash's buttocks, then soaking his hands in the stuff and dipping slick fingers back into Tash's hole to rub and stretch until Tash was whimpering with his thighs spread impossibly wide, his heels dug into the ground, and his hips churning in desperate little circles.

Firae didn't try to cool himself off. He slid his palms back under Tash and let Tash reach between their bodies to guide Firae inside.

They gasped at the intensity: the amplified sensation of their *hubia rija*-slicked flesh sliding against, within, around one another; the lingering zing of the energy exchange from the healing; and... something else. Something sweet and painful and new had woven its way into the very foundation of the attraction they shared.

Firae slid his hands up to the small of Tash's back just as Tash wrapped his legs around him, drawing Firae in deeper, and, without conscious thought, Firae pulled one hand free to cup Tash's face. Their eyes met for one sharp, vivid moment before he closed the distance between their mouths and kissed Tash as if he were trying to devour him whole.

Their bodies rocked together in a tight embrace; their lips were never far from the other's skin. They kept their eyes closed because, Firae suspected, the intensity of eye contact might shatter them into a thousand pieces.

"There is a human *feririar* nearby, isn't there?" Firae asked. He had been trying to understand the strange sensation at the edges of his perception for the past hour, and it wasn't until he caught the faint but unmistakable scent of cooking meat that it slotted into place.

"A human *village*, yes. We should reach the road fairly soon."

Now that Ferae knew the source of the strange feeling, he could sense the road ahead like a tight, aching scar through the heart of the forest.

Firae sighed. "We will need to get dressed for that, I suppose."

Tash laughed and bumped their shoulders together. "We will. Avoiding Tonathe would add time to our journey that we can't spare. And we might find information that could be of use to us."

Firae nodded, tamping down the ball of nerves that arose. "And you truly believe that you can pass as a human," he said, keeping his voice as neutral as possible. Their entire plan was insane, but Tash seemed so sure, and casting doubt would do little for his confidence.

"I do," Tash said. "To be honest, I'm more concerned about you."

"*Me!*" Firae nearly choked.

"You," Tash agreed, and his laugh was so affectionate that Firae smiled despite himself. "I am having a very difficult time imagining you even pretending to be a slave."

"And you believe that you will fare better pretending to be an entirely different *species?*"

"I believe I will fare much better, actually," Tash said in accent-free Villaluan. "I have experience pretending to be something that I'm not. But you..."

"I suppose," Firae grumbled.

"It is not an insult. It is only that I have a difficult time imagining you as anything other than royalty."

Firae considered this as they navigated their way through a dense patch of vegetation.

"Coming from you, that sounds like an insult." Once they were on surer ground, Firae ran his fingers over a scratch on his arm from the prickly bush they had just maneuvered through and wondered if it was worth spending healing energy to repair the scratches at their next stop. It wouldn't take much, but in case they did encounter humans soon, it would be wise to store up as much power as possible should things take a sour turn.

Tash adjusted the pack on his back and hopped onto the trunk of a large fallen tree, then craned his neck as he walked to see if the extra height gave him a better vantage point.

"All I mean is that I cannot picture you in a position of subservience," Tash said, glancing at Firae. He hopped off the log when he reached its end and fell into step beside Firae. "You exude... power."

"And arrogance?"

Tash rolled his eyes. "Do not put words into my mouth."

"That particular word was plucked straight from your mind, Tash. Do not deny it."

"Are you professing to be a dream-walker? Just when I thought I knew the extent of your powers…"

"Ugh, don't remind me." Firae's voice was a childish whine even to his own ears. "I am capable of it, but not gifted in it. I had a tutor who tried to mold what little ability was there into something useful, but all I managed to do after two years of lessons was to convey a few garbled words. Something about apples and grimchins, I believe. It was a torturous process."

Tash laughed heartily. "Well, it seems you do not have access to my mind, then."

"Perhaps not, but I do have my instincts. Admit it: you find me arrogant."

"I find you many things," Tash countered. "I am not saying that 'arrogant' would not have a place on that list, but it would be nowhere near the top."

Firae smiled. "That is an excellent answer. You are well suited for politics."

"I suppose I might have been."

The answer hit Firae like a punch to the chest; if they could not find a way to stop what Tash had put into motion when he began helping the Keshells, Tash would have no future at all.

"We do not yet know what the Gods intend for us," Firae said, his voice quiet. "We may yet fulfill the prophecy."

"And The Border may yet pop like a harmless bubble while music fills the world," Tash snapped. "But in case you have forgotten, Brissa is in enemy hands, and we are naked in hostile territory. The likelihood that either of us will survive, let alone both of us, is less than slim."

Firae clamped his lips tight against the retort that burned in his throat and kept his back rigid and his eyes straight ahead as they moved closer to the scar through the heart of the forest.

"Well then," he said, after long moments in silence, "let us put our clothes on."

THE SUN WAS SETTING BY THE TIME THEY REACHED TONATHE. THE brilliant, ripe colors splashed over the horizon. The wool of his cap irritated the sensitive tips of Tash's ears, his boots were uncomfortable, and the eyeglasses made his temples throb even as they blurred and distorted everything he saw.

Firae was glaring at the ground, that much was obvious even with Tash's compromised vision, but his head was lowered: good enough. Tash could only hope that the men of the village would not catch that spark of defiance in the king's eye. It would draw the sort of attention they simply could not afford.

"Once again," Tash muttered, "tell me what you will do if one of these men asks to inspect you more closely. And bear in mind that burning their internal organs into cinders is *not* an option."

"Nothing," Firae spat in a voice low with tightly controlled rage. His fingers curled tight around the chain that dangled from the collar around his neck. "I shall stand there like a wilting flower on a stem and allow the disgusting creatures to do as they like. Is that what you wish to hear?"

Tash paused to heave a great sigh and rub his temples. "We are not ready. We should have prepared for this hours ago."

"Well, we were naked. Our attention was elsewhere," Firae reminded him, raising his head long enough to shoot Tash a filthy smile. "But I won't hate this idea any less in the morning, so let us face that which we must face."

Tash nodded, but did not resume walking down the rapidly darkening road toward the lights of the village up ahead. "Firae, you are going to hate this," he confirmed, lifting his eyeglasses and ducking to meet the other man's eye. "But please do bear in mind that I am not asking you to allow anyone to *do whatever they wish.* Just to trust me to protect you. Can you do that? Because if you cannot—"

"I can." Firae cast his eyes back to the road. "I will. But if one of them touches me—"

"I will not let anyone touch you," Tash promised. Firae nodded and did not meet his eye, but he did hand the Tash the leather loop at the end of the chain to his collar.

"Very well, then," Firae said, "let us get this over with."

The very moment they stepped into the village square, someone touched Firae.

It was a young woman, probably no more than sixteen, in a lightweight crimson dress with neatly plaited hair, who was accompanied by two older humans that Tash assumed were her parents. A second, younger girl peeked out from behind her mother's skirts, her eyes round.

"Oooh," the girl said, as she touched the tip of Firae's ear, "pretty."

To Firae's credit and Tash's surprise, Firae did not flinch or even so much as grimace. The look in his downcast eyes, however, was nearly murderous.

"Lettia!" Her mother yanked the girl back. "It is not polite to touch other people's things." She cast an apologetic look toward Tash. "I am so sorry about that. Please pardon my daughter; she has never seen one of them up close like this before."

"That's quite all right," Tash said, offering the girl a magnanimous smile. "He is lovely, isn't he?"

"What's his name?" the smaller sister, still mostly hidden behind her mother, asked in a near whisper.

"He doesn't have one yet. Do you have any ideas?"

"Our dog is named Breshee," the girl replied. "I picked it out."

"That's a very good name. I shall suggest it to his master."

"So he is not yours, then?" the father of the family asked. His voice was brusque, and the way he looked back and forth between the two sidhe with narrow eyes made the fine hairs on the back of Tash's neck prickle.

"He is not," Tash confirmed. "He is a gift for the king from one of the humbler branches of the Chrill family. I am merely delivering him to his new home."

"The king is dead," the man said sharply; his eyes narrowed further. "Unless the queen has taken a secret husband that we know nothing of?"

"I—" Tash swallowed and focused on keeping his breaths even and his expression light. "I do beg your pardon, friend. I am not a political person by nature, but rather a simple working man. I was referring to Thieren Panloch."

"It is time that the Panlochs accepted their fate. The queen earned her title when she married that lunatic Dronyen. When my daughters marry, are they not entitled to that which their husband leaves behind?" The man's eyes flashed with righteous indignation, his shoulders were squared, and his posture was straight as a stake in the ground.

"Zaryn," his wife admonished, placing a careful hand on her husband's arm. The man did not acknowledge her, but continued to stare at Tash as if he could drill holes in the other man's body.

"I could not agree with you more, friend," Tash said, subtly glancing around to ascertain what attention they might have drawn. "I am merely fulfilling that which I was hired to do. Now if you will pardon me, I must be—"

"When you see Thieren Panloch, tell him to stay in his family lands and leave Miknauvripal be. His family has inflicted enough damage on the world, and we are grateful to be rid of him." Before Tash could respond, Zaryn put his arm around his wife's shoulders and strode past the two sidhe. "Come along, girls," he called over his shoulder. The girls stared at Firae for a moment before following their father's command.

"And let us go as well," Tash whispered to Firae. "And quickly, now."

With hundreds of human eyes following them, they hurried over the cobblestones of the town square and onto the packed-earth road that would lead them from the village.

"I thought you said you had developed the perfect tale," Firae murmured once they were out of earshot of any humans. Night had fallen completely, and the only light aside from the stars and the dwarf moon was that which emanated from the hearths of the houses on either side of the road. The road was long, straight, and flat, and Tash could see where the homes began to thin perhaps a quarter mile ahead.

"I thought I had," Tash responded under his breath. "I did not think there would be much in the way of support for Brissa's rule in this part of Villalu, but it seems that things are changing—unless that man was an outlier, of course, which is quite possible."

"On a bright note, it does not appear that he knows of Brissa's capture," Firae interjected.

"It does not. And if we are very fortunate in our plan, he shall never know of it."

"Oy!"

Tash stiffened at the voice behind him, but continued on without reaction. There was every possibility that the speaker was not addressing him.

"Oy! You with the elf! We need a word!"

We. Tash did not like the sound of that.

They turned slowly to find a group of nearly a dozen men dressed in the worn boots and simple, sturdy clothing of day laborers. The particulars of their features were difficult to make out in the weak light; two of the men carried oil lamps, but most stood in the shadows. As far as Tash could tell, the oldest of their number seemed near to fifty, and the youngest perhaps twenty.

"May I help you gentlemen?" Tash asked in an even tone. He rested his free hand on the hilt of the dagger at his belt.

"We heard you're bringing that elf to Thieren Panloch," one of the younger men responded. By the sound of his voice, Tash guessed he was the same man who had yelled out to them.

"I am simply passing through, friend, and I had best be on my way, if it is all the same to you."

"Well, it isn't all the same to me, *friend*. Half my family was killed in a Frilauan raid on this village, and I'm not the only one." Grumbles of agreement rose from the men around him. "Way we see it, the Panlochs owe us a lot more than the price of a slave."

Tash swallowed hard. Beside him, the heat of Firae's suppressed power, tinged with fear and laced heavily with aggression, was rolling from him in waves.

"We have all suffered losses at the hands of the Frilauans," Tash said, "but if you take this slave, it shall be me, and not the Panlochs, who suffers for it."

One of the older men in the group chortled. "I believe we can live with that." He stroked his close-cropped salt-and-pepper beard as shadows played across his face in the light of the lantern clutched in his other hand. "You look to me like a boy from the Carzets, not like anyone who has *suffered any losses* at the hands of those Panloch bastards. Hells, you're probably one of Drayez's bastards. God only knows how many he's got runnin' around."

Tash focused on keeping his body still and his head up. He took deep, measured breaths, trying not to let the frantic terror pounding at the door of his conscious mind burst in and destroy of all his control.

He could not have planned this more poorly. It would be unusual to encounter a human as pale as Tash who *wasn't* from the Carzet Mountains, or someplace close to it—the mountains of the Panloch ancestral lands. And worse than that, Tash had had no idea how hated the Panlochs had become, or how ready some villagers might be to embrace their new queen.

He should have listened more closely to Brieden when he told Tash of the raids on his village as a boy. He should have realized just how much of the blood spilled by the Followers of Frilau in the name of King Panloch was still fresh.

Tash racked his brain for a means of escape that didn't blow their cover, half-listened to the man continue to talk, and fought the instinct to take Firae's hand in his own and squeeze it.

"This one'll fetch a nice price at the markets," the man said, holding his lantern higher to better illuminate Firae. "Young. Healthy. Strong.

Pretty if you like that sort of thing. Enough to put extra chickens in all our cauldrons and some new boots on our feet, I'd wager."

"Enough to buy all our wives silken dresses!" piped another man farther back in the group. His voice was young, and eager in a way that made it even more difficult for Tash not to panic.

"Enough to pay for a year at the pub!" called out another. The men all laughed; excitement bubbled up around them as they thought of more and more possibilities.

"Enough for half a stable full of horses," the man who had begun their conversation said, walking several bold steps closer to them. "Perhaps even a bigger cart for the trade market in Mikthonel."

Tash drew his dagger, but the man seemed unconcerned. "If you put that away and leave quietly, you will leave with your life. When you see Thieren Panloch, you can tell him that *he doesn't own us anymore.*"

The man took one more step toward them and reached out to grab the chain connected to Firae's collar. Before Tash had a single second to react, before the man had the chance to pull, he screamed and pulled his hand back.

The chain was glowing red-hot. And then, almost immediately, it melted.

"Firae!" Tash dropped the useless leather loop in his hand just as a waist-high wall of flame shot up between them and the humans. There was screaming from the group in front of them and from the houses along the road, where people must have been watching the confrontation. The barking and howling of dogs joined the commotion, as did the distressed whinny of nearby horses. Firae's eyes burned with fire the color of dark, ripe cherries, and the man who had grabbed the chain was now clutching his heart.

"Firae, stop it!" Tash hissed. "Let him be. No good will come of killing him."

"You say Thieren Panloch owns you no more," Firae said in Villaluan, to the man, completely ignoring Tash. His companions were frozen, suddenly aware of precisely who was in control of the situation, "and yet you wish to own me, to sell me to any who will pay, no matter the cost to my body or my soul." Firae squeezed his hand into a fist. The man howled in pain; his knees buckled as he sank to the ground. Firae held a hand toward Tash to ward off interruption. "So that you may buy silken dresses and a year at the pub." Firae unclenched his hand and let it drop to his side, and the man's screams subsided, though he continued to clutch his chest and pant heavily. Firae walked forward until he was within the flame. Several men gasped, and a few of them sank to the ground on wobbling knees. "You are as bad as they are." Firae's voice was amplified by the fire. "Now leave, or I shall burn your town to ashes."

Tash had never seen a group of humans move so quickly.

Several of those still on their feet turned and fled immediately, letting their lanterns clatter to the ground, while two men pulled Firae's victim between them and left with him. The man stumbled to keep up as they ran.

Firae turned to face Tash. "It is probably best that we leave as well," he said, his voice perfectly calm. Tash stared at him and then burst into hysterical laughter.

He laughed until tears ran down his cheeks, running hand in hand with Firae, running as fast as they could away from Tonathe toward the safety of the forest.

THEY RAN UNTIL THE ROAD ENDED, AND THEN TASH OFF TOOK HIS BOOTS and threw them aside, and they ran into the woods, down a sharp slope, across a small creek, up the side of a few small boulders, and down another slope. It was dark and they had only the weak light of the lone dwarf moon and the innate sense of navigation that came with having their bare feet upon the earth to guide them. But it was enough. They navigated every sharp rock and gnarled root without faltering, and they didn't stop until they reached a clearing that was at least a mile from any human road.

Tash braced his hands on his knees and took deep gulps of air. He kept his eyes closed against the swirling chaos of fear and rage and self-flagellation that had saturated his mind. He could hear Firae catching his breath beside him, and when Tash opened his eyes and looked at him, Firae caught his eye with nothing less than a victorious smile. His cheeks were flushed and his eyes danced as if they were two children who had just gotten away with a fantastic piece of mischief.

And Tash's internal boundaries collapsed.

"What the *fuck* is wrong with you?" he screamed, voice edged with hysteria even to his own ears. He straightened up fully, ripped the pack off his back, and threw it to the ground. "Do you have any idea what you've done? How many people *saw* you?"

Firae's face fell, and for a split second before he snapped his spine straight and narrowed his eyes, he looked like a wounded child. "I believe I was saving our lives, Tash. You did not appear to have a better plan. In fact, the plan you *did* have is to blame for all of this! A gift for *Thieren Panloch*? What were you *thinking?*"

"In another village, it would have worked. How am I to keep abreast of popular opinion in mainland Villalu?"

Firae closed his eyes and took a deep breath. "Tash. You compromised the Non-Interference Doctrine. It was *you.*"

Tash winced at the reminder. "Do you think I could forget something like that?"

"No. But you did not realize that helping Brissa was a violation of the Doctrine before I arrived, correct? Because the magic that binds the Doctrine defines *ruler* not merely as the one who sits upon the throne. For a human to be considered the ruler of Villalu, she must also be seen as such by the majority of the humans who inhabit the land."

A sick feeling twisted in Tash's gut. "If I compromised the Doctrine, it could only mean that support for Brissa has grown significantly over the past year."

Firae nodded. "People consider Brissa their queen, Tash, even if their ruling houses have not entirely settled on the idea. Were that not so, I would still be safely home in Alovur Drovuru."

Tash stared at Firae and then lowered himself to the ground. The rage that had flowed through him so freely now diminished to a mere trickle of irritation, and his annoyance with himself swelled to something bordering on self-loathing.

"It was my fault, he conceded. "You are right. I just thought—"

"You thought that you knew Villalu better than I do," Firae finished for him when Tash trailed off. Firae shed his pack and sat facing Tash. "And you do. But when it comes to the Doctrine—you have spent the last fifty years here, Tash. I have spent them learning to be a king of Laesi."

Tash couldn't help the weak smile that spread across his lips at the phrase *a king of Laesi*. The way Firae said it was always so serious and self-important and unapologetic. Tash was beginning to find that endearing.

Tash sighed. "Next time I have a plan, I shall tell you every detail. I swear it to the Gods. But, Firae, they saw you use magic. And the fact that they respect Brissa's rule does not mean that they will take the words of a sidhe who terrified them to heart. Quite a few humans believe we are demons, and I cannot say that your display would be likely to disabuse them of that notion."

"Well, it's done," Firae said. "There is no point in pouting over wilted blossoms; what can we do about it now?"

"We can—we *must* make every effort to avoid human settlements," Tash said. "Word of this will spread quickly, and it could catch the interest of slave hunters. It is going to slow us down."

Firae sighed. "Well, on the bright side," he said, "this will allow us to spend more time naked, will it not?"

For the second time that night, Tash burst into laughter, but this time it made him feel as light as air. They were in the middle of a strange forest, Brissa was a prisoner, Cliope could be lost to them forever, and it was very likely that Tash would see Laesi again only long enough for a public execution. The prophecy was a puzzle that they so far had no inkling how to solve, and slave traders would begin to pursue them soon.

But Firae looked as pleased as a pixie in a pantry because they would get to spend their days *naked*.

Firae joined his laughter, and for some reason that Tash preferred not to examine too closely, that made him believe that perhaps there was hope after all.

CHAPTER NINETEEN

Brissa held herself perfectly straight, her head up and her shoulders squared, and resolutely ignored the screaming pain in her joints from weeks of sleeping in chains on the journey to Zegripanloch and the bruises from being roughly handled along the way.

She should be grateful for small mercies of the Gods, she supposed. Her captors had made it clear that they had strict orders to leave her virtue—or whatever may remain of it, by their reckoning—intact, and though many of them clearly resented the rule, they had.

She held her head high, though her eyes were covered by a thick strip of cloth, and allowed herself to be led through the echoing stone halls of the manor, choosing to focus on that for which she could be grateful.

She was grateful that she was clean; the blood of the moons had come upon her during the journey, and her captors, all of whom were men, had—*of course*—not planned for any such thing. They had supplied her with disgusted faces and bits of whatever cloth they decided they could spare, but she had still arrived at the Panloch estate last night stinking and caked in dried blood. Her dress had been ruined beyond repair. But she had been given a bath—two baths, in fact, in immediate succession, and warm and fragrant ones at that. She had been attended by serving women, not more men, and she was grateful for that, too. She was grateful that she had been given a bed, and though the straw mattress was one that she would never have found adequate before, it was like a slice of the heavenly realm after weeks on the hard, cold ground and the wooden carriage floor.

She was grateful for the simple dress on her body and the slippers on her feet. She was grateful for the fact that her wrists, though tied behind her back, were fastened with soft rope and not heavy, rough chains. And she was grateful for her absolute and unshakable belief that she would find a way to destroy Thieren Panloch and fulfill the prophecy, even if she had no idea where to begin.

Her guards pulled her to a stop and knocked on what Brissa could only guess was a wooden door. A deep voice from within called for them to enter.

The door creaked open, and Brissa was escorted through and onto a carpeted floor. "Here she is, Your Maj," one of the men said. Brissa forced her expression to remain neutral, though it scraped at her nerves to hear him so addressed.

"Thank you, Cullitch," the deep voice—*Thieren*—replied. "You may leave us."

The sound of retreating footsteps was followed by the snap of the door closing, and then silence, silence but for the sound of calm, even breathing and heavy but muffled footsteps circling her at a relaxed pace.

"The rebel queen," Thieren murmured, his voice thick with satisfaction. "I can understand why Dronyen was blinded to your deceit. You are as beautiful as they say."

Brissa rolled her eyes beneath her blindfold. Before she could think better of it, she replied, "Dronyen was an idiot."

To her surprise, Thieren only laughed. "You may love evil, but even evil can speak the truth. It is true that Dronyen was not fit to lead. Though I have mourned him and my father both, your actions have benefited our family. I have always been meant for the throne."

"Do you refer to the throne your family has lost?" she asked sweetly. "The throne you cannot reach, for Miknauvripal belongs to my family now?"

"If you have not noticed your current predicament, Lady Brissa, you are in no position to reach the throne either." His voice carried a slight edge of irritation.

Brissa shrugged, ignoring the pain that flared in her left shoulder. "Kill me if you wish, and my sister shall take the throne. But it has never been yours, Thieren, and it never shall be."

His footsteps stopped short in front of her. "You shall refer to me as Your Majesty. Your Maj if you are feeling especially friendly. Is that understood?"

"I understand, Thieren, but I shall not comply."

Brissa gasped at the force with which he struck her across the face. She teetered until, without the use of her arms to keep her balance, she fell to the floor.

"You shall comply, eventually," he said from above her. "And it may interest you to know that your sister is nowhere to be found. My sources in Ryovni report that she left the island some weeks ago and has not been seen or heard from since."

Brissa managed to sit up, knees folded to one side, and frowned. If Thieren spoke the truth, those *sources in Ryovni* would need to be located and made an example of as soon as she was in a position to do so. And if he did speak the truth, and Cliope was missing…

There is no reason to trust him, she reminded herself, *and every reason to say as little as possible until I can figure out a way to escape.*

So she said nothing, no matter how loudly her heart screamed.

Thieren retreated from her and began walking about the room and murmuring under his breath. She heard the sound of objects being moved and another sound that could have been the soft click of locks opening, but it was difficult to be certain.

Within moments, Thieren was pulling her roughly to her feet and guiding her deeper into the room. She heard the sound of a key opening a lock—distinct, this time—and then a gruff warning to mind her step as he pushed her ahead of him down a narrow staircase.

"Where are you taking me?" she demanded, careful to keep all traces of fear from her voice.

"To answer to God," Thieren responded.

Once they had reached another room, a cavernous one, Brissa deduced, from the way their footsteps echoed off the stone floor, Thieren startled her by removing her blindfold. Brissa blinked against the dim light, and blinked several times more when she saw what looked like a blurred, quivering column of blue light in the center of the room.

Bring her closer. Brissa looked around wildly to see where the voice—if it could even be called a voice—had come from. But there was nothing but pale torches along the walls. The room was devoid of furniture. The walls were smooth and unbroken save for the doorway she had passed through.

Thieren guided her closer to the column of blue light, and Brissa was too fascinated to resist.

Kneel, the voice said—the voice that seemed to be a physical sensation that was not quite sound and not quite touch and was somehow more invasive and less intimate than either.

And suddenly Brissa had no choice but to kneel. Her knees hit the floor as if by their own volition; the force of the movement made her hiss in pain.

Open to me, Brissa Keshell, Taker of All, Guardian of demons. Show me all you have done to threaten my kingdom.

Brissa stared at the almost-face in the center of the blue light. Nausea crept over her as heavy pressure exerted itself at the base of her skull, pushing upwards as if intent on devouring her brain whole.

"What—" she gasped. Her hands twitched at the small of her back. She was desperate to rub her skull to try and bring herself some measure of relief.

Open to me. Do not fight.

Brissa didn't know whether she was fighting or not; all she knew was that the sensation was akin to trying to breathe underwater: panicky, painful, and impossible.

She gasped at what she could only describe as invasion, like long, cold fingers sliding through her eye sockets and into her brain, pulling out what they wanted. She could feel her deepest and most private thoughts bleeding into the probing strands, the information that she would never share with anyone but her closest advisors and confidantes, every plan and strategy for ultimate victory over the House of Panloch. It left her defenseless and bare and on the verge of vomiting.

But she could not vomit. She could not blink her eyes or move her head. Even the tremors that coursed through her body were beyond her control.

When the entity—whatever it may be—within the blue light seemed to have its fill, it withdrew sharply, causing her to shudder, dry-heave, and eject what little bile had managed to crawl up from the depths of her empty stomach.

"Now you understand why you have had nothing to eat since you arrived," Thieren said, his voice nearly giddy.

The blue light remained silent, but it rippled silver and white and violet, and Brissa knew, somehow, that it was pleased.

Brissa bit her lip until the metallic taste of blood mixed with the bitter taste of bile and did not cry.

Brissa drank the chilled mint tea in small, careful sips. It was helping to settle her stomach, but it was still difficult to force anything down. Her entire body shook from the unfathomable violation she had experienced somewhere in the depths of Panloch Manor.

Everything after that experience had been a blur; Thieren had conversed privately with the entity, murmuring responses to words she could not hear, and then had retied her blindfold, led her back to the room in which he had received her, and handed her back to the guards in the hallway, whom, she gathered, had been waiting there all along.

She wasn't sure whether or not they had any idea what had happened, but neither seemed surprised at the way she stumbled along on unsteady feet all the way back to her cell.

The cell was pleasant enough, Brissa supposed, as cells went: The stone floor was covered with a thin carpet in warm, faded colors, and there were two narrow beds with straw mattresses along the eastern and western walls. On the far wall, directly facing the cell's door, were a small wooden table and two rickety chairs beneath a single, narrow window that was too high for Brissa to peer from, but cast a slice of sunlight into the room. Other than the window, the only light in the room was from the torches along the corridor outside the cell's broad, iron-barred door. In one corner was a small latrine, and a washbasin stood on narrow brass legs in another.

Brissa took a deep, steadying breath and tried to concentrate on being grateful that her wrists were no longer bound; grateful that she had been offered food and a cool drink, even though the thought of eating made her stomach groan in protest; and grateful that Thieren had not seen her cry.

She looked up at the loud series of clicks that heralded the unlocking of her cell door and was surprised to see a woman, escorted by the same two guards who had escorted Brissa from wherever she had been with Thieren barely an hour ago.

But not just a woman. A *sidhe* woman.

She looked every bit the part of a royal house slave: her rich purple dress was luxurious but scant, revealing far more of her body than would be acceptable in a human woman, *especially* on the mainland. Her long, silver-white hair had been brushed until it gleamed and tucked behind her ears with jeweled combs, her violet eyes were lined with kohl, and her milk-pale arms, neck, and earlobes were decorated with polished silver jewelry. She was especially tall and beautiful, even for a sidhe, and Brissa stood to greet her the moment she swept into the room.

The guard closed the door behind the sidhe woman and locked it without a single word.

"Hello," Brissa said carefully, her voice rising as if in question. The other woman walked to the bed on the left-hand side of the room and sat.

"Hello," she responded in heavily accented Villaluan. "It is lovely to finally meet you, Your Majesty. My name is Aehsee."

"Is—I don't wish to be rude, Aehsee, but why are you here?" Brissa asked.

Aehsee smiled. "This is my cell. They brought the second bed in in anticipation of your arrival. It is quite an honor; I am His Majesty's prized slave, after all. The other cells are nowhere near as nice."

"Oh," Brissa said. "But you did not sleep here last night, did you?"

"I did not." The sidhe looked away.

"Oh," Brissa said again. She could think of nothing else to say. She could deduce where Aehsee had been the night before—it wasn't as if the way men liked to abuse their sidhe slaves was a secret—and it did not help the queasiness still roiling her stomach to contemplate it.

"You look ashen," Aehsee said. "I take it that His *Majesty* has taken you to see Frilau?"

Brissa dropped back into her chair in shock. "*Frilau?* The ancient prophet? I don't—what do you mean?"

Aehsee walked to the cell door and glanced surreptitiously down the hallway in both directions before sitting opposite Brissa at the table. "All I know," she said quietly, ducking her head toward Brissa as if they were old co-conspirators, "is that whatever that *creature* that lives beneath Thieren's study may be, he calls it Frilau. I have heard him do it."

"What—" Brissa swallowed. "What did it do to me?"

Aehsee refilled Brissa's glass from the jug at the center of the table and regarded her with a sad smile. "It read your mind, I imagine. That's what it did to me, anyhow. If my powers hadn't been suppressed, I might have been able to fight it off, but—" she sighed, waving a hand. "It takes a toll on the body, though, and it seems to weaken the creature a bit too. You shouldn't be subjected to it again anytime soon, which is why you are here with me."

Brissa raised an eyebrow and took a sip of her tea.

Aehsee studied her. "I am meant to spy on you," she said.

Brissa lowered her glass. "I see. Forgive me, but it does not seem that you are doing a particularly fine job of it."

The sidhe laughed. "No. Thieren believes that I am loyal to him, even though I am no more than a demon in his eyes, because he is *saving my immortal soul* by subjecting me to a life of slavery." Aehsee's disgust was so heavy that it was nearly a physical force. "He is a true believer, Your Majesty, and you would do well to remember that. He is not like his brothers or his father before him. He is like his mother. He would die for his faith and take the whole world with him if Frilau commanded it of him."

"But that thing cannot truly be the author of the T'aukhi scrolls?" Brissa demanded.

"I do not know what it is. All I know is that Thieren believes it is one and the same."

Brissa closed her eyes and breathed deeply. Her predicament—*Villalu's* predicament—was looking worse by the minute. "When is he planning the execution?"

"Execution, Your Majesty?"

Brissa began pacing the length of the cell. "He has all the information my mind can supply, and I am responsible for the deaths of his father and brother and the fall of his House. Were I in his position, my next step would be a very public execution."

"And were he a sane man, it would be his as well. But as I have said, he is devout. And he knows you have support amongst the populace. He is not going to kill you, Your Majesty. If he has his way, he is going to marry you."

Brissa froze; her blood was like ice in her veins. "He is *what?*"

"It is in the T'aukhi scrolls, a fact I am sad to say I know. You are his brother's widow, and marrying you is his responsibility, whether you like it or not. Besides, it will help him retake Villalu if you are his queen."

"I would rather die," Brissa swore. "I would rather he torture me every day."

"Do not say things that you do not understand," Aehsee said sharply. "You cannot imagine what you would do to escape torture."

Brissa bit her lip and looked toward the window, still out of reach. A mixture of guilt and rage swam in her gut, and she wrapped her arms around herself as if they could blanket her from every cruel thing in the world.

"How do you do it?" she asked softly. "How do you live as a slave?"

"By thinking of all the ways I will get revenge one day," Aehsee said, her voice calm. "And ever since I learned that you would be joining me here, I have been thinking of all we could do with the strength of your army behind us." Aehsee walked to Brissa, pulled Brissa's hands away from her body, and took them in her own. Brissa drew in a sharp breath at the bold gesture, but did not resist. Aehsee's eyes, though nowhere near as bright as Brissa knew they would be with her power unbound, flashed sharp, shrewd, and determined.

"I serve no human, Your Majesty, not in my heart," Aehsee continued, "but I do serve *P'ellferbanjin*, the Goddess of Mortal Queens. And I pledge to you, Your Majesty, that I shall do all that I can to help you defeat Thieren Panloch and take your Queendom back."

Brissa could not help but smile, despite the fear that coursed through her body like blood. "Thank you, Aehsee," she said, her voice steady. "Now. Let us have some tea and discuss how to wipe yet another Panloch from the face of the world."

Chapter Twenty

Firae sat in the courtyard behind his sleeping chambers at the Great Hall. The breeze was cool but pleasant on his skin.

"Tea?" he asked his guests pleasantly when the servant came bearing a fragrant tray.

"Do you believe there is time to enjoy tea?" The Truthkeeper asked.

"There is always time," *B!Nauvriija* said, "but the possibilities time holds in her palm are as fragile as a seedling."

"I would love some tea, Firae, thank you," said Sehrys, sitting across from Firae. They shared a smile that warmed Firae's heart despite the niggling sensation that he was missing something—or perhaps several somethings—about this entire situation.

"Sehrys," Firae said. Speaking his friend's name made the confusion easier to bear.

The servant poured tea, and when Firae glanced up to nod his thanks, the servant's face stirred something in his memory. The man was beautiful, with bronze-gold skin, sharp green eyes, and hair the color of fire.

The man continued his way around the table in silence.

"I… why am I not in Villalu?" Firae asked, grasping at the threads of something unclear but important. "I… I was there…" He furrowed his brow.

"And now you are here," Sehrys said cheerfully, sipping his tea. "You have come back to me."

"But... Brieden." Firae was aware that thinking of Sehrys's human usually made something tight and sharp flare in his chest, but that did not happen. He felt nothing but genuine curiosity and the need to understand the persistent sensation that he had forgotten something urgent.

"I cannot have a human husband in Alovur Drovuru." Sehrys laughed. "The law forbids it."

Firae focused on remembering what was wrong with Sehrys's words. The memory came barreling at him with such speed and force that he would have lost his footing were he not already seated.

"You are King Firae, Child of Queen Gira, descendent of Queen Tyzva the Liberator. Do you honestly mean to stand before me and say that you are helpless in the face of the law?"

Sehrys hummed. "I suppose I did say that, did I not?"

"You did not," said *B!Nauvriija*. "I did." Her lips did not move when she spoke, and it took Firae a moment to realize that she was a statue. He could not remember if she had always been a statue, but it was undeniably true now: she towered over them all, covered in fragrant blossoms. Firae suddenly felt very foolish for offering her tea.

"One must follow the law, Your Majesty," the servant said softly. He had an iron collar around his neck and chains connecting his ankles and wrists that clattered as he walked, circling the table over and over again with the serving tray in his hand. Firae wondered why he had not seen the chains before.

"Law is created by sentient beings in an attempt to bring reason to reasonless worlds. And just like all other things on temporal planes, laws run their course."

Firae was not sure if the words had been spoken by Sehrys, *B!Nauvriija*, or himself, but he had heard them before.

"But..." he concentrated, desperate to recall that which his mind, soupy as if from too much nectar, could not seem to grasp and hold. "My soul-walk," he finally realized. "That is where I heard those words. But... I went to Villalu..."

"Unconventional," the servant responded, "but with the full legal blessing of the Council, of course."

"I don't understand—*must* I break the law even if it is unnecessary?"

"You broke the law when you chose to help me," Brissa said. Firae wasn't sure when she had joined them. "But you will not be the one to hang for it."

"What must I do?" Firae tried not to flinch at the desperation in his own voice. "I wish to make the right choice."

"Every moment is choice," *B!Nauvriija* said. "You have more choices than you accept or acknowledge."

"When the journey is long enough, one always ends precisely where one began," said The Truthkeeper.

"Quiet are the *La'ekynog*, those who stayed behind," said Brieden. Firae could not see him, but his voice and the sensation of his presence were clear.

"The scarlet heart requires naked courage," said Sehrys. "When your ancestors whisper into your ear, you must listen."

Their voices blended, rising to a crescendo; their physical forms blurred into swirls of color that closed in on Firae and wrapped him in too much and too little information all at once.

A firm, warm hand wrapped around his forearm and pulled him gently from the swirling chaos. He blinked his eyes and looked into the face of the servant. The man was free of his chains, now, naked save for boots on his feet and an enormous pack on his back. Firae wasn't sure how the man didn't topple under the weight.

"Prophecies are designed to work," the man said, and the familiar words in the familiar voice bathed Firae in sudden comprehension. *Tash.*

Firae wanted to offer to carry Tash's pack, but, as shameful as it may be, he was afraid it would crush him alive. Tash just smiled and reached out his hand. "When the journey is long enough," he said, "one always ends precisely where one began."

THE FIRE CRACKLED SOFTLY AT TASH'S FEET AS HE STUDIED THE MAP. They were in a small, mossy forest clearing a few miles' shy of Belloquepal, near the western banks of Muirdannoch Lake. Firae was curled up beside him, fast asleep after a long day of traveling. Tash could not help but smile fondly from time to time at the smooth lines of his face, the occasional catches in his slow, steady breathing, and the way the night breeze sometimes made his hair dance across his shoulders.

In fact, if he were honest, he was doing more staring at Firae than studying of his map.

It had been two weeks since their failed attempt to pass through Tonathe without incident, and they had lightened their packs in that time. There was little they needed in the wilderness, and it was too risky to attempt passing through another human village until they reached Zegripanloch. They had been making good time; the Great Elchec Forest offered hundreds of miles of uninterrupted wilderness and allowed them to save time by walking along high, thick tree branches where the forest canopy was dense enough to permit it. They had been restraining their physical affections until they made camp. As much as Tash often wanted to reach for Firae when the sun shone on his skin and he saw the muscles in his buttocks and legs, more pronounced from weeks of hiking, he knew that time was a luxury they did not have.

Firae shifted in his sleep; a small smile spread across his lips. Seeing it put a warm blanket around Tash's heart and made him wish he had a real blanket to lay over the other man's body.

Firae sighed as if soothed by Tash's desire to bring him comfort and murmured, "Sehrys."

The warmth in Tash's chest was doused in bitter-cold reality, as if his heart had been plunged into an icy lake.

Sehrys. How could Tash have forgotten? Sehyrs, who was strong and powerful and proud; Sehrys, who was beautiful and compassionate, and would *never* allow himself to do the sorts of things Tash had done; Sehrys, who had been meant to share Firae's throne. Sehrys, who gave up everything for love.

Of course Firae still dreamed of him. He must dream of him often, *think* of him often.

Did he think of him when he touched Tash? Did he wish Tash's green eyes belonged to the face of another?

Tash forced himself to look at the map in his lap, to leave Firae to his dreams of lost love and longing. He tried to think about whether it would be faster to cut through the Carzets or head straight to the Vestech River—the river was a faster route, and it would lead them straight to their destination, but its banks were also more heavily populated, and they couldn't afford any more run-ins with humans, especially as they drew closer to the Panloch lands—but his mind kept straying to Firae, to the way he spoke Sehrys's name and the way he looked at Tash.

He needed to tell Firae the truth. He owed him that much.

When Firae blinked his eyes open less than an hour later, he had barely stretched and murmured a greeting to Tash before Tash was unable to contain himself.

"I need to tell you what I've done," he said.

"Just now?" Firae asked, voice still loose with sleep.

"No. Before. Firae, I... I committed *defmor M'Ferauvise*."

Firae reeled as if he had been struck; his face was a mask of horror and disgust. The term Tash had used meant *betrayal of The Mother Goddess*. In common use, however, it referred to what the humans called rape.

"How is it that you were not executed?" Firae asked, his eyes wide and his voice small. He had increased the distance between them and looked as if he might vomit.

"Not... that wasn't the crime for which I was exiled. But once I was here, I was constantly terrified. I was almost captured by slave traders twice in my first two years. The border cities nearly ate me alive—and there was another sidhe, an exiled home-grower who was able to compel humans by the dozens. He offered me a spot traveling with him, along with one other sidhe, but it did involve... he called it 'clearing entrenched inclinations.' It was sexually preparing humans for their future sidhe masters." Tash felt sick just speaking the words, but he forced himself to continue. "Brec—that was his name—preferred women. My job was to see to the males. Our third companion was a sidhe woman and she prepared them for female masters."

"Humans under compulsion?" Firae asked carefully, his posture settling and his face relaxing.

Tash nodded and looked at his hands in his lap.

"Tash, that… that is not the same thing as *defmor M'Ferauvise.*"

"Is it not?" Tash demanded. "What if he had compelled Brissa? Or Cliope? Would that not be the same?"

"But compulsion requires free will," Firae argued.

"Less than you'd think," Tash mumbled. He looked up to meet Firae's eye. "I never told you how Sehrys and I met."

"You helped him in the border cities," Firae said.

Tash laughed bitterly. "Not precisely."

And since Tash had nothing left to lose by surrendering to honesty, he told Firae all about it: about capturing Brieden, and nearly violating him the way he had violated so many others; about being captured by slave-traders with Brec and Aehsee, which was no less than they deserved; about Sehrys and Brieden saving him; about killing Brec and saving Sehrys and Brieden in turn; about the new start they had offered him in Lekrypal; about the new start he thought he had finally found when Cliope sought him out at Sehrys's suggestion.

They fell into silence. It was both terrifying and a blessed relief to own, without flinching, the damage done.

He looked up at the sensation of a warm hand on his knee. Firae had scooted closer to Tash and then closer still. His eyes seemed warm with pain and understanding.

"After a confession such as that, I believe it only appropriate that I share the tale of how I met Brieden as well," Firae said.

And so he did. He told Tash about how he had tried to kill Brieden immediately upon meeting him and how he would have done so without a second thought or a shred of guilt had Sehrys not stopped him. He told him how he had kept Brieden prisoner in the Northern Tower in

Alovur Drovuru, and how his desperation to have everything the way it had been led him to pressure Sehrys into a marriage that the man clearly was not ready for.

"I was not ready either, but I could not see that. I was not ready to let him go. And then my soul-walk revealed to me that I needed to, for the version of him I longed for was already gone." Firae moved his hand from Tash's knee, and took Tash's hand, lacing their fingers together. Tash inhaled sharply at the sharp points of pleasurable sensitivity in the dips between his fingers as they pressed against the same places on Firae's hand.

"We have both done horrible things, Tash, but the idea… rather, the *fact* that humans are complex people like ourselves, that is… it is new. Even in my generation, I was taught that humans were brutal savages, that killing them could be seen as a mercy, that those living in Khryslee were strange, tame exceptions, that compulsion could be seen as a gift to the burdened human mind as easily as it could be seen as a practice of slavery."

"It does not make anything I have done forgivable."

"The actions are not forgivable, no, but you are. You cannot undo the past, Tash. You can only strive to do good where a past version of yourself might have done evil."

Tash sighed. "You are very young to be so wise, Your Majesty," he said. There was no bite to the words *Your Majesty*, only sincere affection, and Tash relished the delighted grin he received in return. "But I suppose I should give you the opportunity to see how far your forgiveness will truly extend. It is time I told you why I was exiled from Laesi."

FIRAE DID HIS BEST NOT TO REVEAL HOW EAGER HE WAS TO HEAR TASH'S story.

He had been wondering since the day he discovered Tash's identity, but Tash had not been prepared to tell him, and Firae could think of no way to press him on the matter without causing Tash to withdraw into himself or lash out at Firae, the man who had exiled him without so much as remembering his name or his crime.

"I was married," Tash began, "and I was happy. I thought we were both happy, but I was mistaken. My husband and I had chosen the blue bracelet—we were committed to monogamy. But I suppose he changed his mind somewhere along the way and didn't see fit to tell me."

Firae frowned; pairing jewelry was taken very seriously amongst The Sidhe. There was the green bracelet, for those who wished for marriage without the expectation of strict monogamy, or the amber bracelet, for those seeking a long-term union with more than one partner. Or even or the red bracelet, for those seeking sexual partners without any commitment at all. Why on all of Ullavise would a man violate a lifetime commitment without so much as discussing a change in bracelets with his partner?

Tash gave Firae's hand a small squeeze. The firelight caused the lines of his troubled face to look like an agonizingly beautiful painting. "He began an affair with—well, with a royal. Queen Alqii's nephew, in fact. I don't know how long it had gone on for before I discovered it, but when I found him in my bed with my husband—" Tash squeezed his eyes closed and took a deep, shaking breath. "I didn't mean to kill him. I just wanted to hurt him. He was more powerful than me, he was a *royal*. I would never have done something so stupid intentionally, but he was just—remorseless. He found my display of shock and betrayal *amusing*, and I attacked him. I was so enraged I barely knew what I was doing."

Tash took a deep breath and blew it out slowly; the fire in front of them flickered in response to his energy. "I killed him," he whispered, voice trembling with the weight of it. Tash opened his eyes and regarded Firae.

Firae was speechless; he recalled the case now, though Queen Alqii's version was delivered quite differently. According to her, the attack had been utterly unprovoked. But had Firae personally heard Tash's side of things… It would not have mattered, no matter how much he would like to believe that it would. He had played with the children of Alqii's line as a boy, had believed, on some intrinsic level, that the life of a royal was of fundamentally greater worth than the life of a commoner. If he had heard Tash's version, he would not have believed him. Alqii's word—though she had witnessed nothing—would have been enough.

But it should not have been enough. It should not have been close.

"When you spoke of your crime before, you said you should not have been banished for it. You were right," Firae said softly. Tash was looking at him with such naked vulnerability that Firae touched Tash's cheek with his free hand. "A crime of passion such as that—if the victim had been a man of your own caste, you would have labored in the Iron Mountains for perhaps ten years. You would have—you would be home now, Tash. You would be safe. You probably would have found a new mate—"

"Don't." Tash tilted his head to press a light kiss against Firae's palm, making him shiver. He cast his gaze up to meet Firae's.

"I forgive you," Tash said.

Firae felt something dislodge in his chest, and the relief was so palpable that it hurt. If he could have stopped the tears from prickling at the backs of his eyes until they broke free and tumbled down his cheeks, he would have. If he could have controlled the loud, undignified wail that tore from his chest, he would have done that too.

But he couldn't.

Never in his life had Firae's heart been so out of control. He pulled his hand back from where it lay tangled with Tash's on his knee and moved to turn his back to Tash, to shield the other man from his weakness, his *smallness.*

But Tash pulled him back, pulled Firae into his strong, warm arms and wrapped him tight, stroked his hair, and let Firae burrow his face into the junction between Tash's neck and shoulder and sob.

"I do not deserve your forgiveness," Firae whispered against Tash's skin, when his breathing had slowed enough to allow for words. "I cast your life aside like a pebble in my path without even noticing, and now I come find you only to march you to your death—"

"We don't know that," Tash said, but his voice was heavy with the sorrow of knowing Firae was probably right. "Prophecies are designed to work, Firae."

Firae tensed at the words. They were true, and Tash had spoken them before, but something tugged at him, as if to tell him there was significance to hearing Tash speak them *now.*

"And you have my forgiveness whether you deserve it or not. I believe that you do. But I wonder if you can forgive me."

Firae lifted his head to look Tash in the eye. He felt like a child gone without a nap as he wiped the tears from his cheeks, but there was no judgment in Tash's expression.

"What would I need to forgive you for?" Firae asked. "You have done nothing wrong."

"I have done many things wrong, Firae, but I was speaking of compromising the Doctrine in particular. I have put the whole world at risk—"

"You did no such thing!" Firae was shocked by the anger in his voice, but as soon as he heard it, he understood why it was there. It was the same anger he felt toward the Council when he had been forced to beg them to allow him to visit Villalu, the same anger he had felt toward his mother when she had dismissed his concerns about their practice of exile. It was the kind of anger that scared him, because it made things far too clear.

"The priestesses who crafted the Border spell put the whole world at risk," he continued, when Tash opened his mouth to protest. "Tyzva the Liberator put the whole world at risk. *I* put the world at risk, and my mother before her, and her mother before that. I am only surprised that this did not happen hundreds or even thousands of years ago; we cannot banish more sidhe to Villalu each year, ignore the shifts and changes within the human government, and still expect the Doctrine to remain secure."

Tash sighed. "Thank you. But I should have known better, Firae. I should have thought it through. All I knew was that I finally had the opportunity to do something brave, something *good*, something I can be proud of."

"And do you regret your choice to help Brissa? Knowing what you now know to be true?"

"I don't." Tash's eyes went hard with determination. "I will not pretend that I am not afraid to die, but I don't regret it. She—she is going to change the world."

Firae stared at him. *Every moment is choice.* He gently swiped away the moisture that clung to Tash's lower eyelashes and kissed his trembling lips. "We all are," he whispered, between one kiss and another, "and you shall live to see it all."

Chapter Twenty-One

BRIEDEN STOOD IN THE GARDEN IN FRONT OF HIS HOUSE, NEXT to his little plot of soil, and watched a pair of grimchins grow smaller and smaller as they disappeared over the horizon. The creatures always looked a bit like enormous furry dragonflies to Brieden, but from a distance the resemblance was even more striking.

Jaxis shook his head and shot Brieden a glance. "Sree is going to kill him when she discovers that he has brought a human to speak to the Council without consulting her first."

"Sehrys can handle Sree," Brieden said. Sehrys's and Cliope's grimchins were little more than specks in the distance against the clear afternoon sky.

"I imagine he can. I am actually quite surprised at how well they seem to balance one another, at least when they are not fighting like starving wolves over a single kill. Perhaps Firae was not as misguided as I first thought when he assigned them to rule together in his absence."

The mention of Firae made Brieden's chest tighten; the hollow ache that had been there since he woke up grew more pronounced.

"Well, Sehrys has his human," Brieden sighed. "I just hope the Council will listen." He turned to walk back to the house. "May I offer you something to drink?"

Jaxis didn't answer, but he did follow Brieden inside.

Brieden tried to ignore Jaxis's unusually quiet disposition, ignore the way he seemed to scrutinize Brieden as he opened a kitchen cupboard to fetch some of the sweet orange nectar that he knew Jaxis liked. Brieden sat and poured them each a small glass.

Almost from the moment they had met in the Northern Tower more than a year ago, Jaxis had mastered the uncanny ability to see straight through to Brieden's heart. And although the first role he ever played in Brieden's life was that of prison guard, they had never been anything but friends. It had unsettled Brieden at first, how easily Jaxis offered his trust and companionship—not to mention his horrible pranks—but the elf had grown to be one of the most important people in Brieden's life, and Brieden treasured him. Still, sometimes Jaxis's ability to read Brieden as easily as a child's school primer was nothing short of infuriating.

"What?" he finally snapped, when Jaxis did no more than sip his nectar and stare at Brieden through narrowed eyes.

"You tell me, friend. You have *something* lodged up your ass, and not in the way you enjoy."

Brieden sighed and looked away. "Jaxis, I am not in the mood—"

"That is precisely my point! You are *always* in the mood. You have far too much energy and tolerance for nearly everything I do and say."

Brieden drummed his fingers on the table and considered.

"All right," he finally conceded, tossing back the nectar in his glass and pouring himself some more. "Things have been difficult with Sehrys and me. I… I love him, of course I love him, I couldn't stop if I tried, but—"

"But the dew has fallen from the blossom," Jaxis supplied. "Have you stopped boning?" He tilted his head. "Mmmm, no, that doesn't seem to be it…"

"That… isn't it. In fact, that is part of the problem. It's as if sex has taken the place of talking through our problems."

Jaxis sat back in his chair and propped his bare feet on the table. "I fail to see the issue."

"The issue," Brieden said, gently pushing Jaxis's feet off the table, "is that we have promised to be together for the rest of our—well, *my* life. And if we are already struggling to communicate after one year, I find it difficult to imagine how we are going to do it after four hundred."

"You are settling into this life together," Jaxis said. He helped himself to more nectar. "You will work it through. You have done it before. More times than I could count if I spent the rest of my life trying. I know it is human nature to give up easily, but—"

"Jaxis." Brieden put down his glass. "What are you talking about? What have we done before?"

Jaxis stared at him as if he had asked what trees were. "*This.* Desperate love. Commitment so undying it is nearly invasive. To hear Sehrys tell it—" Jaxis stopped himself abruptly. "Oh."

"Oh?"

"Oh. You don't remember."

"Jaxis," Brieden groaned. *"What?"*

"Sehrys's soul-walk."

"The soul-walk he took about *Firae?*" Brieden crossed his arms over his chest and was aware that he was pouting.

Jaxis shook his head. "Why didn't I see this before?" He stood up and clapped his hands. "All right, where are your horses? We've got to get to Glici's nectar shop before she closes for the day."

"Raven and Crow are most likely grazing by the creek," Brieden said, "but we have plenty of nectar here, and I really should get back to the garden—"

"Forget the garden," Jaxis said, pulling Brieden through the back kitchen door. "Any sidhe with a whisper of earth can grow anything from a seed. Sehrys could probably do it in his sleep." Jaxis led him through the already lush gardens behind the house, down the rolling blue-green hills to the little creek where, sure enough, the horses snacked on tall sweet grasses at the water's edge.

"Jaxis," Brieden protested once again. Jaxis let go of his arm and turned to face him.

"The nectar that you need is not in your cupboard, and I cannot grow you the flower that produces it. But you need it, Brieden, even more than you did the last time I gave it to you."

A familiar suspicion crept into the edges of Brieden's mind. "The *last time* you gave it to me."

"Yes. When Sehrys was on his soul-walk."

"That blue liquid that knocked me out cold and made me feel as if I'd fallen off the edge of the world?"

"The world has no edges," Jaxis said, stroking Crow's silky black mane, "but yes. You do not remember because you did not do the ritual, but I can teach you. I can help you. As long as we get to Glici's shop in time." Jaxis leapt up onto Crow's back in one smooth movement, and gestured at Raven, who was already walking to Brieden in anticipation of a ride.

Brieden did not move. "Jaxis. If you expect me to drink that stuff again, you will need to give me more than vague hints. What, precisely, are you going to teach me to do?"

Jaxis grinned. "Well, friend, I am *precisely* going to teach you to soul-walk."

CHAPTER TWENTY-TWO

"WE ONLY NEED TO GET A GUARD OR TWO ON OUR SIDE," Brissa said into the darkness. She and Aehsee were in their beds; their voices were soft in the darkness, their ears primed for the sound of anyone who might approach.

"It is an enormous risk. More than likely it is one a servant would not dare to take," Aehsee responded. Brissa glanced at the other woman's silhouette. She was lying on her side. The jut of her shoulder and slope of her hip were visible in the dimness; her eyes glittered when they met Brissa's.

"I have done it before," Brissa argued. "We took Miknauvripal with the help of more than half of Dronyen's own servants."

"Dronyen was cruel, and you were in a position of strength. There is more loyalty amongst Thieren's people, and you are but a prisoner."

Brissa scowled into the darkness, at least in part because Aehsee was right. Brissa had no leverage at all.

"If we can find a way past the cell door, we might be able to escape the manor, but we will need to plan it carefully," Aehsee said. "The grounds are as well-guarded as the manor."

"If we can kill the first of the guards quietly, we can steal their weapons," Brissa offered. Aehsee laughed softly.

"What?" Brissa asked.

"I suppose I never thought you would be so ruthless. The way people talk about you in the border cities—they call you Brissa the Merciful."

Brissa's heart swelled at that. "Mercy can be a complicated concept."

"I suppose it is."

They were silent; their breathing fell into sync. Outside the cell window, a pair of owls called to one another, and the faint sound of human voices drifted up from the courtyard.

"Are you all right?" Brissa asked, tentative. Aehsee had been returned to the cell limping only an hour before.

"I believe I was clear that I do not wish to speak of it." Aehsee's voice was weary and held little bite.

"I know, but… it is not the same, but I had to submit to Dronyen's lusts in order to gain his trust and overthrow his rule. Sometimes I still feel the need to scrub my skin raw at the memory of it. I cannot imagine what it must be like for you."

"No," Aeshee agreed, "you cannot."

Brissa bit her lip. "Tell me of your life in the Elfin Lands," she ventured.

Aehsee gave a wistful sigh. "I grew up in a small feririar on the Northern Sea, but most of my life was spent at *Sarthan Aloos'ylau*, a great temple of the Goddess *Aloos'ylau* in a large feririar in the mountains. A city, I suppose you could say, in human terms. I was a priestess there."

"What was it like?" Brissa turned onto her side to face Aeshee more fully through the darkness.

"It was wonderful. I led a—I suppose you could say a school, of sorts, for young girls gifted in spirit magic."

"Spirit magic," Brissa mused, combing her mind for all the information about The Sidhe she had learned from the hidden texts in Ryovni. "It was priestesses of the Spirit caste who created The Border, was it not?"

"It was. Spirit magic is the strangest of all sidhe magics, really, but that is what makes it so incredible. It is less innate than elemental powers; it must be cultivated and developed and it grows with practice. Those who created The Border were among the most powerful priestesses in the history of The Sidhe."

"And you?" Brissa asked. "Is your power strong?"

Aehsee was silent for a lingering moment. "Yes," she finally said. "Perhaps too strong. The laws of Laesi have changed over the past fifty thousand years, and the sort of power that created The Border is no longer rewarded."

"And why not?" Brissa craved the details of Aehsee's story like sweet nectar.

"Forgive me, Your Highness," Aehsee said, her voice gone brittle, "but I do not wish to share the story of my expulsion with you." She rolled onto her other side, facing away from Brissa, and said no more.

Brissa watched her through the moonlight from the high window of their cell and wondered just how much she truly did not know.

"There it is," Tash whispered.

They had managed to stay hidden for the most part during their journey through the Carzet Mountains, though Tash was sure that members of a traveling carnival had spotted them along the road several days ago. They had been clothed against the brisk mountain air, so it was likely that they had been mistaken for human at a distance, but it had unsettled him nonetheless. So they had retreated deeper into the scraggly trees, rocky earth, and towering clustered hoodoos of the rock forest that seemed to cover most of the middle Carzets.

But between the edge of the rock forest where they crouched and the iron gates of Panloch Manor was only the open city.

The manor looked more like a castle than Firae had been expecting, though almost nothing like Keshell castle; the structure was wider than it was tall, with a crenellated roof all around. The stone was dark and covered in patches of yellow-brown lichen; the building's fence was high and thick, with black-tipped spears at the top of each picket. There were fewer windows than Firae could imagine living with and most of them little more than tall, thin slits in the stone.

"Who would ever want to live in such a place?" Firae asked. "It looks more like how I might imagine a human prison than a home to royals."

"Yes, well, I suppose it is clear why the Panlochs chose to rule from Miknauvripal when they conquered Villalu." Tash sighed. "But, much like a prison, it looks as if it were built to resist intrusion. And we still have no real plan."

"We could always wait until the dead of night and attack," Firae suggested without conviction. "Kill the guards. Melt the gates."

Tash shifted, frowning at the jagged, rocky earth. "So you have suggested. Repeatedly. But that still leaves us with no plan once we get inside."

"I can handle a sword," Firae argued. "I know you are capable of it as well."

"Against a dozen men?"

"A dozen *humans*," Firae grumbled.

"A dozen humans with *swords*."

Firae hopped down from the rust-colored spire he had been standing on and gave Tash a frank look. "If you have a better plan, Tash, I should like to hear it."

"Castles and manors such as this one usually have underground tunnels," Tash answered. "If we can find an entrance, it may even lead us directly to the dungeons."

"Which will be heavily guarded, I am sure."

Tash brushed a patch of earth in front of him until it was free enough of pebbles to sit upon. "If we are quiet, we shall at least have the element of surprise. Our chances are slim no matter how good our plan."

Firae cleared his own patch of earth and sat next to Tash. "All right. Where shall we start?"

BRISSA CLOSED HER EYES AND BREATHED SLOWLY, DEEPLY, WILLING HER heart not to pound out of her chest.

Thieren had summoned Aehsee again that night. According to Aehsee, it had been happening more frequently since Brissa had arrived, since Thieren would not dream of calling Brissa to his bedchamber before their wedding night. He was too pious a man for that, so pious a man that he called for his slave instead, then sent her back to the cell in the small hours of the morning with tangled hair, drenched in his scent, her eyes bright with tears of rage and humiliation.

Brissa rubbed her thumbs over the smooth rock in her hand. Its surface was warm from her body heat.

Breathe.

Aehsee would be back soon, unless it was one of those rare nights when Thieren kept her with him until morning, and she would need Brissa. She would need Brissa's strength, not her anger; her focus, not her lust for revenge.

Brissa looked at the narrow slit of a window far above the bed where she lay and prayed to the Blessed Guardian that Thieren hadn't hurt Aehsee too badly. He was quite different from his brother. While Thieren lacked empathy, he did not seem to derive the sort of pleasure from the infliction of suffering that Dronyen had. It was little comfort—rape was rape, after all. But at least Aehsee did not spend her days bruised and wincing, as Dronyen's slaves had done.

Brissa stilled at the sound of approaching footsteps. The heavy fall of the guard's boots almost obscured the susurrus of Aehsee's slippers on the stone floor.

Brissa stood and breathed and waited.

And when the door pushed open, she pounced.

The guard—she had never learned his name—let out a howl of pain and surprise as Brissa smashed the rock against his skull with every ounce of power in her body, the blow hitting with a wet, bloody crunch. His cry was cut off when Aehsee slapped her hand over his mouth and then twisted his neck with such speed and strength that Brissa was surprised it didn't separate from his skull.

He crumpled to the floor, blood from his crushed skull spilling into a black pool in the moonlight.

Neither woman wasted a moment. They had spent too long planning this.

Brissa's hands were shaking as she pulled his keyring from where it still hung in the door, and she was fairly sure that Aehsee's were shaking no less when she pulled his sword from its scabbard. But they did not hesitate. After swiftly checking in each direction to see if they had alerted any unwanted attention, they crept quietly down the corridor and toward freedom, leaving a trail of bloody footprints.

Brissa followed Aehsee from one corridor to the next and paused in deep shadows to wait out occasional passing guards with her flesh vibrating and her stomach churning. She was grateful that the other woman had come to know the castle well enough to lead the way; without Aeshee's sure footsteps, she would have been lost.

Brissa had faced men twice her size in battle, had stood, naked and unarmed, in Dronyen's bedchamber and looked into his eyes, knowing full well that he might discover her secrets at any moment. But never had she felt such abject fear, for even if she and Aehsee managed to escape the castle, they would be alone in a hostile land without so much as a pair of shoes between them. To find her way home, to *defeat* Thieren, would be a near impossibility.

Brissa clutched Aehsee's arm as they descended a narrow staircase. Darkness closed in on them, but Aehsee's steps were no less sure.

"This will lead us through the kitchens," Aehsee whispered, her voice barely a thread of sound, but jarring enough in the stillness to make Brissa's shoulders jump. "We should be able to slip out the kitchen door, but the courtyard will be well guarded. Stay close."

Moonlight poured through the windows of the kitchen. The jarring contrast to the dark staircase made Brissa tighten her grip on Aehsee's arm. Aehsee nodded toward the thick double doors just ahead. She paused at a butcher block on the counter near the door to pick up a large knife with a heavy wooden handle and a thick blade, pried Brissa's hand from her arm, and handed her the knife.

"You may need this," she said softly, then furrowed her brow as she examined Brissa's face. "Your Highness, you are shaking."

"I am terrified," Brissa admitted with a small, breathless laugh. "If we should fail—"

"We shall not fail."

"How can you be sure of such a thing?"

"Because," Aehsee said, fingers tightening on the hilt of the sword she carried as she continued toward the door, "they are only men, and we have nothing left to lose."

They emerged from the kitchen into a little alley that stank of decaying kitchen scraps and human waste. "This way," Aehsee said, leading Brissa to a wooden gate at the end of the alley. Brissa tried not to think about the wet, slimy things beneath her bare feet: all that mattered was the open air, the moons above, and the tantalizing promise of freedom that was nearly within their reach.

The lock on the gate easily smashed with Aehsee's sword, they emerged at the back of the castle. "Now, I am not entirely sure, as it has been some time since I was last permitted to step outside, but I believe there is a little door—"

"Oy! Who goes there?"

Both women froze.

"I said—" The guard came into focus as he moved toward them. He was very large; much taller than either woman. His shoulders were three times as broad as Brissa's. Brissa stared, frozen, for a moment that seemed to stretch into eternity.

And then the rage hit.

It hit her like a stampede of wild horses, like the deafening roar of a dragon from the farthest edges of The Border in the Eastern Sea. This man, *this man*, who was utterly complicit in all that poisoned the heart of Villalu, stood between Brissa and freedom, between Aehsee and the power that was her birthright.

With the steely calm focus of a warrior in battle, Brissa raised the knife and threw it with all of her strength. It landed squarely in the man's throat with a wet, crunching thud, the stillness of the night pierced by the mangled sound he made as he crumpled to his knees.

Brissa walked up to him and looked him squarely in the eyes as his life drained away.

"I shall tell you who goes there," she hissed, wrenching the blade free from his neck, so that blood rushed out like the swell of a river after heavy rain. "It is your fucking *queen*."

"Ah," Aehsee breathed behind her. "There you are. Brissa the Merciful."

Before Brissa could reply, the shouts and thunderous footfalls of at least a dozen guards, summoned by the choking screams of their fallen brother, advanced in their direction.

Aeshee grabbed the queen's hand, and they ran.

IT SEEMED THAT THE LITTLE CITY HAD FINALLY GONE TO SLEEP.

Tash and Firae had waited through the clang of dinner bells and the shouts of children running home as the sun began its lazy decline into evening, and through the parade of freshly scrubbed humans marching along the dimly lit streets, chattering as they walked to the Frilauan temple at the center of town for the evening service. The two sidhe had waited through the quiet that had settled when lamps were blown out for the night, and then through the surge in noise when the taverns began to fill. And after the last tavern had shuttered its door, and the last hollering drunkard had found somewhere to collapse until the sun rose, they crept through the darkest and narrowest streets they could find until the iron from the great fence around the whole of Panloch Manor was close enough to make them dizzy.

"I..." Firae concentrated on the packed-earth road and did his best to ignore the nausea-inducing ripples of energy drifting from the thick iron pickets of the manor fence. "I believe there is a hollow space to the west," he whispered, gesturing toward the corner of the building where he could perceive a large, artificial bubble in the earth. "But it does not seem to be a corridor, more a large cavern."

"That could be the dungeon," Tash whispered back. "It seems like an odd place for it, but—"

"Let her go!"

"Fetch Ednec! Fetch His Maj!"

The voices were followed by a crash of metal against metal, a scream, and an influx of angry male voices.

Firae and Tash turned to stare at one another for the briefest of seconds, until one voice, rich and powerful, rose above the rest: "Kill me if you dare, but make no mistake, I shall plunge this sword into my own heart before I live another day as that man's slave!"

They didn't realize that they had begun running toward the melee until they were already halfway there, for that voice was unmistakable. It could not belong to anyone but their queen.

They found Brissa in a pool of torchlight with her back to the manor's front wall, blocking, bodily, what appeared to be a sidhe woman behind her. She was surrounded by a group of guardsmen, all of whom made occasional attempts to move toward her, but between the sword she held pointed toward them and the dagger she held to her own throat, they seemed at a loss.

It was a predicament that Tash did not share. "Melt the gate," he said, voice sharp and steady. "Kill the guards."

Firae was surprised at how little the command bothered him. He grabbed Tash's hand and focused with all the rage that seeing Brissa cornered like a hunted animal instilled in him. Tash's power raced through him, blending with his own, strengthening into something else. Every inch of his skin burned with it; every drop of his blood sang it. It was almost no effort at all, like lighting a single candle, to melt the gate into a river of liquid iron, which then parted to let the two men through.

Every guard in the courtyard was completely still. Tash fixed his eyes on the door to the manor, melting just enough of its locks and metal trim to fuse it shut. Firae could feel him do it. It was almost like the connection he had felt with Firae at The Truthkeeper's cave, but there was no pain and nothing standing between them. Firae gripped Tash's hand even tighter.

"Leave us," he said to the guards, "and don't let anyone else out of the manor." Firae's ability to compel was weak but serviceable, but he knew, in that moment, that he barely needed it at all. The power he shared with Tash had grown so that the men were nearly choking with it, and between their palpable fear and the bit of compulsion Firae was directing at them, the men would have no choice but to obey.

And they did.

Brissa lowered the sword and dagger slowly; her eyes were round as tea saucers. "Please tell me I have not gone mad," she whispered, drinking them in as if they were the most amazing things she had ever laid eyes on.

"If you have, then it is a shared affliction." Tash's voice wavered with emotion.

Brissa threw her weapons to the ground and ran at them, launching herself into their arms. Firae realized that he and Tash were still gripping one another's hands, but he did not let go. He simply wrapped his free arm around Tash so that Brissa was sandwiched between them and allowed the sobs of relief to break free from his throat.

"You found me," Brissa whispered, face pressed into Tash's throat. "And just when I thought there was no way I could leave this place alive—if you had arrived even a few moments later—"

"Of course we found you," Firae said, smiling into her knotted curls. "There are eight, and we are three, after all. Our fates are woven together on one loom."

Brissa laughed, bright and wet. "I suppose that is true, Your Majesty."

"It is, Your Majesty," Firae returned. Tash just tightened his arms around them.

"Ahem." The voice was delicate but strong, like an indestructible silver bell. Firae looked up to behold the sidhe woman Brissa had been protecting. "I am very happy for the three of you, and for myself as well, if I am honest, but I do believe it is past time that we left."

Firae opened his mouth to agree, but then closed it when he followed her line of vision. Beyond the melted gate, perhaps a hundred feet away from where they stood, was a small crowd of city dwellers. Firae glanced up to see the outlines of faces in far too many windows. Tash looked up as well.

"Aehsee?"

"Hello, Tash," she said, her voice sweet and even. "So nice of you to finally notice that I am here. Now shall we go before we are forced to start killing these people? It would be a shame to give them yet another reason to refer to our kind as demons."

The townspeople gave them a wide berth as they made their way out. Several held up iron pendants as if to ward off the three sidhe. Firae was tempted to melt some of them, just to see what particular horrified reaction that might elicit. A few of the braver humans yelled pleas to them to surrender, to undertake slavery so that they might rescue their immortal souls.

"Frilau is a lie," Brissa yelled, "and your king is a fraud! The only demons in this city are those that dwell in the hearts of Frilauans!"

They hastened their departure; Aehsee was right. These people may fear them, but it was only a matter of time until fear turned to violence, and Firae had no desire to confirm their worst suspicions about The Sidhe.

None of them noticed the patch of earth near the west wall of the manor as they rode out of town on stolen horses. They did not see the ground begin to bubble and turn an angry steel blue, and they did not hear the wrathful hiss that rose through the bubbling earth from the cavern below.

CHAPTER TWENTY-THREE

ARE YOU *SURE* THIS IS GOING TO WORK, JAXIS?" BRIEDEN TRIED not to jostle the little drawstring sack he carried as he followed Jaxis down the narrow footpath.

An abrupt gush of water crashed over Brieden's shoulders, as if someone had tossed a pailful onto him from the trees. He dropped his sack to the ground.

"I told you what would happen if you asked that question even one more time, friend," Jaxis said mildly, continuing his steady pace.

"You—" Brieden narrowed his eyes and, without thinking twice, ran at the other man. Just as he was about to close in, Jaxis burst into a gleeful peal of laughter and ran as well.

Brieden chased the elf along the gnarled forest path, cursing his human deficiencies. Jaxis moved across the earth like a swan upon water, avoiding every loose rock and bulbous tree root. In comparison, Brieden, despite an admirable degree of physical prowess and years of training in combat, thrashed about like a dragon foal just out of the nest.

"I know where you sleep, elf!" Brieden yelled after him.

"Between your fiancé's thighs? How clever of you to notice!" Jaxis shot back, and Brieden could not help but snort.

"Well, it won't be between Cliope Keshell's thighs, I can tell you that much!"

The path ended at a small, mossy clearing, and Brieden almost ran straight into Jaxis, who had stopped running and turned to face him with a frown.

"Did she say that?" Jaxis demanded.

Brieden fixed his face in a contemplative expression. "Hmm. You know, she just may have. Then again, she may have said something else entirely. I can't seem to recall…"

He looked around the clearing and noticed, at its heart, the small statue flanked by two small reflecting pools thick with water lilies. It was the smallest sidhe shrine he'd seen yet, and something about it made him feel soothed and protected.

"What did you say her name was?" Brieden asked Jaxis, as he walked past him to the statue.

"*Bislhia Talysis,*" Jaxis said. "Protector of All Young Lovers. She is one of the minor divinities and is easier on virgin soul-walkers than are the old Gods."

Brieden set down the cloth sack containing his offering and walked closer. The figure in the statue was perhaps two-thirds his size, and depicted in repose upon a mound of giant mushrooms, flowers, and vines. Some of the flowering vines curled around her naked body. She seemed young, and was lithe, with small breasts and slim hips. Her face was a picture of sharp elfin beauty. Her chin-length hair fanned out behind her head. One hand was cupped beside her head, and in it she held a single large rose. Her other hand lay between her breasts, and in that one she held half a passionfruit so intricately carved that Brieden swore he could see juice from the fruit dripping onto her skin.

"Why… do I feel so instantly at ease in her presence?" Brieden asked.

"Most likely because of the lilies. They emit a calming vapor. She was most often visited by very young sidhe entering into arranged marriages before they came of age, and it was meant to help them through the experience. Arranged marriages fell out of fashion centuries ago, of course, but there are those who seek her still."

Brieden turned to gape at Jaxis. "You brought me to a *child's* shrine?"

"You may have your pride or your soulmate, friend, but you cannot have both." Jaxis crossed his arms over his chest and met Brieden's eyes.

"Very *well*." Brieden stalked back to pick up the sack of offerings.

"Excellent," Jaxis said, in the tone of a long-suffering school teacher. Brieden had to fight the urge to push him into a lily pond. "Now. Let us return to the matter at hand. Did Cliope actually *tell* you she does not desire to bone me? Because the sense I got—"

"The offerings are wet now, you realize," Brieden interrupted.

"That doesn't matter." Jaxis dismissed that with a wave of his hand. "It won't affect anything, and they're going to get wet anyhow. Now, did Cliope—"

"Jaxis. Cliope is my friend," Brieden said.

Jaxis furrowed his brow. "You don't want to help your friend get laid?"

"I… I want Cliope to do whatever she likes, and I don't know what that is. But Jaxis, humans are different than sidhe. And human women… don't expect her to figure out the significance of the red bracelet, all right? You will need to explain it to her clearly. You will need to make sure that she truly understands."

"Of course, friend." Jaxis's voice was soft. "I seek only to share pleasure if it is a pleasure she truly craves."

Brieden smiled. "All right, then. Just… if you two… if it happens, I do not need to hear about it, all right?"

Jaxis laughed. "Of course you do. Do you recall how much time I spent listening to you moan about Sehrys back in the Northern Tower? If that lovely human lady does share her bed with me, then you, my friend, are going to hear *every detail*."

Brieden closed his eyes and inhaled, seeking the calming effects of the water lilies. "Remind me to have Sehrys cover you in marriage tattoos while you slumber," Brieden grumbled. "Now, shall we get on with this? I—I need to know—" Brieden swallowed the lump in his throat and allowed his mind to return to the reason he was at the shrine. "I need to know that I did not give my heart and my life to a foolish dream."

Rather than reply, Jaxis tugged the cloth sack from Brieden's hands and knelt to begin pulling out the carefully wrapped roses and passionfruit.

"Once you drink the nectar, it is important that you remain focused on the task at hand," he said, and pulled a vial of pale blue liquid from the purse at his hip. He handed it to Brieden along with a small, sharp knife. "Alternate roses and fruit until all are gone just as I told you. Your guide should be here by the time you are finished with the ritual."

Brieden nodded; his fingers were tight around the vial.

"I will stay nearby in case you need any help, but you won't. If you grow uneasy, just remember that I am here."

Brieden nodded again and shot Jaxis a grateful smile. Jaxis rose to his feet and gave Brieden's shoulder a friendly squeeze before going to the edge of the clearing.

Brieden turned to the statue and took a slow, shaking breath.

"Goddess of lovers, I seek your guidance," he spoke, and then uncorked the vial and gulped its contents.

He winced at the bitterness of the liquid; this was a concentrated and uncut form of the nectar Jaxis had pushed on him in the Northern Tower a year ago. It had been one thing to find himself drawn into Sehrys's soul-walk and emerge with no memory of it, and it was quite another to undertake a soul-walk of his own.

Brieden picked up the first rose and concentrated on his heart: on the way it lurched when Sehrys gave him that tender smile that cut through to his very core; the way it fluttered when he awoke to see Sehrys's eyes, warm and sleepy and drenched in love, gazing at him in their shared bed; the way it ached whenever he felt Sehrys slipping away from him, from *them*.

He raised the rose to his lips, inhaled its scent, kissed it softly, and dropped it into the pool to the left of the statue.

Next, Brieden cut a passionfruit in half; its sweet, tangy scent made him hum with pleasure. He placed one half on the ground and held the other, concentrating on the physical desire that surged in his groin when he looked upon Sehrys, emerging warm and naked from a fragrant bath; the way his pulse raced when Sehrys moved in a way that put his bare, muscled arms or the breadth of his shoulders on display. He remembered the desire, so constant and acute he thought it might kill him, in the early, desperate days of their relationship, when all they had was intense passion and a thin hope that they might survive. He bit into the fruit; the juice exploded in his mouth as his teeth scraped against the thick rind. When he was finished, he dropped the rind into the pool to the statue's right.

Brieden repeated the movements until he was lost in the ritual, as if his body were continuing to kiss the flowers and eat the fruit, while his mind drifted into a waking dream. Images and thoughts and feelings, all centered upon Sehrys, swirled about him, bore down on him, penetrated him so completely that he had to clamp his eyes closed.

After a deep, steadying breath, his eyes fluttered open and he gasped.

"*You*? But—but what—"

Before him stood a sidhe whose name he did not know, but whose face he would never forget. The elf was pale and lithe, with midnight blue hair and dark, bright eyes, and somehow appeared to be bathed in moonlight, though it was the middle of the day.

"That—that doesn't make any sense," he muttered. Had he made a mistake? Somehow performed the wrong ritual? He had been under the impression that the guide would appear in the form of someone very important to him, and he had expected his mother or his brother, or perhaps even Sehrys.

"There is no mistake," the elf said, his musical voice a delicious exaggeration of a true sidhe voice. "And do not think that I lack significance in your life. Was glimpsing me not the very thing that set you on your current path?"

Brieden could not argue; this man, the first sidhe he had seen, had captured and altered his heart in a way he still could not understand. After first beholding him in the moonlight on the riverbank near his home as a boy, Brieden had returned to that same spot nearly every night for more than a year.

The guide turned and stepped into the pool to Brieden's right. The lilies moved swiftly aside, framing the edges of the pool while the water in its center moved in a slow, steady clockwise motion, then picked up speed until the entire center of the pool was a shimmering whirlpool. The water had turned pale pink, and the air was thick with the scent of roses.

Without so much as a single backward glance, the elf walked into the center of the whirlpool and sank into its depths.

Brieden hesitated before following him, and when he took the first few steps toward the pool, he stopped; it felt as if his body were completely solid and insubstantial as smoke at the same time. He turned around, shocked despite Jaxis telling him that this would happen. It was too strange *not* to look.

There on the grass was his own body. His eyes were glazed in trance; his legs were crossed in front of him as he faced the statue with a rose cupped in his right hand and half a passionfruit in his left.

He still didn't understand, nor was he convinced that what was happening was real, but he did know that any answers were at the bottom of that pale pink vortex in the reflecting pool.

He stepped into the pool, and everything changed.

He was in the middle of the night sky, if the night sky were a million night skies all at once. All around him were darkness and bright points of light, and a feeling of overwhelming familiarity. He began moving—not walking, not precisely, but something close to it—and in little more than time for a breath, he was someplace that felt like *his*.

"So. Tell me what it is that you seek," his guide said, appearing beside him.

"I… I need to know that I am following the right path, that Sehrys and I can truly make a life together."

"You seemed quite sure of it until recently," the guide pointed out.

"Yes, but—" Brieden took a deep breath and finally admitted what he had been afraid to say. "I am afraid he is only just beginning to realize what he lost in rejecting Firae."

"And what was it that he lost?" the guide asked, voice gentle.

Brieden settled himself in a nest of stars. "Sehrys is…" he cast about for the best way to express the lingering unease in his heart. "When Sehrys learns of a great risk to the world, his first instinct is to act: to scream it from the mountaintops and dare anyone to claim they cannot hear; to blaze a path toward justice and confront all those who stand in his way. When I learn of such a risk, my first instinct is to protect those I hold close. The world could end at any time, but even as it crumbles, people still must eat. Children must be watched; animals still need tending."

"And you do not believe that Sehrys prizes such instincts?"

"I believe Sehrys loves me. But I believe I may not offer him nearly enough. I am… I am happy living the life of a farmer. But perhaps he needs more than that. Perhaps I need something less. At times I feel as if we are like the pairing of a God and a pixie."

The guide cocked his head. "You have seen the relief at the capitol."

Brieden nodded; when he had first seen the carving at the Khryslean Hall of Governance in Vizerche, it had stolen the breath from his body. It was an enormous depiction of sidhe and human founders of Khryslee in celebration on the banks of Merkhryslin Lake, swimming and dancing and playing music. Above them all was The Gatekeeper; her wings spanned from one edge of the relief to the next.

The relief appeared before him, and then its edges dissolved into the inky sky until all that remained were two figures, a grimchin and a small boy.

"If you were to see no more than this, would you not think this was a carving of a grimchin and a child and no more?" the guide asked.

Brieden nodded.

"Each immortal soul is much like a child's puzzle. Each mortal life that the soul experiences is but a small piece of that puzzle, and the truth is impossible to discern by treating each piece as if it were the whole."

Brieden nodded again, as a recollection that he could not grasp scratched at his mind.

"It is time that you remembered," the guide said, scooping up a star and holding it out in his palm. Brieden gingerly reached out his hand, and the moment the star touched his fingertips, he was overwhelmed by a sharp sensation of freefall.

And then something snapped into place in his mind, like the sudden recollection of a long forgotten dream.

He was in a place like this one, but not entirely the same. It wasn't his, but it was Sehrys's, and he felt safe.

"Sehrys, where are we?"

"We… we're someplace you probably won't remember, Brieden. We are at The Heart of All Worlds."

This was Sehrys's soul-walk, the very soul-walk he had taken before his intended marriage to Firae, the soul-walk in which Brieden had found him, and in which Sehrys had showed him the truth.

As each of the little stars, which were not stars at all, showed Brieden another piece of the puzzle, the puzzle that was not merely Sehrys or himself but something larger, something utterly *them,* he understood.

In this lifetime, Sehrys was a force of nature, while Brieden was a simple farmer, but that did not matter. It did not matter that Brieden was no more than a disgraced criminal in his homeland, while Sehrys was all but a king in his, for each of them was always precisely what the other needed.

"And so you see," the guide said. His voice sounded more realistic. His hair was still midnight blue, but his eyes were now the same bright green as Sehrys's, and dancing with love.

"And so I see," Brieden agreed. Warmth flowed through him in ribbons as he touched another of the little light-points to learn another story of another lifetime spent in Sehrys's arms.

Sehrys stroked the grimchin's soft head as it nibbled on the feast in his garden. He didn't know the creature's name, but he could tell it was the same one that always came to him when he summoned a grimchin from the hive. The creature that had carried Cliope to the World River Valley alongside him was one he hadn't seen before, but based on how it interacted with his grimchin, Sehrys would guess that the two were mated. That thought made him yearn for Brieden: Brieden, who had always been so sure about the two of them; Brieden who had sacrificed everything for him; Brieden who looked at him as if he were the most perfect being in all of creation.

It was not Brieden's frustration with him that ate away at Sehrys; he knew he could be single-minded, sometimes selfish toward those who loved him in favor of championing those who suffered. He didn't blame Brieden for finding fault with him for that. But to contemplate *giving up* on them—

Sehrys bit his trembling lip for the dozenth time that day and willed himself not to cry.

"We still have time," Cliope said, turning her attention from her grimchin to give his arm a conciliatory squeeze. "I couldn't understand what any of them were saying, but you said that a couple of them seemed swayed, and no one tried to kill or compel me, so I see that as something of a personal victory."

Sehrys tried to smile. "I suppose it could have been worse," he conceded.

"Anyhow, cheer up. At least you'll be able to sleep in your lover's arms tonight."

Cliope winked. Sehrys let out a violent sob.

"Oh. That was… supposed to cheer you up."

"I'm sorry," Sehrys said, swiping at his damp cheeks with the back of his hand. He couldn't bring himself to meet Cliope's eye, but he laid his hand over hers where she was still touching his arm. "It has just… things have been difficult lately."

"Do you… wish to talk about it?"

Sehrys shook his head. "Thank you, but no. I should find Brieden."

"And now find him you have!" Jaxis called out merrily, as he rounded the house with Brieden in tow. Brieden looked a bit... well, Sehrys couldn't quite put his finger on it. It was like a deep state of concentration coupled with slight inebriation. When he looked up and locked eyes with Sehrys, Sehrys felt as if he were pinned in place by the sheer weight of his fiancé's gaze. Their hands went to their promise pendants at the same time, as if the same puppet master were pulling each of their strings in precisely the same way.

"Lady Keshell, might I interest you in a stroll through the forest?" Jaxis asked, extending his hand to Cliope.

Cliope blinked. "I just finished a two-day grimchin ride," she said dryly.

"All the more reason to stretch your legs, then. Or... find someplace nice to sit. We could visit the lake just down the road—a nymph lives there, and sometimes she comes out to sing."

Cliope opened her mouth to respond and then closed it after looking back and forth between Brieden and Sehrys.

"Oh," she said. "Of course. Let us go to the lake."

Sehrys intended to bid them goodbye—he truly did—but Brieden's eyes had consumed every bit of his concentration, though he was quite sure that he heard Jaxis casually ask Cliope what color bracelet she thought she might wear if she were a sidhe.

"Brieden?" Sehrys managed to ask softly once they were alone.

"I did a soul-walk," Brieden blurted, his eyes still pinning Sehrys in place. "Jaxis taught me how, I... I visited the shrine of *Bislhia Talysis*, because she likes roses and passionfruit as an offering, and we have some in the garden, and she..." Brieden trailed off, staring at Sehrys as if he were seeing him for the very first time.

"She is the guardian of young lovers," Sehrys finished softly. "And did she—what did she show you?"

He strode to Sehrys and pulled him into his arms.

"She showed me everything," Brieden said, before claiming Sehrys's lips with his own, kissing him for the very first time with the true, deep knowledge of all that they were to one another, all that they had always been.

"I did not remember. Why did you not tell me?" Brieden asked, peppering tiny kisses across Sehrys's forehead and the apples of his cheeks and down the bridge of his nose.

"I… I thought you knew," Sehrys said, tears rolling down his cheeks. "You—you always seemed to simply *know* the very thing that I needed a soul-walk to understand. I didn't realize that you might need one, too."

Brieden kissed Sehrys again and pressed their foreheads together gently. "You must not forget that I am only human, Sehrys. In this lifetime, at least."

Sehrys wrapped his arms tightly around Brieden so their promise pendants pressed into one another's chests. "And I am only sidhe," Sehrys said. He pulled back far enough to meet Brieden's eyes. "And I am sorry that I have not shown you the respect you deserve. After calving season, will you come with me to speak to the Council? I can't be sure, but I think Cliope may have frightened them."

Brieden laughed. "I would be honored, Ambassador," he said, and kissed Sehrys again.

Chapter Twenty-Four

Tash did his best to provide small luxuries for Brissa as they traveled south through the Panloch lands, following the Vestech River at a distance and on foot. They hadn't been able to keep the horses; the creatures were too conspicuous, and unable to navigate the deep woods.

This difficulty extended to their human companion as well.

They risked stopping outside a village so that Brissa could purchase a pair of boots. No one seemed to recognize her in her plain dress and frizzed hair, and so they stopped again a few days later so that she could barter Tash's eyeglasses for food that was more nourishing to her human constitution than leaves and berries and edible blossoms.

And Tash did what he could. He crafted a heating surface from a flat stone to lay over their fire so that Brissa could cook, and he built the softest beds he could from leaves and spongy moss so that she might sleep comfortably through the night. It was not luxury fit for a queen, but it was the best he could do.

It also distracted him from the way Aehsee's eyes seemed to bore into the back of his skull as they walked, and the way Firae frowned at her, as if trying to place how he knew her.

Tash had some idea why Firae might know her. Aehsee's crime had been so horrific that she was nearly put to death. If she hadn't been such an influential priestess, she would have been.

But Tash wasn't going to tell him. They were drawing uncomfortably close to The Border, and Tash had his own fate to worry about without inciting more problems.

"Why are you traveling with us?" he finally asked Aehsee when he fell into step beside her one day about a week into their journey.

"Where else would you propose I go?" she asked, not meeting his eye. "I am still bound by verbena, and even once I am free of it, I have sworn allegiance to the queen."

Tash laughed bitterly. "You have sworn allegiance to yourself, Aehsee. Do not try to tell me that you have developed loyalty to a human after all you have done."

"And you have?" she asked sharply, levelling him with that same stare she had been sending his way all week. "If I recall, Tash, we both hurt humans for pleasure."

"I don't deny that I have committed evil, and I do not beg the Gods for forgiveness where I do not deserve it. But you—you have been hurting those weaker than yourself since before you left Laesi. Why should I think you will treat Brissa any better once your powers are restored?"

Aehsee slowed to a stop and looked him directly in the eye. "She is a mortal queen. And we have suffered together. There is no bond greater than a bond forged through suffering."

Tash narrowed his eyes and watched her turn and walk ahead to fall into step beside Brissa. The queen seemed delighted by Aehsee's company. Tash supposed he would have to carry enough distrust for both of them.

The third time that Brissa ventured into town, she was recognized.

She returned to them on horseback, with two carriages and four men clad in gold and white uniforms.

"We are saved!" Brissa said, beaming, and threw open one of the carriage doors.

They had crossed into Lord Lottechet's lands and, once Brissa realized this, she had looked for his local guard detail. This close to the Panloch lands, she knew he would not leave any good-sized village without defense.

And when the men were confronted by their queen, they naturally followed whatever orders she chose to give them.

And that was how, less than two weeks after escaping Zegripanloch, Tash found himself seated at a long, ornate wooden dining table in Lottechet Manor trying to decide if he liked the mushrooms although they had been cooked with cow's butter.

It wasn't a decision he would be able to arrive at easily; everything tasted like ash in his mouth.

The manor was pleasant enough: airy, like Keshell castle in Ryovni, but with the dark woods and detailed carvings that were more typical of mainland Villaluan opulence. The Lottechets themselves were almost aggressively friendly, repeatedly remarking on their support of the border cities—while neglecting to mention the healthy taxes paid to them by those cities—and looking as if they were memorizing every word the three sidhe spoke to them so they could repeat them at dinner parties.

But all Tash could think of was how close they were to The Border. And they were no closer to understanding the prophecy than they had been when The Truthkeeper shared it with them in Ryovni.

The simple truth was that Tash was going to die. And it was going to be soon.

After the meal, Tash slipped away.

He knew Brissa would want to discuss strategy with the Lottechets, and Firae—Firae was more than he could bear at the moment.

Tash found his way to the gardens behind the manor; they were well tended, with a variety of flowers and fruit trees. Ropes of flowering jasmine sent a sweet fragrance wafting from a trellis.

Tash made his way to a large tree in a shadowed corner of the garden. The base of its trunk formed a cupped seat that was perfect for Tash to settle into and feel blessedly invisible.

"Tash?"

He sighed and opened his eyes to see Firae, whose eyes were shining beneath the light of two full moons.

"What are you doing out here?" Firae asked, his voice uncharacteristically soft.

"Thinking," Tash said. "Hiding."

"What are you hiding from?" he settled beside Tash in the shadows.

"The future, I suppose," Tash admitted with a shrug. "Or lack thereof, in my case."

Firae took his hand. "I wouldn't be so sure about that."

Tash closed his eyes. "I know I said that prophecies are designed to work, but prophecies fail sometimes too, Firae. I think... I think we have run out of time to fulfill this one."

Firae continued to hold his hand. "I don't care about the prophecy," he said.

Tash blinked his eyes open and looked at him. "What do you mean?"

"I mean..." Firae rubbed his thumb over the pulse of Firae's wrist. "I mean, I think I understand what The Truthkeeper was telling me. She was telling me *not* to look for the prophecy, to let it go."

Tash furrowed his brow. "I'm afraid you're going to have to explain that to me."

Firae smiled. He picked a dandelion that was brushing his knee and twirled it slowly in his free hand.

"The scarlet heart requires naked courage," Firae said. "And my ancestors... my ancestors were rebels. Radicals. They risked everything, their power, their reputations, *everything* to change the world for the better. I... I have been afraid to do the same, Tash. I have been a coward."

Tash leaned forward, clutching Firae's hand more tightly. "That isn't true, Firae. You... you came to Villalu by yourself, not knowing—"

"I came with the permission of the Council. It took a degree of courage, I will admit that, but not the kind of courage that would compromise my legacy. Not the kind of courage that ignores the law when the law itself is unjust. You are not meant to die, Tash. Not now."

Tash blinked, startled. "My life is not worth every other life in Villalu, Firae."

"Your life is precious. And you are part of the prophecy. You are *meant* to live, Tash. I… I told myself I was being selfish by wanting to spare you, that I must sacrifice you for the greater good. But the truth is, that was never selfish. What was selfish was letting my own fear blind me to how important you are to the fate of our world."

Firae tucked the dandelion behind Tash's ear and took Tash's other hand, his left hand, pressing their palms together just so.

Tash gasped.

"No, Firae, you can't. I am not worthy of this. The law—"

"A wise being once reminded me that law is created by sentient beings in an attempt to bring reason to reasonless worlds," Firae said. "It is not inherent."

And before Tash could protest any further, Firae began the chant.

"*Esil supalin vormikente nau'at. Malinan vornanu bil feririar. Malinan vornanu bil zershe. Malinan vornanu bil thitherog. Malinan vornanu bil zershe…*"

As he repeated the words, a soft golden glow traveled from Firae's heart to his shoulder and from his shoulder down his arm and into his hand where it lay over the invisible mark that hid Tash's shame. The mark that kept him imprisoned in Villalu was so deeply embedded in Tash's skin that he couldn't see it if he tried, couldn't remove it even if he burned off his own flesh in the attempt.

Tash gasped when the light hit his body; it was different from sharing power with Firae. It didn't zip through his veins, but rather washed over him all at once like a warm bath. Tash's hand twitched against Firae's; the pleasure was almost too overwhelming to bear, as the mark melted into nothing and his skin hummed with the gift that Firae had bestowed upon him.

Tash hadn't realized how heavy the mark had been until it was gone. He felt as though he could float away.

"You are not a criminal anymore," Firae said softly. "You are no longer bound to Villalu. You are free to go wherever you like."

"Firae," Tash whispered, because it was all he *could* say. And it was all there was to say; Firae was everything.

Firae began to release Tash's hands, but Tash only held on tighter. He loosened his grip just long enough to lace their fingers together.

"I will cross The Border alone and deal with The Council, and you can stay here with Brissa," Firae said. "Help her find the *La'ekynog*."

Tash held on to Firae's hands. He wondered if Firae could feel the hammering of his heart through his palms. "Firae..." Tash ventured, "when you said it was selfish of you to want to keep me alive..."

Firae swallowed and looked at his lap. "You must know, Tash. You must have figured it out by now."

Tash stared at him, at his lovely pale golden cheeks, visibly flushed beneath the light of the moons, at his sparkling eyes and the sweet slope of his throat. He could not begin to hope, to even *imagine*—

Firae chuckled. "I suppose you are going to make me say it, aren't you?" He looked up to meet Tash's eyes, and his innocent vulnerability made Tash's throat tighten. "Very well, then. I am in love with you. But—but I know it doesn't matter, because you are my equal, Tash, and you're free, and I know you don't belong to me."

Tash forced himself not to argue, not to reject the words, even though Firae *couldn't* love him. Firae was a brave and beautiful king, and Tash...

Tash was what Firae wanted. Though he knew he didn't deserve anyone's love, let alone *this* man's love, Tash could not reject Firae's words; there was nothing on his face but naked honesty, and there was nothing in his voice but naked courage.

"Firae," Tash said, releasing his hands. Firae cast his eyes toward the ground, then looked startled when Tash lifted his hands to frame Firae's face. "Whatever gave you the ridiculous notion that I don't belong to you?"

Tash barely had time to register Firae's wonder-wide eyes before he kissed him, softly, sweetly. "I love you too. And I am crossing The Border with you whether you like it or not."

Firae attempted to protest, but Tash kissed him again.

"No," he said when they parted. "We are in this together. Anything you must face, I shall face by your side. Whether that is the Council or Thieren Panloch or the *La'ekynog*, wherever they might be, or… or an army of sphinxes."

"But—it might not be safe—" Firae protested.

"You shall keep me safe," Tash said. "You are a king of Laesi, after all."

Firae pressed his smiling lips to Tash's again and again and again. And it was then that the words of The Truthkeeper finally fell into place.

The violet heart requires freedom. You must not hide from the mirror of your soul.

His soul had never changed, after all, merely his body. The mirror of his soul had always been Firae.

"I cannot believe you left Sree in charge of the entire Queendom," Jaxis said, shaking his head.

"Well, *I* cannot believe that you are voluntarily going back to Villalu," Cliope chimed in.

Sehrys looked at them from his perch next to Brieden on the very carriage that had brought them to the safety of Laesi nearly two years before. Jaxis and Cliope were on their own carriage. It was smaller, but it would do the trick. Their horses were a pair of brindle mares.

Sehrys gave Brieden a smile. "Well, you did say something about the purest heart tethered to the greatest power. It sounds as if we are needed." But despite the placid look on his face, Cliope could see the white-knuckled grip he had on the reins. "And besides, we need to find Firae. Time is running out, and it doesn't seem that the Council has any intention of reconsidering their decision without him."

"Yes, well, I suppose I *should* reassure Brissa that I am alive," Cliope sighed, ignoring the pang of guilt lying to her sister had caused her.

Jaxis smiled his crafty, lopsided smile at her, and the guilt subsided rather nicely.

"Well," Brieden said, running a soothing hand over Sehrys's back, "lead the way."

It was less frightening this time; she had barely managed to get through on her own in her first Border crossing, and without Tash's essence and Blue Shell's guidance she probably wouldn't have managed it at all. It was still disorienting, but at least this time she did not have to keep herself awake through sheer force of will. Jaxis's constant stream of flirtatious words and touches kept her so wound up that she almost didn't mind the momentary sensation of being without a physical body or the wave of nausea that hit her the moment they burst through onto Villaluan soil.

The portal they had chosen was a relatively hidden one, and Cliope was relieved that she did not have to use any of her weapons immediately upon their arrival. They were in a small clearing in the woods, not far from the Western shore of Tyzkin Lake. Bird chatter and a softly trickling stream were the only sounds Cliope could hear.

Cliope and Jaxis moved their carriage out of the way to offer the others a wide berth, and not a moment later, Brieden and Sehrys's carriage followed.

It was empty.

To Be Continued in the *Heart of All Worlds* series
Book Three: *The Sixth Anchor*...

GLOSSARY

Iₙ THE FOLLOWING DEFINITIONS, ELVISH WORDS ARE ITALICIZED.

defmor M'Ferauvise. Sidhe term for rape, literally Betrayal of the Mother Goddess

Durstan. name of star

elcei. Elfin name for a tree

es lemeddison rubrio. Elfin for Non-Interference Doctrine

Esil supalin vormikente nau'at. Malinan vornanu bil feririar. Malinan vornanu bil zershe. Malinan vornanu bil thitherog. Malinan vornanu bil zershe... Chant in Elfin—a spell of release, a promise of freedom.

Esilog supanauvo nau'at ul zersheog esilog filameton wa peristorn nau'at telfidan nauefa feririar. We welcome you to the lands that we guard and invite you to treat them as your home.

es Muirdannoch. the Merrowfolk (a singular merrowperson = *muirdannoch*)

ferban. queen

grimchin. flying beast used for transport

hubia rija. Elfin flower prized for its lubricating oil

immervish. incorruptible

karanoviches. Ryovnian sweet treat

lackente. Elfin name for a tree

La'ekynog. the Blessed Guardian's helpers, who tend to the small things

Lekianoche. Ryovnian term for *La'ekynog*

L'auvkinlea. the Blessed Guardian of Small Things, Bearer of Seeds

Merkhryslin. Lake in Khryslee

Mikrigday. your majesty, literally Great King

muirdannoch. a single merrowperson

nomkin. pet name, short name of an elf

novichene. Ryovnian plant with sweet nectar

P'ellferbanjin. the Goddess of Mortal Queens

posselke . Elfin name for a plant similar to milkweed

presmij. oil or extract

rigday. king

Rigday Firae efa es Alovur Drovuru Feririar, Silerth Valusidhe efa Ferban Gira efa es Alovur Drovuru Feririar ala es Fervishlaea efa es Yestralekrezershe. Firae's full name

Rijamiknauvriog. Flower Forest, a place in Khryslee

sarthan. temple

Sehrys Silerth Valusidhe efa Naisdhe efa es Zulla Maletog Feririar ala es Fervishlaea efa es Vestramezershe. Sehrys's full name

Sree Silerth Banvalusidhe efa Seledhe efa es Alovur Drovuru Feririar ala es Fervishlaea efa es Yestralekrezershe. Sree's full name

simblini. a flower-tree of the Western Sea Lands

srechelee. flower-trees

Tash Tirarth Valusidhe efa Lesette efa es Zulla Melleva Feririar ala es Fervishlaea efa es Sola Pelzershe. Tash's full name

tochet. tree in Ryovnia

verlokinlee. Elfin name for a plant that repels pixies.

walwasha. Elfin name for a plant whose blossoms have calming properties similar to lavender

For a complete language guide and Sidhe cultural terms, please visit charlotteashe.com.

ACKNOWLEDGMENTS

I CANNOT PROPERLY EXPRESS MY GRATITUDE FOR ALL THOSE who have helped me bring this book to fruition in a year of great difficulty and personal loss.

First and foremost, I must extend my gratitude to the Interlude team for their tireless help, support, input, and flexibility: Annie, for being everything I needed and more in an editor and friend, from a source of nurturing support to a source of much-needed tough love—you help me become a better writer with every draft; Candy, for always being enthusiastic, encouraging, and entirely on the ball; Sarah, for bringing my characters and world to life in the most exquisite way; Choi, for somehow making Sarah's masterpieces even more breathtaking; and Nicki, for quite literally giving my sidhe characters a voice with your incredible linguistic skills. You are all amazing. I also have to give posthumous thanks to Lex, one of my very first champions, who loved *The Heart of All Worlds* and who I dearly wish could read this book. It hasn't been the same without you, my friend.

I also need to express thanks to my friends and family, both those who read and celebrated my first book and those who couldn't handle the idea of magical lube flowers but supported and encouraged me anyway. Stoney, Riah, Ellen, Tanya, Chris, Ben, Noel, Tim, Link, Neil, H'Rina, Bunch, Christine, Victor, Kelly, Adam, Ryan, Alysia, Max, Mary, Rick, and all those I will regretfully forget to name here—thank you. You can't possibly imagine how crucial each and every one of you have been to me. Even when I go far too long without seeing some of you, it is an incredible source of comfort to always know that you are there.

And of course, as always, I give thanks to and for Pepper and Tilly, my fuzzy, dictatorial little muses. Thank you bringing joy into my life even on my worst days.

Finally, thank you to all my readers. It is you who motivate me to write, who push me to develop the detailed, vibrant world that my characters deserve. Without you I wouldn't be doing this, so thank you, so very much, for allowing me to do what I love.

ABOUT THE AUTHOR

CHARLOTTE ASHE WORKS IN THE NONPROFIT WORLD BY DAY and writes romantic fantasy by night. A long-time fan of speculative fiction that skews feminist and features LGBT characters, Charlotte loves writing stories that are sexy, heartfelt, and full of magic and adventure. She has put her BA in literature and creative writing to use over the years as a writer of fan fiction, and her most popular work has drawn more than one million readers worldwide, been translated into several languages, and been featured in online publications including *The Backlot. The Sidhe* (2015) and *The King and the Criminal* were named Foreword INDIES Book of the Year finalists.

interlude**press**™

 interludepress.com
 @InterludePress
 interludepress
 store.interludepress.com

interlude press™
you may also like...

The Sidhe by Charlotte Ashe
The Heart of All Worlds, Book One
Foreword INDIES Book of the Year Finalist

Brieden is captivated by the magical Sidhe who live outside his homeland of Villalu and objects to their enslavement by Villalu's elite. Enamored with the mysterious sidhe slave Sehrys, Brieden vows to free and return him home. They find love as they navigate a treacherous path to freedom. If they survive to reach the border, Brieden must choose: the love of his life, or the fate of his world.

ISBN (print) 978-1-941530-33-7 | (eBook) 978-1-941530-50-4

Céilí by Moriah Gemel

When Devon stumbles into a club called Céilí he discovers a community of mystical people, and that he found it only because he is Fae himself. With help from Eldan—a powerful Fae Lord protecting his kind in the city—Devon discovers his magical abilities. His life appears to be back on track—until a member of the Faerie Court is murdered and the secret of their world is threatened to be revealed.

ISBN (print) 78-1-941530-65-8 | (eBook) 978-1-941530-66-5

The Star Host by F.T. Lukens
Published by Duet, an imprint of Interlude Press

Ren grew up listening to his mother tell stories about the Star Hosts—mythical people possessed by the power of the stars. Captured by a nefarious Baron, Ren discovers he may be something out of his mother's stories. He befriends Asher, a member of the Phoenix Corps. Together, they must master Ren's growing power, and try to save their friends while navigating the growing attraction between them.

ISBN (print) 978-1-941530-72-6 | (eBook) 978-1-941530-73-3